THE
RAINCROW

Books by Jane Gilmore Rushing

WALNUT GROVE

AGAINST THE MOON

TAMZEN

MARY DOVE

THE RAINCROW

THE RAINCROW

by

Jane Gilmore Rushing

DOUBLEDAY & COMPANY, INC.
GARDEN CITY, NEW YORK 1977

Walnut Grove: The landscape and the customs are of a country known to me, but the people and the happenings are complete fabrications.

Library of Congress Cataloging in Publication Data

Rushing, Jane Gilmore.

    The raincrow.
    I. Title.
PZ4.R9524Rai   [PS3568.U73]   813'.5'4
ISBN: 0-385-13059-7
Library of Congress Catalog Card Number 76-52223

TO JIM

THE
RAINCROW

ONE

Once I thought I would never go back to Walnut Grove, but of course I do. I drive most of three days to get there, a thousand miles across the Great American Desert to my childhood home on its eastern approaches. I don't much like the long drive, but it is the only reasonable alternative to the long-drawn-out intimacy of a bus ride, which I dislike even more. Years ago, trains stopped at Walnut Grove, and even after I moved to California I could still take a train and be met at Sloan City. I could fly now, of course, but the major airlines would not bring me within a hundred miles of Walnut Grove; and though my mother would be entirely willing to meet me at the airport, I don't like asking that much of her.

Perhaps, on the whole, I really don't mind the drive very much. It is a long way back to my mother's house, and the long straight western highways underscoring the distance have sometimes been a satisfaction to my mind. Really, it is a figure of speech to say that I go back to Walnut Grove. I turn off the highway where a sign pretends to point there; but a stranger seeking the place would be hard put to tell when he reached it, for the last structure marking where a town tried to be was removed years ago.

My journey ends at a weathered-gray house sparsely shaded by trees we always called Chinese elms. I don't know how long this has been the only one of Walnut Grove's old box houses that anyone lives in—it may even be the last one left standing. I have not been in the habit of examining very carefully the remains of Walnut Grove. For years I drove through the community as if I were wearing blinders like those my grandfather used to put on his old gray mule that I almost remember.

I come to my old home along a bright white caliche road, drawing behind me a cloud of fine white dust. Mother wishes they would pave the road, but I remember it when it was graded red dirt and appreciate the all-weather topping. Paved roads crisscross the county now, but our place always was a little out of the way. I wouldn't care, if I lived there. The old house doesn't belong on a pavement.

As I pull off the road onto the packed red earth in front of the house, I imagine Mother watching, having followed with her eyes the white cloud moving toward her, guessing it is time for me to arrive if I got an early start from Alamogordo. It is strange to think that this year my son may be watching too.

By the time I have stopped, Mother has pushed open the screen door and is standing on the front porch, at the top of the steps, a slender figure in a lime green pants suit. At this distance no one would guess she is nearly sixty-five. We hurry together, and pause on the graveled walk for a brief hug and kiss.

"Where's Paul?" I can't help asking.

"He's plowing," she says. "We've had so much rain—this was the first day in a week he could get in the field. He said he'd quit early."

We go into the house to drink the coffee she has waiting. This is what we always do, and no need to discuss it. I will bring my things in later, or perhaps Paul will get them.

"I'm surprised at this room all over again every time I come," I say as we walk through the living room.

When I lived here with Mother and Mama, we had a nine-by-twelve linoleum rug on the pine board floor, faded brown-flowered paper on the walls, and marquisette panels (ordered from Sears) at the tall double window. Now there are good green carpet in a tweedy pattern on the floor, paneling with a dark wood finish on the walls, and tweedy green draperies that pull back to reveal all of the window and let in more light than the room ever knew in Mama's time. The old leatherette davenport and assorted rocking chairs where we sat so many evenings listening to the radio have given way to a set of maple-armed furniture upholstered in rust and brown.

I pause before something new—a Franklin stove, installed where in my earliest childhood a potbellied coal stove stood in winter. The last time I was here Mother was still using an open butane heater.

"This is Paul's idea," she says. "After I had central heating installed last winter, he said he missed having a glow to stand by. I did too, so we just went to town and got us a stove and me and him put it in."

"You were lucky to have a chimney already."

"That's what he said. I never thought about houses nowadays not having flues, but of course they don't."

"You didn't write about it."

"I guess I was saving it for a surprise. I wish we'd have a cool spell so I could light a fire in it for you. It's almost like having a fireplace."

In the kitchen things haven't changed. They have hardly changed since Mama's time, except for the institution of modern appliances. It is still the most inconvenient kitchen I have ever seen—too large, and completely unplanned. In the beginning it was a dining room. I remember Mama telling me that when she finally got an oil cookstove to replace the wood stove she had cooked on so long, she decided to move the kitchen into the dining room so she wouldn't have so far to go back and forth between cooking and eating. She put the round oak table in the middle of the floor, and the arrangement seemed beautifully convenient to her.

Mother keeps the same old oak table and the same arrange-

3

ment: the sink on one wall, under a window looking out on the back yard, and now in recent years the wall filled out with modern cabinets; opposite it, the electric range; on another wall, the refrigerator; on the fourth an old-fashioned kitchen cabinet, and in one corner a ceiling-high cupboard faced with bead-and-tongue plank.

"The arrangement might be a little more step-saving," I have sometimes observed to Mother.

"Oh well, I'm used to exercise," she says.

She is used to exercise. She has farmed the Messenger place for over forty years.

We set out coffee mugs on the yellow-plaid vinyl table cover and draw up heavy oak chairs.

"I can't imagine Paul plowing," I say.

"That boy's a born farmer. I had the right hunch when I wrote to him."

It is Mother's plan that Paul will take her place and farm the Messenger land now that she has reached retirement age. I never had the slightest idea of Paul wanting to be a farmer, though it is true what I tell Mother now: "I've always said I wouldn't object to any kind of work that gave him satisfaction, but I did hope he'd finish college." It is true that this is what I've always said, but the only thing I never dreamed of was that he would ever be a farmer at Walnut Grove. I can't help believing, anyhow, that he will go back to college. He has always agreed with me that a person needs a good liberal education for living, and job training is something else again.

"I never would've wrote," Mother says, "if he hadn't already left college. And you said he wasn't satisfied with his daddy's business, after working there so many summers."

"No, he certainly wasn't," I say. "And Ted wasn't satisfied with him. One reason he left college, I think, was a hassle over Ted wanting him to major in business administration. You know he'd come home to stay with me, and although I was glad to have him again, he was so depressed about his future we really weren't having a very good time together."

"I sort of thought that was the way of it. And I remembered how much he used to like this place when you'd bring him in the summers."

"But of course it had been a good while since he'd been here," I say, "and I just didn't know—"

"Five years," Mother says, interrupting. "I missed him enough to know."

"Well, of course he always wanted to come," I say, "but Ted had made him think he had a duty to work in the store every summer and prepare to go into the business. He used to like this place so much, but I was afraid he was just remembering it in a glow of childish illusion and would be discouraged when the reality of West Texas farm life struck him. I think you did have sandstorms this spring?"

"As bad as you ever saw, till it started raining in May. He plowed right through some of the worst of them, with never a word of complaint. Yes, Paul's a born farmer."

I don't think Mother knows Paul as well as I do. And isn't it a little soon to be recognizing a born farmer?

"Well, if it works out for you both I'll be glad," I say. I think I mean it. "I do like the idea of the old place staying in our family. But what does Hugh think about your arrangement?"

Hugh is Mother's brother-in-law, son of my grandmother Messenger—who was always Mama to both my mother and me. He encouraged Mama to leave the farm to Mother, because she had lived there and looked after Mama and the place for so many years and hadn't anywhere else to go. But it was nearly twenty-five years ago when Mama died. I wonder how he feels now.

Mother puts down her mug and settles back in her chair with an air of physical comfort, like a cat come in from the cold. "Hugh likes my plan just fine," she says. Then she straightens and I see a little fire of mischief leap in her almost yellow eyes. There is something catlike about that too. "Stanfield is not the happiest thing in the world though, I understand."

My cousin Stanfield—Hugh's son. I never see him when I come for my two-week summer stay, but I understand he is an exceptionally well-to-do farmer in an area where all the farmers are doing very well indeed. "He wouldn't expect to get the place?"

"I believe he thought he could take it over this year, and when the time came to sell have first chance to buy it. I don't imagine he ever thought of you or Paul wanting to keep it."

"And you think Paul will?"

"I think he will."

"Well, I suppose I hope so. I'm still not used to the idea of Paul as a farmer."

"Wait till you see him."

"I hardly can. Do you think he'll come soon?"

"I expect he will. He may have seen your car from the north field."

"How do you think he'll feel if I spend the whole summer?"

"*Are* you, Gail?" she leans toward me, reaching a hand across the table. She is tense again now, I can't think why. After all these years, to care so much how long I stay? And yet of course she has written that letter, not urgent really, just asking, but she has never done that before, never said more than (once, a long time ago) "come when you can, and stay as long as you will." Mother would never beg.

"I have made arrangements to stay away all summer," I tell her. "I have decided not to teach in summer school."

"Oh, I'm so glad."

There is intensity there—but why? "Are you all right, Mother? Are you well?"

She certainly looks well. Her skin is still rosy and firm, her hair still glossy and brown, just gray enough that you can be sure she isn't dyeing it. I envy her figure.

"Oh sure," she says, dismissing that. "I'm always well."

"Something's wrong though?"

"Nothing's wrong. I just hoped you'd come. I thought you would like it, with Paul here. I knew I would like it. I didn't see why I shouldn't have my little family together once, and long enough to enjoy."

"Well, I plan to stay."

She takes my hand and presses it. I wonder, I wonder. But then—I know she has been lonely all these years.

"I think I hear the tractor," she says.

Yes, there is a roar. "I didn't recognize it," I say. "I guess I still expect it to sound like our old Poppin' Johnnie."

"I still buy John Deere," she says absently.

The tractor is coming in. I look out the window and see it pulling up between the house and barn. Paul jumps down and comes toward the house. What a sight! His medium-length sun-burnished hair sticks out all ways from the billed cap he has pulled down hard on his head. (The cap has a John Deere emblem on the front, as I discover later.) He has lost weight and is long and lank now, in his dust-caked Levis and half-buttoned chambray shirt.

"What do the neighbors think about the way he looks?" I wonder.

"He looks just like the rest of the youngsters," Mother says.

"Good heavens." But of course Walnut Grove boys don't wear crew cuts any more.

He is on the back steps and I run to meet him, into the little room that was once Mama's kitchen, then a catch-all, and at last (in my teen years) became part bathroom and part back hall.

"Hey, Ma!" he shouts.

I run to embrace him but he holds me off. "I brought half the field in with me," he says. "Wait till I shower."

"Oh fudge," I say, and we're embracing. I'm kissing his cheeks and tasting red dirt and sweat.

I stand back and look at him. He is certainly not Mother's baby boy. "Well," I say. "Rites of passage."

"You'd better believe it," he says.

I do believe it. Something has happened to Paul—just getting to be a farmer, perhaps. He said it would happen. When he got Mother's letter he said it opened up in a flash of light everything he ever wanted in life.

"Back to the soil!" he cried. "A dumb cliché, but, Mother, it's what I want. I want to get my hands in the dirt and know I'm making something real. Live among real people who can see the results of their work. I'm tired of Dad's installment plans and interest rates and imitation wood furniture. I feel like Gran's just touched me with a wand and made me come alive—come wide awake for the first time in my life."

"Paul," I said then, "you haven't been to Walnut Grove in years, and you never did know what it was really like. Gathering eggs for Grandma, hunting bird nests in the pasture, wading in the creek after rains—that's not the usual life at Walnut Grove, even for children. You've got some romantic picture out of the nineteenth century Middle West in your mind, and this is twentieth century West Texas you're talking about. Most of the time it doesn't rain, and the creeks are dry. Farming is mechanized—it won't be much different from a furniture store. Walnut Grove is no pleasant little village; in fact, there isn't any village. From what Mother says, most people seem to spend their time driving to towns fifty or sixty miles away or more, just to do their shopping. They don't even bother much with Sloan City, where everybody went on Saturdays when I was a child. I don't know how you'd ever even get to know all these people that are doing such real things."

"I'm going to try it," he said.

He certainly did. Perhaps I was wrong. Anyway, something has happened, probably something good.

After supper, we sit on the porch in the rocking chairs from the old living room, looking south across dark land to a pale sky. There is nothing against the sky now but tall poles, where once I used to see clumps of trees rising like islands, and windmills reaching high. The trees have all been cut down to make farm land, and the windmills replaced with pumps powered by the force that flows along the lines between those poles. If we turn our heads to the east, we can see something else—the lights of the microwave tower and the faint silhouette of the tower itself. But what has that to do with Walnut Grove?

"Is it what you expected, Paul?" I suddenly ask, out of a time of silence.

"I'm not sure what I expected," he says. "I like it, I'll tell you that." He is quiet a moment. A bird calls—a mockingbird tuning up for the night. Scissortails with their snipping night noises come to roost in the Chinese elms. We see carlight, moving along a road a mile to the south of us.

"Look a-yonder," he says. I'm sure I never heard him say that before in his life. Can he be already learning to speak Walnut Grove's ancient language?

"Look a-yonder. It shore ain't no L.A. freeway."

"It shore ain't," I agree.

He laughs. We all laugh together.

"I really like it, Mother," he says then, serious as a little boy. "I can go to town if I want to, if I want the lights and noise; but they don't come to me."

I let myself sigh. It is a temptation to think I have wanted this a long time. It is a temptation to think I could have it and it would be enough. To sit on a porch in the deepening dusk, with slivers of birdsong and glimmers of light.

"Well," I say, "I shall stay the summer and then I may understand the appeal."

For a moment he doesn't seem to understand what I have told him. Then he swings his bare feet down from the porch rail and comes up behind me to grab my head in his hands, an

9

old way he has. "Hey Ma, that's great!" he cries. "Hey Grandma, did you know Mother's staying all summer?"

"Won't we have fun?" Mother says.

We go to bed early. Paul is a workman, and I am tired from my trip.

"You can sleep late if you want to," Mother says to me.

"Oh, I'll get up and help get Paul off to the field," I say. "I aim to be a country girl again."

"Mother, I believe you could," Paul says. He seems delighted to think it.

I sleep, as I always have done, in the room at the northwest corner of the house, under the Chinese elms. It is a little low-ceilinged room that used to be a shed room or a porch, opening off the kitchen, and the kitchen is still the only approach. There is an old, dark-varnished dresser where I put my folded clothes away—the dresses must hang in a curtained-off corner, where Mother always meant to build a closet. The books of my childhood still stand in the pine-board bookcase that Mother built and painted green for me when I was ten—I thrust among them the volumes of Renaissance poetry that I have brought to read this summer, for a change from the familiar works in my academic field and a possible inspiration for the kind of verse I think I'd like to write.

I turn down the white spread and sheets on the little white-painted iron bed with knobby curlicues, where I slept every night of my childhood. Sometimes in my teens I used to wonder what I could do about that old-fashioned bed. But then what difference did it make? Who would have known if I had a bedroom straight out of the *Ladies Home Journal*? I lived a singularly private life at Walnut Grove. Some day I suppose I shall try to tell Paul how it really was. And yet I wonder as I lie in my little white bed if we have already been closer than we ever shall be again. Nothing but natural, I suppose, nothing but normal if we have. Still I could tell him. Sometime I'll tell him.

But didn't he wait just a little too long to be glad I am staying the summer? Does he wish me away? Is there something wrong about Paul? If Mother is all right, with no problems, then perhaps the thing wrong is to do with Paul.

What thing? Must there be something wrong? I wonder if I have in fact grown so fearful I can't accept my mother's invitation to make a long summer visit without suspecting trouble.

Well, I shall stay the summer. If it yields only half a dozen nights on the porch with my mother and son, watching the twilight fade and the stars appear, feeling the great loneliness come down with the old peace we knew in my childhood, I shall have a bargain. And wherever stars look down, there is trouble.

II

The scissortails wake me early, as the elm tree by my window begins to fill with their sharp metallic cries. When I was a little girl I thought the sounds came from their busy scissoring tails. The tree is like an alarm clock gradually increasing in volume. I shall not go back to sleep. I wonder if I'll be waking at daylight every morning—in spite of what I said about getting Paul off today, this is not exactly my idea of a schoolteacher's summer vacation.

A rooster crows somewhere far-off sounding. I wonder where. Most people don't keep chickens these days, Mother has told me. She has a few hens, enough for the eggs she needs, but she hasn't had a rooster for years. A diesel locomotive hoots on the track a mile or so away. I am glad I remember the long lonesome whistle of the old steam trains in the night, but I like the sound of the diesel too. There is nowhere it could be going that I would want to go, but I listen with heart yearning to its call.

Bird voices rise everywhere, coming with the soft cool honeysuckle air through my two wide-open windows. This is the reason of course—the open windows are the reason—why I am having my morning serenade. We have birds in California, too. I even have a pleasant back yard, with a small fountain and a stone bench beside it, where I sit sometimes in the evenings. It is a walled garden, really, in a faintly Spanish style, matching the faintly Spanish, 1920ish house, which has been converted to a duplex and so thoroughly modernized that I live the year around in a sealed-up apartment heated and cooled as the season dictates. So I never feel fresh air on my face or hear bird noises when I lie in bed in the morning, and I don't even go into the garden as often as I thought I would when I moved there. It is such a tiny, closed-in place—the original back yard of the house was not large, and now it is cut in two by a stuccoed wall with an arched doorway in it, and a locked door. The key is in my keeping, and I used to wonder if opening the door would provide any effect of spaciousness. But no city garden could seem very spacious to a girl who grew up with a three-hundred-acre back yard; and besides, I suppose the neighbors want their privacy as much as I do mine.

The scissortail tree is quieting down, as gradually as it filled with noise. I can hear the flutter of wings as the birds begin to fly away on their morning's business. About the same time I hear a stir and bustle from Mother's bedroom, which is next to mine. I lie waiting to hear her patter across the kitchen to the bathroom, turn on the faucet, flush the toilet. The plumbing in my mother's house is rather primitive, but I can remember when we had none at all.

I am about to sit up on the side of the bed and consider joining the household when another outdoor sound arrests me. A single hoarse cry, it is repeated several times at intervals while I try to think what it is. I have heard it before, long ago—it is a strange sound. I think first of a dog—not Mother's old Spot, but a hound perhaps, a hound on a hunt sending notice of its prey. From a tree? For surely it comes from a bush or tree not far away. A strange and mythical hound, lost like Thoreau's long ago. No, it's a bird of course. It must be a bird. Yes, I know. I remember now. It must be over thirty years since I first heard it, and I never heard it more than two or three times in my life. But I know now. It's the raincrow.

I was twelve or thirteen years old. It was a Sunday in a rainy June, and we were all seated at dinner around the table in the kitchen: Mama, Mother, and I, and Hugh and Stanfield. In those days Hugh and Stanfield came for Sunday dinner one time a month—third Sunday, I think; it was an arrangement carefully worked out and followed. We were eating fried chicken and stacking the bones on the oilcloth by our plates (nobody—not my mother, not anybody, could ever fry chicken as good as Mama's was when she piled it up on her old chipped blue willow platter and set it in the middle of the table where we all could reach the pieces we wanted). On those Sundays there were at least two pulley bones so Stanfield and I wouldn't have to fight over them, though if Hugh would let him, he would grab them both.

We had good, pleasant, easy times on those Sundays. Stanfield and I fought, as boy and girl cousins near the same age must do, but often we joined the grown folks' conversation and sat as long as they did at the table, drinking iced tea as long as they did, and eating the sugar that settled in the depression at the bottom of Mama's big old heavy glass goblets. Perhaps we had already finished the meal and were just sitting there talking, eating sugar and drinking tea. We often did that.

At least I know we were at the table when the call of the raincrow came. I remember how everyone looked up and someone said, "What's that noise?" and at first no one remembered.

Then Hugh spoke with a suddenness and a kind of awed surprise. "Why it's a raincrow," he said.

13

"Oh, of course," Mama and Mother said, exasperated with themselves for not recalling.

You don't hear a raincrow very often in West Texas. They all agreed to that. They thought it had been at least ten years since they heard one—"More than that," Mother said. "I know Gail was a baby in my arms, and we'as all around the table, just like we are now."

"But what *is* a raincrow?" I demanded. That was what I wanted to know. Was it really a bird? A kind of crow? I had never heard the name before, and I considered myself something of an authority on birds. I had written a bird book (in a Blue Horse composition book) when I was ten, and I had a good bird egg collection. I had never heard of a bird called the raincrow or read the name in any book.

Nobody knew. "It's a sign of rain," Hugh said.

"We used to hear them pretty often," Mother said, "when I was a girl in East Texas. But I never heard of anyone that saw one. I don't know what it is."

Stanfield was already running out of the kitchen, and I jumped up and followed him. "Don't scare it!" I begged. We heard the cry one more time and thought it must have come from one of the elm trees, but we couldn't be sure which one. Stanfield ran about under the trees while I attempted a stealthier plan of watchful waiting. Neither was any good. We never heard a flutter of wings or saw a shadow move. We never heard the raincrow any more that summer, but I thought about it a lot. "What is it really saying?" I wondered. I remember I tried to write a poem about it and finally gave up, believing that only if I could interpret the bird's cry would I ever succeed. I wonder if I believe so still.

Drinking coffee in the kitchen while Mother fries eggs and bacon for Paul, I speak of the raincrow.

"Have you heard it before?" I wonder. "I mean in recent years."

She has heard it several times this spring and she thinks at least once or twice a summer for the past four or five years.

"Well, do you know what it really is?" I ask importunately, almost a child again, lost in mystery. "Not a crow, surely."

"No, I never see it," she says. "And I've looked, too. It always seems just a little farther away than I think it is, although I'm pretty sure it's in the elm trees sometimes."

"Do you remember that time Stanfield and I ran out to look for the raincrow, when we heard it during Sunday dinner?"

"Oh yes, I remember that time. I remember another time, too. In fact, I guess it was the only time up to then that I'd heard a raincrow in West Texas. It was me and Hugh run out to look that time, and I remember how mad Estelle got. She claimed it was because of me talking about believing in the sign. She said it was superstition and a sin—because of course our Church does believe that way about superstition. But she was jealous, was what it was. She was a jealous-hearted woman."

I can't remember ever hearing Mother talk that way about Hugh's wife. It embarrasses me, upsets me, and I hurriedly bring us back to speculations about the raincrow.

"Why do you suppose there would be such long periods of time when you didn't hear it?"

"I imagine they come in rainy times. After so many years of drouth in the fifties, I'm surprised we ever heard one again."

"Well, I'd like to know what it is," I say. "It can't be just a voice."

Paul comes in. He has been in the bathroom and is shaved, but still in his pajamas. "Why can't it be a voice?" he says, already wolfing his bacon and eggs. I have never seen him eat breakfast like this—the most I ever saw him eat before was two Pop Tarts.

"We're talking about the raincrow," I say.

Oh yes. His grandmother has told him about the raincrow. "I wish it would hush," he says, "till I get this plowing done."

15

Mother says, "I remember back in East Texas they used to say if you turned your shoes upside down when you went to bed it would make the raincrow stop crying. And I suppose keep the rain away."

"Well, I'll remember and try that," he says. He pays attention to his eating. I am having toast and orange juice; Mother is having what she calls a real breakfast, but not as much of one as Paul.

"What are your plans for the day, Mother?" Paul asks me.

"Just be lazy and help Grandma a little, I suppose. I don't seem to want any plans this summer if I can avoid them."

"We're fixing to pick beans," Mother says.

"I hope it won't rain anyway," Paul says.

"There's moisture in the air," Mother says, "but no clouds in the sky that I can see. I expect the raincrow works like these little houses where a little fair-weather person comes out when its dry and a little rain person comes out when there's a lot of humidity."

"You're smart, Gran." He kisses us both and hurries to dress and get to the field. "I'll see you at dinner," he says.

"Does he take his lunch?" I ask Mother.

"No, he means noon dinner, just like we always had," she says. "I think a workingman needs his big meal in the middle of the day."

The sun is hardly up over the chicken house when we go to the garden to gather Kentucky Wonders. Everything is wet with dew and the morning birds are still singing. We don't hear the raincrow though.

"I expect Paul scared it off, getting the tractor started," Mother says.

The sun is still not very high when we go to sit on the front porch and "fix the beans." Mother wants to get them on early

—she belongs to the old school that cooks vegetables all morning in plenty of water with a good-sized hunk of salt pork.

"Paul likes 'em that way," she says, "as long as he's got plenty of corn bread and butter."

He probably likes them better than any vegetables I ever cooked, being so careful to preserve the color and nutrients by using only a few drops of water and cooking only until done.

I love the front porch. It stretches across the front of the house like an old southern gallery. I seem to remember that Mama would sometimes call it the gallery. Mother keeps the floor planks painted to preserve them, but the exterior walls of the house have never been painted. They are like the weathered barn plank that city people pay any price for, to put on the walls of their dens. Now in the morning, screened by the honeysuckle from the rays of the sun, the walls are dark, but I know that when the sun strikes them they will turn luminous silvery gray.

There is a hummingbird after the scarlet sage by the gate, and orioles are flashing in a mesquite at the corner of the yard. In and out of the honeysuckle fly some brown birds with long curved bills, carrying sticks and straw, dropping as much on the porch as they leave in a crotch of the honeysuckle vine.

"Them silly cuckoos," Mother says. "They're so messy, I wish they wouldn't try to build there, but they won't ever give up. Their nest's been blowed down twice this year, when we've had clouds come up, but they just keep right on."

"Why, Mother," I say, "we never used to have cuckoos. Are you sure that's what they are?"

"Yes, I'm sure," she says. "I've got me a good bird book—a field guide to Texas birds. It's not like that little kid book with all the pretty pictures that I got you that time. You could find out all about bobolinks and robins, but I don't think there was more than one or two birds in it that we ever see around here."

"I don't think I knew there was such a thing as a cuckoo outside of English poetry," I say.

17

"I don't know about that, but these are cuckoos." Mother insists on it. "I've noticed them around here for several years now, and Hugh says he used to see them on the creeks once in a while—only he didn't know any name for 'em. Anyway, you'd be surprised the birds I see that we didn't use to. And varmints. I bet you don't remember coons and foxes being here either."

"Just coyotes," I say.

"Well, we've got coyotes and coons and foxes, too, now. I've caught 'em all in my hen house, different times."

Is it because the population in this area is dwindling as the farms grow larger? I don't know, and neither does Mother.

I keep sitting on the porch when she goes to put on her beans. She says she'll go see about the chicken water too. I'm sure there are a dozen household tasks that I could offer to do, but I feel lazy. I feel happy. I smell the flowers and hear the birds and watch a few fluffy clouds float across the soft sky. I try not to think of anything at all beyond what I can see and hear and smell from my rocking chair on the porch, but the thankful thought comes into my mind that I don't have to go and get down a book and prepare a dry lecture on preromantic poetry. I like the period—I am fond of the poetry—but, yes, it would be a dull lecture—thorough but dry. I know I give dull lectures. Once in a while I used to try to bring in stories showing my personal responses, the little pieces of myself that would go to make me the kind of teacher that brings everything to life. Makes it seem relevant. Whatever the current phrase may be. It was painful. I cannot give pieces of myself away to a roomful of strangers who do not especially want them anyway. I have even known myself to blush upon telling a story about Robert Burns's love life. And it is not (is it?) that I am so modest and old-fashioned about sex. It is simply the fear that I have told something that shouldn't have been told and thus made a fool of myself.

I do not have to go and prepare to tell anybody anything. To Mother and Paul, who do not usually appear to me as strangers, I may speak or not. They will not care. They may listen or not when I do. It doesn't matter. It almost seems to me that I can sit on this porch all summer and never need to speak to anyone. I hear a car coming down our road. I had almost forgotten how it is here—we used to know the sound of every car that passed our house, and guess if it would stop. But I don't know the cars of Walnut Grove nowadays, and probably they all sound alike. I can tell this one is slowing, and I feel my heart contract a little, for there is no time to run and hide. But then I see it is only the mail carrier, stopping at the box in front of the house. I look down and never know if he waves his hand as he drives off, the way old Eddie Porter used to do.

I shall go and get the mail in a little while, I suppose. But not yet. There might be a letter. It might even be for me. It might demand an answer. I do not want a letter from the world, nor do I wish to send one. Not yet. All I want is to sit on the porch, hearing from the birds, all summer long, perhaps even—

Do not speak it yet. There is a fantasy coming, and it can be dangerous to entertain fantasies unless they are warded off by a certain ritual long known to me. You have to be careful about the way fantasies sometimes come true. I do not wish this to be true, do not expect it; it would be a very foolish thing for me to attempt it. There. It is said. I do not know whether the gods believe me.

And what if I were to stay here always, in this house, with my mother and my son, the only persons in the world not strangers to me? And we would live as my mother and grandmother and I used to do, only better, because now the old community of Walnut Grove is gone and we would never be bothered by school or churches or old Mrs. Bailey, whose husband kept the store. All gone, and only the three of us here together. I would sleep in my little old room and on summer mornings be awakened by the birds. I would walk the old paths of my childhood—the mesquite pastures, the banks of the hackberry creeks. The winds and birds and insects would speak to me. And sometime I would follow the call of the raincrow, until at last I understood that cryptic cry, and then maybe— but this is fantastic, indeed! be careful!—I would write it down, what I knew, in words so few and spare that nothing foolish and surplus would be told. And I would call it poetry, and someone somewhere would read it and be something more than they had been before.

Before I learned better I used to send some poems off to magazines. One even was printed, years ago, in a thin little literary journal published by a college in the South. I never showed it to anyone, never even sent a copy to my mother. I meant to at first, and then I knew she wouldn't understand it, and then I knew it would be better if she didn't understand it. In the end I simply prayed that no one I knew would ever see the poem.

But here at Walnut Grove now, long empty days, and the words hoarded and counted, saved from foolish wasteful uses. . . .

Mother comes back, and I am rescued from absurdity.

"I'm still sitting here," I say. "I'm sorry to be so lazy."

"Set there," she says. "I want you to rest."

She has done most of the farm work here as long as I can remember, and I don't know when she ever rested. But she believes teaching involves some mysterious drain on the energies far more devastating than driving a tractor all day.

"The mail has come," I say. "I'll go and get it, to prove I can still put one foot in front of the other."

"I'll go," she says.

"No, I'd like to." She sits down, with a little secret sigh, in the rocking chair by mine. Of course she gets tired.

I bring the mail and put it in her lap. She has the newspaper and a farm magazine and two or three envelopes. "Junk," she says. She flips through the paper, stopping to look a minute at some pages, paying no attention to others. "I read the obituaries now," she says.

"And the funnies, too, I see."

"Like Mama," she says. "She never did get too old to read the funnies. And you know, she never got over thinking some day Marigold would come back and marry Uncle Bim."

"Or at least they would hear some word of her. It seems like hearing some word was one of her constant hopes. You remember all those years when Uncle Nezer used to talk about finding Rosabella."

" 'He'll hear some word some day,' she used to say. And sure enough one day he did."

I do not like to think, though, about Nezer and Rosabella. "Is it time to start the rest of the dinner?" I wonder.

"In a little bit," she says.

There is another car coming. I think it is slowing down.

She lifts her head, holds it a bit to one side like a listening quail. "That's Hugh," she says, a pleased affirmation.

I have seen Hugh now and then through the years, not every summer though. I have got over hating him, but I haven't got over remembering I once did. I know he understands how I feel, for he is a kind and forbearing man, but I can never think of much to say to him. Ours is one of those relationships where the usual topic of conversation is the past, the far past.

I get up and shake hands. It is hard to believe, but Hugh must be nearly seventy-five years old. He is tall and erect, sun-browned and twinkling-eyed as ever, although I know he has had at least one heart attack.

"How are you, Hugh?"

"I can't complain," he says. "You look better than you ever did in your life."

"She does, don't she?" Mother says. "I like her with a little more weight on her."

We all sit down. "And how do you find Walnut Grove?" Hugh asks, with his twinkle.

"Well, to tell the truth, Hugh," I say, guessing what he wants, "I don't believe you *could* find Walnut Grove."

He laughs heartily, but when he is done the twinkle has faded from his eyes. "Did you notice they've tore down the schoolhouse?" he asks.

"I never do come that way," I say. "But I believe Mother wrote me about it."

"Well, it's better so, better than standing there falling to ruin, with the caved-in roof and all the window lights broke out. But I hated to see it go—I remember how hard my daddy worked for that school, to get it consolidated I mean, get an accredited high school. And then later on we got the brick building, and didn't use it no more than five or six years."

"You'd think some use could have been found for it," I say.

"Well, I don't know what it would've been. I did think one time they might use it for one of them community centers, but the county's put them metal buildings up for that."

"Oh, does Walnut Grove have a community center?" I ask, not quite pleased. I prefer that nothing should be left of Walnut Grove.

"Folks here uses it," he says, "but I believe they call it the northeast county center—something like that. It's over on the highway."

"The schoolhouse might not have done very well for that anyhow," I say. "And didn't one of the Stanfields buy it?"

"Bob Stanfield. He made a bracero camp out of it for a few years there before everybody started using mechanical cotton pickers. For a while he said it would cost too much to have the building tore down, but he says now he just can't afford to own any land he can't raise cotton on."

"I've always been glad you and Stanfield got to graduate from Walnut Grove anyway," Mother says.

"Yeah, that was the last year of the school, wasn't it?" Hugh says. "Well, I voted against consolidating with Herley."

I am sure this is the first time since that graduation night that it has been mentioned among the three of us. And after all this time the thought of it changes my pulse rate. I suspect there is some reason why it is mentioned now, but I can't imagine what it is and I prefer to change the subject.

"Hugh, is there anything at all left that you could call Walnut Grove?" I ask him.

"Well, there's the switch on the railroad," he says. "They've got a sign there that says Walnut Grove."

"There's a sign on the highway that points to Walnut Grove, too," I say, "but I think it's a joke."

"Walnut Grove always was a joke, in a way," Hugh says.

"Yes," Mother says. "You remember how Earl never did quit going on at me about what I said the first time I saw it. He stopped over yonder where them two farm-to-market roads corner now, about where the land starts that long slant down to the railroad. He said 'There's Walnut Grove,' and I said, 'But where's the grove?' I never did see why he thought that was so funny. I didn't know what this country was like—where I come from we *had* groves."

"Anyway there was *something* to see then," Hugh says. "There was the depot and section houses down at the railroad, and Mr. Bailey's store and their house. I reckon that was before the gin burned, too, wasn't it?"

"Oh yes, the gin was there, and they still had two church houses then."

"Oh, Walnut Grove was quite a town once," he says. "I remember the townsite opening, when I was ten years old. I never had seen anything like that in my life. Come to think of it, I don't guess I've seen anything like it since."

"Mama always talked about the balloon ascension," I recall.

"Oh, gosh, yes," Hugh agrees. "That and horse races and soda pop all over the place. And you know, they had streets graded off and even concrete sidewalks along in front of some of the buildings."

"But no grove," I say.

"That's a funny thing, though," he says. "In the beginning, when we first come to settle here, there was a kind of a grove, right in front of where the schoolhouse was then—the old one-room school I started in. They told a story about an old woman that had walnut trees sent from back in Tennessee I think it was, and made the trustees name the school Walnut Grove, after the place where she come from."

"That was Nadine's great-grandmother," Mother says. "She was about the earliest settler."

We have all heard the story. I used to nearly cry when they would tell about the last living tree being cut down to make way for the sidewalk in front of the schoolhouse. At one time in my life that act appeared to me as a symbol of Walnut Grove values. I think I tried to write a poem about it.

"Some folks wanted to get a new name when the railroad come through and they'as fixing to build a town," Hugh says. "But others said Walnut Grove was just the name of the place and wasn't supposed to mean anything. Seems like my daddy was one that favored the change."

"I bet Papa did," Mother says. "Trees meant so much to him—I can guess what he felt like."

"He wouldn't have wanted to take their name in vain?" I suggest.

Mother draws in just a little. That is how I have always described to myself her reaction to certain words or intimations that she doesn't quite like. I have always known this; I remember Uncle Nezer's jokes were apt to bring about that reaction.

"He sure liked trees," Hugh agrees. "People thought he was crazy for putting out all these Chinese elms. Gosh, fifty years ago, that must've been. Some feller come through peddling these trees, said they was just the thing for this country: didn't take a lot of water, growed fast. Said there'd be shade in no time."

"Was there?" I ask.

"Oh yes. He told the truth, as far as he went. They got to be right popular trees—a good many planted a few of them. But then they turned out to be pretty sorry trees, too, coming up like weeds all over the place, but breaking up easy in the wind or ice. I swear, Laura, I don't know how you've kept these in as good shape as you have. I think everybody else that ever planted any got rid of 'em thirty years ago."

"I've worked to save 'em," Mother says. "You know I had the county agent out here to look at 'em several years ago. He was the one told me they're really Siberian elms."

"But now I tell you, Gail," says Hugh, "backing up a little to what you asked about Walnut Grove. The truth is, about all that's left to go by that name is the cemetery."

They haven't plowed it up to plant cotton yet? I am tempted to say that, but I don't. "I guess graveyards last the longest of anything about a community," is what I say.

"Well, that's right," he says. "But this is more than just a weedy old country graveyard. It's well kep' up, and folks keeps right on a-burying in it. You'd be surprised how many that moved off maybe twenty–thirty years ago will come back to Walnut Grove to bury."

"I want us to go to the cemetery, Gail," Mother says. "I don't know how long it's been since I took you to see our graves."

"Yes, all right," I say. "There'll be time for more things this year. Yes, I'd like to see the graves." I suppose I would. At least I am willing.

"Say, Gail, are you fixing to stay all summer?" Hugh takes it as a happy surprise.

"I've made arrangements so I can," I say.

"Got somebody to see about your things, have you?" he says.

I remember hearing that phrase in my childhood, when somebody (never our family) went off on a fishing trip some-where, or visiting relatives. Milk the cow and feed the chickens was what it meant then.

"Well, I don't have much to see about, Hugh. I get my mail and paper stopped, and there's a man comes once in a while to see about the yard."

"I guess folks don't neighbor out there in them California towns like they do here in the country."

Really for the first time it occurs to me that some people probably do ask their neighbors at least to keep an eye on their houses and gardens while they're gone. But of course I've never had time to get to know my neighbors. To be sure, the little old couple on the other side of the duplex always greet me when we meet, but that would hardly be sufficient grounds for asking favors of them.

"Oh, I don't know, Hugh," I say. "I think they do, in their fashion. Anyway, I'm fixed up to stay awhile."

"Well, that's fine," he says. "That's sure fine." I don't know why he would be quite so happy.

"Was that the clock striking?" Mother suddenly says.

Yes, it was: Mama's old clock that Mother still keeps on its shelf by the living room stove. I am still noticing every time it strikes, but I suppose I will soon be used to it again.

"Lordy mercy," she says. (That was one of Mama's expressions.) "It must be time to put the corn bread on. I don't know how long we've set here." She is getting up, but turns back to Hugh. "You'll stay and eat with us," she tells him, and he makes no objection.

He picks up the paper that Mother has left on the floor by her chair and prepares to read while the womenfolks go and get dinner ready.

"Hugh doesn't seem to change much," I say, as she stirs up the corn bread and I prepare to warm some slices of ham left from last night.

"He has always been a good man, Gail," she says with great solemnity.

At dinner Hugh tells what he came for.

"Stanfield and Tommye Jo want us all to have supper with

them Saturday night. Stanfield said tell you they'll make a freezer of cream, Gail, and y'all can lick the dasher."

Lick the dasher! Good Lord, how long since I've thought of that—of me and Stanfield, waiting by the tub on the porch for Mama to draw out the dasher, laden with heavy yellow buttery ice cream that we can scrape off with a spoon.

"Well, what do you think, Gail?" Mother is saying. I have the distinct impression that she is not surprised at this invitation, that it may even somehow be her doing. And she has always known I never meant to go to Stanfield's house, and never have, in more than twenty-five years. This is the first time I have ever suspected that she herself might care to go.

It is hard for me to think. There must be a way out though. "Paul may have plans," I say. "On Saturday night."

But he fails to get the message. "No plans," he says. "I'd like to go, it sounds like fun."

Fun? What does he know? Has he even met Stanfield? I have a good many questions to ask later on, but right now I can't think of any excuses. I may be sick—I may really be sick —on Saturday night.

III

"Mother, what on earth is going on?" We are alone together now, washing the dishes.

"Nothing is going on," she says softly, not looking at me.

"You knew it was coming, didn't you? Invitation to supper at Stanfield's."

"Hugh had talked to me about it," she admits.

"But why? After all these years—couldn't we just be left in peace? I don't want to see him any worse than I did the day after graduation, and I can't imagine why he would want to see me."

Mother speaks slowly, her attention on the dishes in the sink. "It wasn't—really—what he did, or you did. Hugh and I have talked about that. We're getting old. Yes"—at a suspicion that I am about to protest—"I'm getting old too. You're all we have—all that's left of the Messenger family, after we're gone."

"This wasn't Stanfield's idea, or Tommye Jo's?"

"They go along with it."

"Great reconciliation in the Messenger family."

"Isn't it time?"

Could it ever be? I don't try to answer her question.

"Mother," I say at last, "do you visit Stanfield's family?"

"Oh, I've been there once or twice," she says, "with Hugh. We're not what folks used to call *thick*, exactly."

"Has Paul been there too?"

"I don't know, maybe a few times. I haven't been myself for three or four months."

"But Paul knows them?"

"Oh yes, I think he knows them. Why?"

"I don't know. I just had an intuition when he said what he did."

"He has met Cyndi, I know."

That is Stanfield's only daughter, I remember. "Cindye with a 'ye'?" I ask.

"Cyndi with an 'i'—C-y-n-d-i. The 'ye' was for her mother's generation."

"Of course." I remember now that Tommye Jo changed from "Tommie" to "Tommye" during our junior year. "Tommye Jo is always up-to-date, I'm sure."

"Wait till you see."

Yes, I think I shall probably have to see. "Cyndi must be about the age of Paul," I say.

"Just about."

"And so what are you telling me?"

"Just that they've met."

"How would they?"

"How not? They're young kids, living in the same community."

"This isn't a real community—there's nowhere *for* them to meet. Besides—what does Cyndi do? She's out of high school, I guess. Does she live with her parents?"

"She's been in college this year—the last two years, I believe. I think Paul met her when he went to a chili supper at the community center and she was home for the weekend. Like I say—kids just naturally meet."

"So they met."

"He took her to the show once, that I know of. She's only been home from college for a few weeks."

"Does he know they're kin?"

"He seems to think it's kind of funny for them to be second cousins. I thought you'd call it third, myself, but he says second. Of course he guessed from her name she was kinfolks, and he asked me about it. Gail, I don't believe he even knew you had a cousin."

"He never knew it from me."

"I don't guess Cyndi knew who he was till they had that date and she told her folks who she was going with."

"And they let her?"

"Evidently. I have no idea what they may have said."

"Well, I don't suppose they're asking us to supper because they want to make a match."

"I'm sure they're not, and I don't imagine the kids have ever thought of such a thing. I think Cyndi has a boy friend at school that they're hoping she'll marry."

"She goes to the Church school, and he's in the Church?"

"Of course."

"Well—"

"Just come for my sake, Gail," she says.

"For your sake: I don't think I understand that."

"Don't try—just come."

I tell her I will go, unless I am sick. "Things like this really make me sick sometimes, Mother. I can't help it, they do."

"It will be all right," she says.

TWO

I have made up my mind to walk to the back of the pasture. "I believe I'll take something to eat," I tell Mother. She is pleased, for this is the sort of thing I used to like to do. She has cooked an old-fashioned breakfast and gives me leftover biscuit-and-sausage to take for my lunch.

"Like old times," she says. "Stay just as long as you want to." Then as I cross the back yard she calls after me, "Now be careful and don't step on a snake!"—echo from my far childhood. I will watch for the ominous movement in the grass and listen for the quick buzz of warning. I like our pasture, but it isn't paradise.

We have not discussed the invitation to Stanfield's any more. Perhaps I shall go—I don't know. But today I don't want to puzzle over Mother's importunateness or the extent of Paul's interest in Cyndi. This is one of the reasons I came for the summer at Walnut Grove—our pasture; one of the reasons I allow myself (though I know it is foolish) the fantasy about coming here to live.

The Messenger place, to my mind, is better if less prosperous than most of the Walnut Grove farms. It is at the edge of the divide, and about half of it is too rugged for cultivation. Mother has always run a few cows in that part, and Paul tells me he is hoping to improve the herd. No doubt he remembers the walks we used to take there when he was a little boy coming with me to Grandma's place. But he sees the land now with the eyes of a farmer.

Cow trails that lead me forth on my pasture walk slope gently down through summer-brown grass and scattered mesquite to the head of a shallow draw where the grass (in a rainy season) stays green all summer long. On any day after school I might come this far. On many a summer morning I was led here, to dream beneath the twisted branches of an uncommonly ancient mesquite tree, as I gazed at the sky through the delicate tracery of its slender leaves.

But one experience in particular—one awakening—comes back to me now. I cast myself down on the soft silky grass and embrace it, rest my cheek on it, as I call back a morning in April, fresh with the smells and sounds of spring. Nadine Carlile was with me—Nadine, a person of importance in my life, my mother's only friend outside the family. I remember when she came back into our lives.

We rarely had visitors. Mother and Mama didn't pay visits themselves. "It's just our way," Mama said. Whenever we heard a car slow down, as if turning in at our house, one of us would always run to look out the living room window. Usually the caller would be Hugh, but in those days I think of now it could have been Uncle Nezer Kelso, Mama's brother, who lived by himself in a little house on our place and helped with the work of the farm. The house—built for my mother and father when they married—was just down the road, and usually Uncle Nezer walked up through the pasture and in at our back door, but he might be stopping by on his way from town or the Walnut Grove store. If it wasn't Hugh or Nezer, it was usually a stranger, and we seemed to do a good bit of running about the house, consulting with each other. We would peer through the thin curtains as we tried to guess the stranger's business: a "peddler," as we called all salesmen, some candidate canvassing, or—if they carried a portable phonograph—"them Jehovah's Witnesses."

31

The day Nadine came was a Sunday—not one of Hugh and Stanfield's days—and we were alone, eating popcorn by the living room stove. It was March 1941, not long after my tenth birthday, and although it had seemed like spring only a few days before, so that Mother and I were able to go for my traditional birthday picnic under the big mesquite, this day was blustery, with a fierce wind bringing little flurries of dry, sugary snow. Snuggled up on a pallet with my popcorn and book, I wasn't missing spring at all but wishing for enough snow to keep the school buses from running next day. Among the sounds of the sweeping wind, the purring coal fire, and Sunday afternoon music on the radio, no one heard a car on the road until Mama saw it turn in.

"Somebody's coming," she announced with mild astonishment.

We jumped up as if threatened and hurried to huddle together by the window.

"I don't know that car," Mama said. "I can't think who would come in this weather."

It was a shabby, rattling car. "About a '34 Ford," Mother said. "We don't know anybody that drives a car like that."

There was a woman getting out of the car. With her head tied up in a square of plaid wool and her body enveloped in a big loose coat, she was unrecognizable, even to Mother and Mama, who had known her well. As she came into the yard, opening and closing the gate, straining against the wind, a flurry of snow screened her so that when she knocked at the door they still had no idea who she was.

Mother went hesitantly and opened the door. "Nadine!" she exclaimed, and stood as though amazed, letting the cold blow in.

"Can I come in, Laura?" the visitor asked, waiting outside the screen door.

"Oh. Yes. The screen's fastened." Mother fumbled with the hook.

Nadine is a little younger than Mother. She was in her late twenties and to me then very beautiful. She was removing her scarf as she came in, letting her thick dark curly hair spring free, and then she flung off her coat, revealing a girlish figure in a pink sweater and a plaid wool skirt.

"Gosh it's cold! That wind!" she said, hurrying to hold her hands toward the heat of the stove for only a moment before, rushing to where Mama sat, she bent to kiss her cheek, saying, "Oh Mrs. Messenger, you look so good, I'm so glad to see you." She seemed to move about everywhere, filling the room with some excitement I wanted to respond to but didn't understand.

I stood up. "This is Laura Gail!" she cried. "You're so big!"

"Gail, do you remember Nadine?" Mother said.

I shook my head and stayed behind the stove. I knew I used to see her when I was three years old, but I didn't remember her. She had just come back, divorced, to Walnut Grove, and everyone wondered what her grandma would say. That was really all I knew about Nadine.

"Oh, you like to read," Nadine said suddenly, and picked up my book from the quilt on the floor. It was *Pollyanna*, a recent birthday gift; I was on my third reading of it. "I have ten books," I decided to tell her.

"That's really nice," she said. "I have some books at home from when I was a little girl. I'll have to hunt them up and we'll see if you'd like to read them."

"Gail would like that," Mother said for me. "She don't get many books."

"Haven't you got a library at school?" Nadine asked.

"Not for my grade," I said. "Just for high school." I had a grudge against the school about that; it took away my shyness for a moment.

"Oh, it was the same when I went to Walnut Grove school," Nadine said. "And not many books for high school, either."

"Set down," Mother said, "and tell us about yourself."

Nadine sat down, then got up and went to her purse—which

she had flung, with her coat, on an empty rocking chair. She took out a packet of cigarettes, drew Hugh's smoking stand near a wicker rocking chair, lit the cigarette with a match from the cat-face holder on the wall behind the stove, then said, "Oh, do you mind if I smoke?"

Mother and Mama shook their heads. I stared. I had never seen a woman smoke before.

"I guess I picked up some bad habits in the big city," Nadine said.

"You worked in Fort Worth," Mama said.

"I did when I first left Walnut Grove," Nadine said, "and then you know I married and we moved to California."

"Well, you've got the brogue," Mother said.

"That's what everyone says," she said.

California accounted for it, of course. I should have known, for I had known one or two California kids at school, but I had been associating the lilting rhythm of her sentences, the vivacity of her voice, with the energy and youthful good looks that made her so attractive to me.

"Are you going back?" Mother asked.

"I don't know. I like California—or I think I would if I was married to a decent man. I couldn't take the way I was having to live any longer, and when I got out all I wanted to do was get home to Walnut Grove. But I'm not sure the folks are very glad to see me. You can guess what Grandma thinks. She always seemed to think a waitress was about the same as a fallen woman"—she looked around swiftly, as if embarrassed to use the phrase—"and now a *divorced* waitress. But Mama and Daddy say I can stay at home as long as I behave myself. Lord, I don't know what else I'd *do* at Walnut Grove—not that I want to." She looked around again, fearing she had scandalized Mama, I supposed.

"But you do want to marry again," Mama said.

"Oh, I do. Maybe I oughtn't to—Grandma says the Bible allows one mistake, and that's all. Divorce itself is not a sin, she says, if it's on what she calls biblical grounds. It's bad, but it's not a sin. It's remarrying that makes it—well, you know, breaking the Commandment." She seemed embarrassed again, a condition I thought must be uncommon in Nadine. "But nobody believes that any more. I want to be married, only not to a man that thinks he's got to make a show of his life, with a long string of different leading ladies. I need a nice, kind, steady sort of a man—oh, I could settle down at Walnut Grove or anywhere with him."

She took another cigarette from her purse and lit it from the one she was finishing. I had never seen anyone do that before. She inhaled deeply and blew out white smoke. For perhaps a minute, we all watched her.

"Do you know what I want?" Nadine asked suddenly. "I want to know where Buck is."

Buck was Uncle Nezer's son. He used to come and stay for a little while at Walnut Grove and then go off again, hunting a job.

"He's in the Army," Mother said. "I don't know where they've sent him."

"Not married?"

"No, he's never married."

"Oh, thank God," Nadine breathed out with the smoke from her cigarette. "Laura, I want his address."

"Do we have it, Mama?" Mother asked.

"No, but I guess Nezer does," Mama said.

"All the time I was thinking about Walnut Grove," Nadine said, "I kept hoping he was here. If only I'd come back sooner —I think I could have stopped him."

"From joining the Army?" Mama asked.

"Yes. I wish he hadn't done that."

"Hugh says we'll be in the war anyway," Mother said, "and all the boys will be drafted."

"At his age, he could have kept out."

"He wouldn't want to."

"If he had a wife he might."

"You couldn't change him," Mama said. "He'll do what he'll do."

"Get his address for me," Nadine said.

"You could get it from Uncle Nezer," Mother said.

"I'd feel funny asking his daddy," Nadine said. "I'll come back in a day or two and maybe you'll have a chance to get it."

"Come and eat dinner with us and stay all day," Mama said.

I was surprised—we didn't have that kind of company very often.

"I'll be plowing as soon as the weather's fit," Mother said. "But you come. I'll be home to eat dinner, and Mama will be glad of your company for as long as you can stay." Something about what Mother said, or the way she said it, sounded unduly formal.

I wished I could be there when she came.

"Why, did you especially like her?" Mother asked when I told her that, after Nadine was gone.

"She talked to me, but not too much," I said. "She left me alone to read my book. I like the way she talks, too. I like to listen to her."

"I thought you'as buried in that book," Mother said.

"I was," I said, "but I listened some. Did she use to go with Buck?"

"They went together a little," Mother said. "When your daddy was alive, all four of us went around together some. But then Buck left, and stayed gone a long time, and Nadine got restless at Walnut Grove. She wanted some other kind of life. So she left, and met this man—his name was Raymond Benedict, a kind of a handsome man, in a movie-star sort of way; I saw him once."

"I thought her name was Nadine Carlile," I said.

"It's Benedict," Mother said. "Or maybe she took her name back, I don't know."

I never did know. We always called her Nadine Carlile, even

after she married Buck. They have a way of keeping to a woman's maiden name at Walnut Grove.

Nadine came fairly often to visit. One Saturday morning, several weeks after our first meeting, she came asking for me. "It's such a pretty day," she said. "I thought we'd go to the creek."

I had been wanting to go, for there had been rain in the past week and I knew the creeks still held water and pastures were green and blooming; but in those days Mother often didn't like the idea of my going all the way to the back of the pasture by myself.

"Can I?" I asked Mama eagerly. (Mother was already in the field plowing.)

"Well, put your bonnet on," said Mama. In summer or spring she said that, whenever I left the house. I took it off as soon as I was out of sight.

As we started off, Nadine called back, "Oh, by the way, don't worry if we're not back by noon. I've got a bite of lunch in my pocket."

She patted the big patch pockets of her light corduroy jacket, then stopped and gave me a big hug. "Oh we'll have a grand time," she said.

We started off slowly, down my familiar trail. The sky was soft April blue, with fleecy, drifting clouds. "It looks like a baby blanket," Nadine said.

I hadn't seen many baby blankets and would never have thought of the comparison, but it struck me as beautifully apt.

The whole world was soft and lovely that day. The mesquite trees had new leaves, limp and lovely, the softest, tenderest yellow-green.

"Do you like mesquite leaves?" I asked, wanting to make some striking statement too, not knowing quite how. "I used to have a Crayola that color."

"I love them this way," Nadine said, "when they're so new

37

and tender. It always makes me want to snatch off big handfuls and squeeze them."

"Me too!" I cried. "I do that—or at least I used to," I added, suddenly seeing it as a very childish thing to do.

"Well, when we're very little we think we can have it," Nadine said; "the thing that makes them so pretty. Then we know we can't, and it hurts because we think there must be something we can do about it, and there never is."

The hillside we had reached then, the one sloping gently to the head of the draw, was covered with a leafy green plant blooming with flowers of red-violet.

"I'd almost forgotten filaree," Nadine said.

"Mother says it's good grazing," I said. "I always used to want to pick all the flowers before the cows ate them. But they're not pretty when you pick them off and carry them home. They wilt so quick."

"No, there's no way of having it," Nadine said.

Most of the pasture's green came from weeds like the filaree, but part of it was from different kinds of grasses. Under this big old mesquite tree then veiled in chartreuse, the grass grew thick and tenderly soft, almost as tender as the drooping leaves of the tree.

Nadine stood still a moment in the grass, and I watched, wondering, while she thrust her hands in her pockets and gazed at the sky. "It's too early to eat," I thought. But Nadine wasn't taking anything out of her pockets. Suddenly she drew out her empty hands and flung out her arms, then cast herself down among the soft grass.

"Oh, world!" she cried, she almost moaned. "I cannot hold thee close enough!"

Understanding her in a way, for I had often laid myself down that way beneath the sky, still I felt startled at this behavior in a grownup.

Nadine turned over and lay on her back, looking up through the pale leaves and dark branches. I lay beside her.

"That was a poem, Gail," she said. "Did you ever hear it?"

"No," I said.

"No," Nadine said, "they don't say that one much in grammar school, I guess. Would you like to hear it all?"

I said I would, and Nadine recited it. Although it seemed to be about fall instead of spring, it sounded beautiful and full of meaning as birdsong.

"That's one way of having it, a little bit," Nadine said.

"Having it?"

"Making it part of you, in a way, not letting it go. Beauty, I guess, is what I mean; I can't think of any other word for it."

I had sometimes tried to write poems (they were secrets, from everybody, in a Blue Horse composition book kept in a box under my bed). For the first time, I guessed at a reason for them.

But Nadine abruptly (in a way grownups have, I knew, when they have carelessly said almost too much) jumped up and began striding briskly along the gently sloping bank. "Let's get to the very back of the pasture before we eat," she said.

Now in June the pasture is different from what it was that April day. The mesquite leaves are firmer, deepened to a pure apple green. The flowers are gaudier—red Indian blanket, a thick deep-yellow odorous flower that Mama always called tallow weed. There are still some algerita berries; I pluck one or two from among their prickly leaves. A mockingbird flies from a clump of chaparral, and I go almost automatically to discover its nest, admire its brown-speckled green eggs. I used to count a pasture walk in summer lost unless I could find a bird nest or two.

Beyond the first draw, I come near the north field as I follow my accustomed path. The tractor is halfway across the field, coming my way. I wait and have a word with Paul, who stops at the end of the row and leaves the tractor to come and stand near me, wiping the sweat from his brow as he takes off his cap.

"I won't be home for dinner," I tell him. "I'm off for the back of the pasture, with biscuit and sausage in my pocket."

"The old Snake Den," he says, smiling. I used to take him there.

"Have you been to it?" I ask him.

"Oh, sure. Read all the old initials, you know. Gosh, they used to seem ancient as Indian petroglyphs to me when I was a child."

"I don't guess you do much aimless walking now, though."

"Not much, and I don't especially miss it. You know I really like to plow, just like I thought I would. I even like the dirt in my face."

"Well, it's your work, and I mustn't keep you," I say. "I'll see you tonight."

"Have fun," he says, and climbs on the big machine to plow away from me. I can hardly believe those muscles playing under the thin knit shirt.

As I walk on I am thinking of one of those times when I was trying to make him see what farming really is.

"Yes, farming is like the furniture business," he admitted. "I remember my grandfather actually caressing a chair. He loved good wood and clean lines—his delight was really in finding the right person for that chair—bringing the chair and the person into some kind of partnership. Dad laughed at him, I know —his way is something else. But I remember Granddad's way, and I don't believe any work is worth doing unless you can feel like that about it. Listen, Mother: food and fiber! Aren't those eloquent words? Really with my own hands, my own caressing hands, to coax into being those two basic needs of every person in the world. Isn't it the greatest possible communion?"

He wouldn't talk to me that way now, of course. I don't suppose he needs to.

Past the field, the landscape changes. This is where the

Breaks begin. Low rocky hills appear, and the canyon between them, which we always called the creek, is rocky, too. China trees and hackberry grow on its banks and now and then a little bunch of wild plum. The birds are different. We always saw cardinals down here on the creek but never had them around the house. I wonder if Mother does now.

I step along the rocks that border the stream bed here, staying just out of the reddish-brown water. I could slip and fall in —in the past, I have done so—but I feel fairly sure-footed in my crepe-soled oxfords. Now I reach a bend in the creek where the bank is high and gravelly, colored a peculiar yellow ocher. This is a treasure-trove of fossils, and I stop to pick up a handful of little curling shells. When I was a young child I used to wonder about those shells and how they came there, but when I asked Mother and Mama they said they were just funny-shaped rocks.

Then in sixth-grade geography came a marvelous revelation. We had an unusual sort of teacher that year—a young man (imagine a man teaching in grammar school, everyone said). Mr. Thornhill was a veteran, wounded and discharged already in that first or second year of war, and the community welcomed him with sympathy and curiosity. Qualified teachers were scarce everywhere, and he could easily have gone to a much better school. I heard him say once he wanted to find himself, but I never knew why he thought that self could be discovered at Walnut Grove.

Kids liked Mr. Thornhill because it was so easy to get him off the subject. He often forgot to assign any lesson at all, and in subjects like history and geography he would just mention some topic in the textbook and then start talking about a hundred things not in the book. (As I always read all my textbooks whether they were assigned or not, I was onto Mr. Thornhill better than most of my classmates were.) One day he told about dinosaur bones, which he said he had seen in a great museum in New York. We knew about dinosaurs and more or less accepted them but had never guessed they bore any relationship to any other beings in the world. That day, in trying to explain their significance, Mr. Thornhill let drop the word *Evolution.*

At first everybody laughed. We all knew what Evolution meant: people descended from monkeys. We didn't know anybody took that joke seriously. Mr. Thornhill turned a little pale, as he did sometimes—or so we imagined—when his war wound pained him. Then he began to tell an earnest, impassioned tale, beginning with one-celled animals swimming in prehistoric seas, sketching this story of life through the time of the great dinosaurs—they were *real*, then, I marveled—and on through the immediate ancestors of man. He told how the record of fossils in the rocks had revealed this wonderful story—how we were lucky enough to be living in an area where we could find the kind of evidence he spoke of along ditches and creek banks. "No," he cried, "man did not descend from monkeys. And if you think it belittles God to believe He evolved His finest creation through this plan of almost incomprehensible magnitude, instead of mumbo jumbo, like a stage magician, turning a handful of dust into a human being, then I am sorry for your pitiful deprivation."

He said far too much, I know now, even considering the words he used that went over the heads of most of his class—or perhaps because he did. The whole school—teachers as well as pupils—was buzzing by the end of the day, but I wasn't much aware of this reaction. I was thinking all the time of my yellow bank and what I knew now of the little shells and the other unexplained shapes and patterns in the rocks that I found there. The next day was Saturday. I couldn't wait to get to them.

At recess I talked to Stanfield. We didn't talk to each other much at school: he was almost a year older than I, though in the same grade, and still at the age where being a boy made him almost too superior to recognize my existence in public.

But I wanted so much to ask what he thought of the shell bank on our creek that I risked being snubbed. He was excited, too, enough to stand talking on the playground for a minute or two.

"Listen," he said, "me and Daddy's coming over there tomorrow morning. Let's me and you go down there and see what we can find."

We took a shovel and bucket. "We're going fossil hunting," we told our parents. I don't think they paid any attention to what we said—Hugh just told Stanfield not to be gone over two hours. In the short time we had, we collected half a bucket full of objects we took to be fossils—shell shapes, cylinders, spirals, all bearing signs, so we thought, of having lived in the old sea that once covered this land.

We were late getting back to the house, and Hugh was ready to go, so we didn't have time to divide the fossils. Stanfield agreed to get his part the next day, which was a Sunday when he and his father were due at our house for dinner. (Stanfield's mother did not come to our house, and in those days I never wondered why.) That afternoon I spread them all out on a bench in the back yard and spent a long time trying to classify them, guessing what they had been when they swam in our sea. Excitedly, at noon dinner, I told Mr. Thornhill's story to Mother and Mama, and begged them to come and look at what we had found. Mama did come and look, and I think she was interested, though all she did was shake her head and say, several times, "Well, I declare." Mother scarcely looked at the collection. She turned away from my excitement with slightly pursed mouth and a stiffening of her body—the drawing in that has been a signal to me all my life of a disapproval which I often fail to understand.

When Hugh and Stanfield arrived for dinner next day, I knew something had happened. It was time to sit down to the table already, for Stanfield had to go to Church with his mother before they could come, and nobody said much for a while, through the first hungry eating.

Finally Hugh said, "Has Gail told you what that feller Thornhill's been teaching at school?"

"A little," Mother said. "I'm not sure I understand it very well."

Stanfield looked up. "Brother Jeffcoat preached against him," he said. "He called him an atheist, whatever that is."

"I guess it's somebody that don't believe the Bible," Mother said.

I had looked up the word. "An atheist is a person that doesn't believe in God," I said. "Mr. Thornhill believes in God, he said so."

"If he don't believe the Bible, he don't believe in God," Mother said. "I don't know what you think you're talking about."

"Well, the way I see it," Hugh said, "if he's teaching this evolution business he don't believe the Bible. I don't hold with a lot of beliefs in that Church, but I don't know but what I might come around to agreeing with Brother Jeffcoat this time."

"Brother Jeffcoat says Mr. Thornhill has got to be fired," Stanfield said. "He said this is the devil's work at Walnut Grove, and has got to be stopped and stopped fast."

"I hate Brother Jeffcoat," I said.

"Gail!" Mother said.

"Well, ain't no use in going on about it," Mama said. "We can't fire the poor man."

We talked about other things. After dinner, I offered to divide the fossils with Stanfield.

"I don't think Mother would want me to bring them home," he said.

"I don't see why not," I said. "If they're not fossils, they're *something*, and they've been here all the time."

"Brother Jeffcoat said you could find things like Mr. Thornhill talked about, all right, but you didn't know but what the devil put 'em there to confuse people about the works of God."

"Oh, that's silly," I said.

"It's not," Stanfield said. "The devil can do anything."

"Couldn't God keep him from it?"

"Of course He could, He just don't want to."

"That's silly."

We had a long argument about God and the devil and fossils and Creation, consisting mostly of phrases like "That's silly" or "That's not so." And Stanfield left me our whole collection of fossils.

"I want to take these tomorrow and show Mr. Thornhill," I told Mother that night.

Mother drew in. "I wouldn't do that," she said.

"But he's so interested," I said. "Maybe he could come and look at the creek bank where we found them."

"No," she said, "we won't have anything to do with him. He's fixing to get in bad trouble."

"Just because that old preacher preached against him?"

"That's part of it," she said.

"I hate that Church," I said. "I'm glad we don't go."

"Hush," Mother said.

"Is that why we don't?" I asked. "Because they preach such silly things?"

"I told you a long time ago I believe in the Church teachings," Mother said. "It was just a question of what they call interpretation that made me stop going to worship. I'm as good a Christian as I ever was, and I aim for you to be. Now I don't want to hear another word about that Mr. Thornhill."

All the churches in the Walnut Grove school district preached against Mr. Thornhill that Sunday, I soon learned the next day at school. I never heard of anyone who came to his defense, though in my bed at night I imagined how I would go—one lone little powerless girl—and beg on my knees to the school board. He left at the end of that week, and for the rest of that term our teacher was an old lady who had an emergency teaching certificate based on her attendance at a summer normal school some forty years before. I have always had a feeling that someday I might encounter Mr. Thornhill again; he must be teaching somewhere, opening minds as he opened ours —or mine, at least—at Walnut Grove, and not being punished for it. At least I hope this may be so.

I am glad to have been reminded of him by the yellow fossil bank at the bend in the creek.

Just around the bend a little tributary comes in, the creek deepens and widens, and rocks reassert themselves. The stream bed is strewn with rocks, and on my left the bank is a low sandstone cliff, hollowed out so deep it is almost a cave. Above it an outcropping of sandstone forms a flat pavement behind which a low hill rises. On the opposite bank is a thicket of plum.

This is my destination, the back of the pasture. Across the creek stretches the Circle K fence, barbed wire weighted down with heavy stones, the border between cotton farms and ranch country. Beyond it is No Trespassing—wild bulls, perhaps, men riding with guns to keep out invaders. I never saw wild bulls or armed men there, but in my childhood I believed in them and I always stop at the fence.

We used to call this place the Snake Den. It was said to be a place where rattlers hibernated in the winter and crawled thick as caterpillars in the spring. Actually I never saw a rattlesnake there, but I believed in them with considerably more reason than I ever had to accept the scary stories about the Circle K. I watch carefully as I step from rock to rock.

One of my earliest memories—my earliest, I believe—is of this place. Mother and Mama had come together, having driven around the edge of the field to a spot perhaps a quarter of a mile from here, as close as they could drive to the plum thicket. I think I walked part of the way here but was mostly carried, the women taking turns, until at last I was set down in the creek bed, with a collection of pretty colored pebbles to play with and an injunction to stay right there, not to move, until Mother came for me. They took their buckets up on the bank where the plum bushes grew, bright with red fruit. Mother brought me one to taste of right away, so I would know how sour it was and not be tempted to run away into the plum thicket, always a likely place for rattlesnakes. She was wise about that, but she forgot how hot and bare the creek bed was. She didn't see how cool and deep a shade, how cozy and protective a little hollow, there was awaiting me under the rock cliff. I tired of my pebbles and crept there, back against the rock, in deep shadow. I was sleepy from the sun and tired from the unaccustomed rough walking I had done along the way. Soon I took off my little sunbonnet, made a pillow of it, and curled up in a ball and went to sleep.

"Gail! Laura Gail!" my mother was presently screaming— frightened and frightening screams. I could not think what was wrong, and I began to cry. I sat up and cried and cried in my cozy place under the rock, until at last Mother heard me and came. She came running and snatched me up. She was crying herself and scolding at the same time. "I told you not to move," she said, "I told you not to move. Don't you ever get back under that rock any more—it's full of rattlesnakes in there."

I would not dream now of taking shelter from the sun under that overhang of rock. I feel a slight shiver as I think of the snakes that must await me there, should I be so foolish. And that was over forty years ago, and I have never seen a snake there yet.

I climb up the bank, in an open sunny spot where I can see that only a green lizard lurks, onto the flat pavement of rock. This soft sandstone is always a temptation to wanderers who want to leave some record of their presence, and many have carved their initials here. I know where my father's are, carved with the date when he was thirteen years old, and my father's and mother's together, with a date sometime in the first year of their marriage. I used to scratch my name or initials in the rock almost every time I came here, but as I never had any better tool than a piece of sharp flint picked up in the creek, the signs I left have mostly worn away. But here is a G.M., carved big and deep, in the same style as an S.M. nearby. They are circled together and dated 1943. Stanfield carved them of course, with the big bone-handled pocket knife he always carried. I remember that knife.

I don't quite remember, though, an occasion when he circled our initials together. It doesn't seem like him, somehow. I suppose I have seen them in fairly recent years, for I came once or twice bringing Paul when he was a little boy, but then my attention was on him and the questions he was always asking. Now I wonder. Of course Stanfield might have been alone—it need not have been an occasion I would remember; but that seems unlikely. In fact, I am almost certain he never walked alone to the back of our pasture. Stanfield likes company. We sat here together, I suppose, as we did many times, gazing across the hazy low hills that follow our creek as it flows through the Circle K ranch land. I sit as I know we often used to do, legs folded under me, and look at the hills. They are not hazy today. I wonder why I thought of them that way. Sometimes, especially in autumn, their outlines are softened and the whole landscape seems obscured by the lightest of smoke. Sometimes in summer mirage lifts them, making of them shimmering mountains. But I think of them now in autumn haze. I sit and let myself drift in it, until gradually the time comes back to me.

It was September or October, I think. After Sunday dinner, having been trapped in school all week, we wanted to get out of the house. We didn't plan to go far, or I would have changed my new skirt for an old pair of slacks. But I suppose the loveliness of autumn lured us: I still remember chinaberries hanging like amber beads against the gauzy sky.

I soon wished I'd changed clothes, for I scratched my legs as we went through some bushes or dried weeds into the creek bed. But there was no going back then: the creek led us on, and after a while we found ourselves at the Snake Den. We sat, legs folded, and in a little bit Stanfield took out his knife and began idly carving. I watched a hawk and presently, to see it better, lay down on my back across the clean smooth rock, liking the way the warmth of it crept through my body. The hawk wheeled ever higher and farther over the Circle K until it was out of sight in the mild blue.

"Look," Stanfield said.

I turned over on my side and saw what he had cut into the rock. "Good," I said, or something like that. They were deeper than we had ever cut our initials before.

He put his knife back in his pocket and then, still somehow part of the same motion, let the hand that had held it (his hot and sweaty hand) rest on the calf of my leg. While I still pondered the meaning of my cousin's strange action, he let the hand move upward, past my knee, up under my plaid gingham skirt.

I rolled away from him and sat up. I didn't know why, exactly. That is, I knew exactly that I didn't want Stanfield's hand under my skirt, but I didn't know why he would want to put it there. He didn't try to put it back, or say anything about what he had done. For a little while I felt strange and unsettled—I know I thought of the time when my mother had surprised and frightened me as I slept so innocently among her imagined snakes. I knew that, both times, I had received a warning, but I wasn't sure what it was. Soon though we got up and started home, walking slowly and naturally, as we had done on the way to the Snake Den. When we got there Hugh was ready to go and they scolded us for staying away so long.

I think it crossed my mind that I might ask Mother about what Stanfield did. But without understanding why, I knew it was something I never would mention to her. I was probably the only twelve-year-old girl at Walnut Grove school who wouldn't know why a boy tried to put his hand under her skirt. Perhaps I guessed, perhaps I didn't. I honestly don't know now. What I do know is that I put the incident almost immediately out of my mind. Oh, I might have thought of it once in a while for six months or so, but by the time of my graduation from high school I had forgotten it completely. I could almost swear that today is the first time I have thought of it in more than thirty years. I am not sorry I have remembered, but I am a little sorry to think why it has been buried in my unconscious all this time.

It is midafternoon when I reach home, and I realize I haven't eaten my biscuit and sausage. And I realize I am hungry. "Come sit on the porch with me," I say to Mother, "while I eat my lunch."

She wants to give me something better, since I haven't eaten for so long and must be starving, but I tell her if I had been starving I would have eaten. I make myself a cup of coffee though.

Then we sit together while I have my lunch.

"How come you not to eat?" she asks.

"I don't know," I say. "I was remembering things. Do you remember the time you nearly scared me out of my wits at the Snake Den? I wouldn't go back there for years."

"My, I was silly," she says complacently.

What would Mother say if she knew I was remembering the time Stanfield stuck his hand up my skirt? I will never know, for it is as impossible to speak of such matters to Mother now as it was when I was ten or twelve years old.

Once when I was about sixteen I tried in an offhand way to ask Mother if she didn't think it was about time she told me about the birds and the bees.

"I expect you've heard it all from the kids at school long ago," she said, drawing in.

I hadn't. I never talked to anybody about sex. Nobody ever

talked to me about sex. Sometimes when I heard allusions to something that brought snickers I snickered too and pretended to know the rules of that game.

"You'll learn when you need to," Mother said. I suppose I did.

THREE

I find myself able to go to Stanfield's. Mother and Paul are pleased with me, and perhaps for that reason I feel well, keep free of my anticipated headache. I dread going still, as though to a house of strangers (better no doubt if it were), but I can go.

Paul drives Mother's LTD (a favorite car with the medium-prosperous farmers of the community). He knows the roads like a native, and when Mother says "Let's go by Walnut Grove" he takes a left turn instead of continuing on a paved road that would take us to Stanfield's in a little less time. Now we are in the heart of the divide—the flat black land—and for miles around it seems there is nothing but plowed earth, open to the cloudless, luminous sky.

"You know what I miss most?" I say. "The pastures people used to have around their houses."

"People used to keep milk cows," Mother says. "Nobody does that any more. They make more money raising cotton than pasture for cows—and like Hugh says, it's easier just to go to town and get a box of milk."

Paul laughs. "Is that what he calls it? I like that."

"You like Hugh?" I ask Paul.

"Sure I like him. He has a good time—gets a lot out of life."

"Here's Walnut Grove," Mother says, and I look and see its ghost.

Paul slows down, as if he knows I want to get a better look. We are driving along the road now where—to the left—Mr. Bailey's store, with the post office in one corner, was located. We usually went to the store at Herley to buy our groceries, though. It was my understanding that Mother didn't like Mrs. Bailey, perhaps (I used to think) because she was so hard on her granddaughter, Mother's friend Nadine. Mama seemed to think well enough of her, however, and when I got old enough to drive I used to bring her sometimes when she needed "just a thing or two" from the store. On our right two churches stood, gone long ago. I don't miss them much. It's the absence of the school building that strikes like a blow. Yet why should I care if the last vestige of Walnut Grove is gone? There was a time when I wanted to wipe it off the face of the earth.

Paul remembers the schoolhouse. I brought him here once and showed him what was left inside the brick shell that still stood then. He couldn't believe the postage-stamp size of our school library, when I pointed out where part of a wall still divided it from what had been the study hall. I am glad I went back to see the remains of the library, anyway. It was the only corner of Walnut Grove school where I ever belonged.

"So it goes," says Paul, a Vonnegut fan.

That is as good a thing to say as any.

"It's all Stanfield country now," Mother says.

"Stanfield country?" I don't remember ever hearing the phrase.

"That's what your daddy called it," Mother says. "It used to start just beyond the schoolhouse."

"How many Stanfields are there?" Paul asks.

"Too many," I say.

"I don't think I could tell you now," Mother says, "but I remember being told the first Stanfield had six sections of land here. In time they had divided every section into two farms at least, some into four. Every son and daughter got a farm out of that land, and for a while every grandchild that wanted it."

"Stanfield?" I ask.

"Yes, he was one of the oldest, and his grandpa let him have eighty acres that he'd kept next to Hugh and Estelle's part. Of course he give land to all his children, but I believe he let Stanfield buy his cheap, with some kind of a long-term loan. Then when he died he left it to him clear."

"And that's where Stanfield's house is?"

"Right in the middle of Stanfield country."

"You never called it that," I say. Of course she never spoke of it.

"I guess I did once," she says. "I remember the first time I saw it, the time Earl sort of introduced it to me. 'Well, here's Stanfield country,' he said. It was my first Sunday at Walnut Grove, and he brought me over here to go to worship with Estelle. Of course the Church still met at Walnut Grove then, and it was out of the way to go to Hugh and Estelle's first. I remember Estelle offered to come after me, but Earl said that would be too far, there was no use. He would go and visit with Hugh while the womenfolks went to Church, and then we would all go back to Mama's for dinner."

"The men didn't go to church?" Paul asks with mild interest.

"The Messengers were Baptists," Mother says, "but Earl never did join that church and I guess Hugh quit going when he married Estelle. She tried hard to make him go with her and join—obey the Gospel, as we called it—but he was stubborn about that."

"Don't Baptists obey the Gospel?" Paul asks.

"Not to our way of thinking," says Mother. "Earl knew how I felt and didn't care. Of course I prayed about him a lot when we was courting and first married, but he never deceived me about how he felt. I think he sort of held Estelle out to me as compensation. Having her to think about helped a lot, too, when I was making up my mind to marry and come 'way out here."

"Was she a help," I ask, "after you got here?"

54

"Some," Mother says. "But Estelle was funny. From the first I always knew she was funny. She had a way of laughing—a dry little laugh more like a cough—after nearly everything she said. It would make you wonder whether she meant what she said, or just the opposite." She paused, looking back I suppose— assessing Estelle. "But no, she did help. Whether she meant to or not, she helped, because I felt like I had her to lean on. A sister-in-law that was also a sister in the Church, you know."

"There's Hugh's place." I haven't seen it in years, but it looks the same. Even the mailbox proclaims HUGH MESSENGER in the same straggling block letters. There is still a small pasture, and the white frame house is fresh among green shrubbery.

"Was that the house they lived in when you came that day?" I ask Mother.

"Yes, they had it built when they married. Estelle insisted on it, Earl told me. He said Hugh didn't want to go in debt that much, but she had to have a fine house. They called it fine, you know, and it's true there wasn't another house like it around Walnut Grove then. Frame construction—when everybody else lived in box houses—and painted on the outside. Nicely papered on the inside, too, and furnished in *suits*. You remember them bedroom suits, with chest of drawers and what they called a vanity dresser. Estelle was so proud of hers. All the Stanfield sister-in-laws was jealous."

"And when Stanfield married, did Tommye Jo insist on a fine house too?"

"No, and I think that bothered Estelle. But Tommye Jo knew what she wanted; Hugh says she was talking about a brick house from the first. They lived in a little house on the old Stanfield place awhile, and then moved to a better house on the Bill Phillips place when Stanfield rented, and finally they built the new house on that land he inherited from his grandfather."

"How old is the new house?"

55

"Five or six years, I think, maybe more. But it's still the new house."

"There it is," Paul says. I find I resent a little the fact that he has been here.

We have not been able to see it a long way ahead because it is concealed by Hugh's pasture; it bursts upon us with the full effect of a four-bedroom Roman brick ranch house completely surrounded by plowed earth. Though I have been prepared, I am astonished. I can't believe such a house at Walnut Grove. I have seen similar houses throughout this farm country—"long bricks," Mother calls them—but I have not visited one before. Perhaps it is the sense of its having sprung full-blown from a cotton patch that astounds me. Besides Hugh's car (a brown LTD), there are in the driveway a red pickup with a gun on a rack across the back window, a yellow Continental, and a pink Volkswagen bug. I wonder why they keep all these vehicles in the driveway when they have an attached three-car garage—no doubt they are pleased with the impression they make, especially conjoined with the two enormous tractors for which there is just room between the house and the planted field. One of them, Paul points out with what strikes me as a trace of envy, has a glass-enclosed, air-conditioned cab, with AM-FM radio.

"But you prefer the dirt in your face," I remind him.

He grins. "Sure. But when I'm as old as Stanfield I may not."

"He does his own plowing?"

"Some. He's got a hand, of course, that lives on a place Stanfield has two or three miles from here. They've been plowing this place and Hugh's—the reason the tractors are here. He keeps his equipment at the farm where his hand lives."

We park behind the Continental, then follow a curved walk that cleanly divides a small but incredibly well-kept lawn of a deep, even green.

"I wonder who takes care of the lawn," I say.

"Feel of the grass," Paul says.

"What?"

"Reach down and feel of it."

I do that. "My God, it's Astroturf," I exclaim under my breath.

"I think it's one of Kevin's chores," Paul says. "All he has to do is hose it off."

Paul pushes the bell button, and we hear chimes ring inside. The house is tightly closed for air conditioning; otherwise someone would have heard us drive up and flung the door open by now—at least that was the way we used to do with expected company.

I don't know who I hope will open the door. I try to stand behind Mother and Paul, but Paul courteously steps back to let me go ahead of him and Mother moves to one side. So I am face to face with Stanfield when he opens the door.

"Well, dad gum," he says, his voice mellow with an effect of pleased surprise.

I am glad to register at once the impression that I'd never have known him. He is twice his old bulk, rather gray and a bit weather-beaten, and he looks a lot more like the Stanfields than the Messengers.

In the entrance hall, he hugs Mother, shakes my hand warmly, and says, "How are you, Paul?" No, I'd never have known my cousin, if I'd met him anywhere else, but I'd have known he was a Walnut Grove-style farmer, with his boots, his khaki work pants, his short neat haircut, and his eyes with the look about them that comes from staring a lot at distant horizons while plowing through West Texas wind and dust. Of Tommye Jo, now presenting herself, I am not so sure. I could meet her in any upper middle-class suburb and suppose her right at home. She has stayed slender and her hair (which I am almost sure used to be a dull light brown) is colored a pale ash blond and set in an up-to-date style.

She embraces us, Mother and me, speaks pleasantly to Paul,

and leads us past a small unlighted parlor to the family room where the children await us. Naturally, my eyes go at once to Cyndi. Long shining hair, a cute nose, a nice smile—jeans and a T-shirt printed with Greek letters. Why did Paul have to come to Walnut Grove to find her? We are introduced: she has poise and a manner that I am sure the girls describe as sincere. Stanfield brings ten-year-old Kevin across the room to me. "We finally got us one of this kind, to go with Cyndi," he says proudly. Mother has told me that after waiting ten years for another child they adopted him because Stanfield wanted a boy so much.

Kevin looks up at me out of ingenuous blue eyes. "Hey, are you a professor?" he asks.

"Yes," I say, "what do you do?"

He points with great seriousness to a row of deer antlers over a gun case on the end wall.

"Are you a hunter?" I ask.

He nods. Stanfield tells for him. "Kevin killed that un right there, last fall just before he was ten years old."

I ask where they hunt.

"You won't believe this, Gail," Stanfield says, "but right down yonder below your mother's place a couple of miles. I don't know if you remember, it belonged to an old man that had a whiskey still there during Prohibition and still bootlegged when we'as kids. Well, I got a chance to buy it a couple of years ago, I was sure needing a place to put some cows, and you wouldn't hardly believe the deer we see on it, especially in the winter and early spring when they come up from farther on down in the Breaks. Why, you had to go a hundred miles to kill a deer when we'as kids, didn't you?"

"I imagine so." I don't remember wanting to kill a deer, but I know we didn't have any around here then.

"I'm go'n take ol' Paul down there this year and give him a chance at a buck."

Paul smiles. "I'm not much of a hunter," he says.

58

Now Tommye Jo seats us in an arrangement around the fireplace, which is filled with green plastic plants. A silence falls, and I think what a good time it would be for a drink, but I don't expect that. What Tommye Jo thinks is that it is time to bustle in the kitchen, and this works just about as well. I get up and offer to help, but she says Cyndi is all the help she needs, and there isn't much more to do.

Presently she comes out of the kitchen (which is almost separated from the family room by a bar and cabinets at one end) bearing a big platter of fried chicken, which she sets on an extended maple table.

"Stanfield always wants to have steak," she says, "but I told him I bet fried chicken would seem more like an old-time Walnut Grove supper to you."

"Especially with homemade ice cream," I say.

"Look out on the patio," Stanfield says from across the room.

I peer through the sliding doors and see an old-fashioned wood ice cream freezer sitting in a number three washtub.

"We've had an electric freezer for years," Tommye Jo says, "but Cyndi found this old thing over at her great-aunt Lillian Stanfield's house. Aunt Lillian didn't want it, and nothing would do Cyndi and Stanfield but they fix it up and start making cream in it."

"Well, it's just a whole lot better that way," Stanfield says argumentatively, a way I recall he was always inclined to speak, whether anyone wanted to argue or not.

For a meal at which there are so many things no one wants to talk about, this one goes rather pleasantly. We speak of the schools the children go to, the weather, how long I plan to stay, and again of the weather—past, present, and possible future.

We go to the patio to eat the ice cream.

"How about that, Gail?" Stanfield says. "Ain't that just like Grandma Messenger's?"

"Just like it," I say. If it is, Mama's didn't taste as good as I remember it.

The patio is pleasant in the June sunset (though we cannot see the actual setting of the sun from behind the eight-foot board fence). The enclosed ground is covered with squares of aggregate interspersed with squares of petunias and what I suppose you call ground cover. There is one small, slender tree, I think a poplar.

"How about this?" Stanfield says. "It's not much like Walnut Grove, is it?"

"You-all have a beautiful place," is the answer I give him.

"We had a feller come out here from Sloan City and landscape it," he says. "I guess you saw our front lawn?"

"It looked like the real thing to me," I say, "till Paul told me."

"Shoot, we haven't got a blade of grass to worry about anywhere," he says.

"As I remember Walnut Grove," I say, "we didn't have any grass to worry about then either."

"Not in the yard," Hugh says. "I never saw anybody try to have a lawn out here till after the war. It took too much work and too much water."

We sit eating ice cream as twilight comes on. The kids are lined up on a glider under the tree, Kevin in the middle. Paul and Cyndi don't seem to care, and I wonder if this is a good sign or a cover-up. I am ashamed of myself for the question—I never expected to go all suspicious about any girl Paul happened to look at. But I never expected him to look at Cyndi Messenger.

Tommye Jo, I don't know why, decides Hugh is chilly. He admits it. Eating ice cream outdoors after sundown gets to him these days.

"Laura, I bet you're chilly, too," Tommye Jo says. "Why don't you and Hugh go on in, and we'll come in a little bit, when everybody gets through."

There is a certain timbre in Tommye Jo's voice that reminds me she was captain of the basketball team in high school. She is still used to having her directions followed. Hugh says it seems funny to him to go into an air-conditioned house to warm up, but he obeys his daughter-in-law and Mother goes along with him.

"I guess it does seem funny to the old folks," Tommye Jo says, "to keep the air conditioning going when we do of course have pretty cool nights."

"Daddy's always going on about it, but you can't air condition a house right if you keep it open half the time," Stanfield says.

"And I'd rather not have the dust blowing in," Tommye Jo says. "Our windows won't even open, and I like it that way."

Cyndi wants to serve everybody more ice cream, but no one seems to care for it. Actually, I am a little chilly myself, but I don't think Tommye Jo wants me to go in yet.

"Why don't you kids go in the garage and play ping-pong?" Tommye Jo asks. (That must be why the cars were left out.)

Now we three of the middle generation are left alone, and I wonder if there is some design in Tommye Jo's directing. All I can think of is Paul and Cyndi, but I can't believe we need to talk about them. At least I am not ready to. I believe it is time to start remembering the class of '48.

"Whatever happened to Gloria Nell Babcock?" I wonder.

We remember all fifteen members of the class, for about half an hour. Kevin gets tired of ping-pong and comes back to sit with his daddy. We never get around to any talk that could possibly be considered significant of anything, and I suppose I have simply imagined a reason for the manipulating of the guests.

Soon after Kevin appears, Tommye Jo decides we are all getting chilly and had better go in.

"Just look at them," she says in a low voice as we go through the sliding doors. She nods toward Mother and Hugh, who are sitting together on a love seat at the other end of the room, working the day's crossword puzzle. Her tone is that of one mother to another, upon the happy discovery that their three-year-olds play well together.

"Hey, let's make some coffee," says Stanfield as he comes in behind us.

"Why don't you show Gail the house while I fix it?" Tommye Jo says.

The four bedrooms and three baths are about all there is to the part of the house I haven't already seen. I protest about invading the children's privacy, but Stanfield says, "Oh, we're in and out of each other's rooms all the time."

On Cyndi's dresser there is a picture of an earnest-looking young man whose rather full, long sideburns are his concession to modern hair-styling. "What a good-looking boy," I say.

"Yeah, that's Cyndi's sweetie-pie, Bob Fillingim," he says, full of pride. "Hey listen, he's really a good un. He's on the football team, and makes the Dean's List, and everything. He's fixing to go to law school."

"You'd better hang onto him," I say.

"I sure aim to." He exaggerates a tendency to say "shore"—I have noticed already that his West Texas speech style seems a good deal more pronounced than I remember it. "We shore like him. We've been to see his folks—his daddy's a preacher at a little neighborhood Church in Dallas."

Cyndi has calico curtains and bedspread to go with her set of maple furniture that includes a well-filled bookcase. These are the first books I've seen in the house.

"I don't believe I heard what Cyndi's majoring in," I say.

"Oh, English," he says. "I kind of wish she'd take something where she might make a little more money, but then we don't hardly expect her to work anyway. Unless she maybe teaches just a year or two."

"While Bob goes to law school," I say innocently.

"Well, I kinda figger that's what she's got in mind," he says seriously.

"It's a good plan," I say.

A very good plan. I suppose they are right, and it really is Cyndi's plan. There is no reason in the world to imagine Paul and Cyndi would see anything in each other except casual friends and distant cousins. I put out of my mind the idea I have had that the reason for my coming here tonight is something to do with Paul and Cyndi: the encouragement of a courtship or a conspiracy to break it up.

In the master bedroom I stand looking at a collection of family photographs hung in a well-considered arrangement on the wall opposite the king-size bed. Tommye Jo has had what appear to be wedding pictures of their parents colored in oils and framed. I am fascinated by the picture of Hugh and Estelle. I can remember seeing Estelle only one time—at our high school graduation. Hugh took me to speak to her, and she said, "So this is Gail," and laughed, a toothy "tuh-huh-huh." I think I blushed—I supposed she was laughing at me, but I didn't know why. As I remember it now, I know what Mother meant by her description of Estelle's laugh. It held an unsettling note of irony.

By her drop-waisted, long-skirted dress and her hair drawn into a Psyche knot, I am reminded of the fact that—even though Stanfield and I are about the same age—Hugh and Estelle were married almost ten years before my mother and father. Mama told me once Estelle lost her first baby and was in bad health a long time afterward. She never meant to have another and blamed Hugh when she did. Mama thought she had turned him out of the marriage bed.

"I wonder if Mother and Daddy was happy then," Stanfield says, at my side.

I don't know. I don't answer. But there is something about her little puckered smile—something akin to the humorless

63

laughter—that makes me doubt it. A mistake discovered early, probably, and regretted a lifetime.

"I thought him and Laura would marry, didn't you?" he says.

"I really never thought about it," I say. Of course he knows that's a lie, but he understands what I mean by it and changes the subject.

"Do you think Paul will stay with her?" he asks.

"I don't know," I say. "I never would have guessed he would come in the first place."

"He seems like a good kid," Stanfield says.

"I think he is."

"I'as kind of figgering on getting a-hold of that place, but if Paul wants to stay here I'm glad. I really am, Gail."

"I am too, if he wants it. I always said I wanted anything for him that would make him happy; but to tell you the truth, Stanfield, I didn't want another link with Walnut Grove."

"Forget all that, Gail," he says. "Forget all that; it's all wiped out, just like Walnut Grove is wiped off the map."

"I don't know," I say. "I think I believe in ghosts."

"I know what you mean," he says. "But try to forget, Gail—I really wish you would."

I wonder if this is what I have been brought here for tonight: to hear him say "Forget."

"We had better go drink our coffee," I say.

The kids come in for Cokes. "Don't you want coffee, Paul?" Tommye Jo asks, but Paul doesn't drink coffee.

"Neither does Cyndi," Stanfield says. "I don't know what's the matter with these modern kids." He laughs, with an irony reminiscent of his mother's, but happier. He intends to convey that this is what people are saying about modern kids, criticizing them all the time, but as far as he can tell, about the worst thing you can say about them is that they don't drink coffee. At least he finds no fault with his own children—this seems abundantly clear.

"Say, Hugh," Tommye Jo says as if just happening to think of something, "did that woman with the tape recorder ever find you the other day?"

Hugh laughs in self-deprecation. "Oh yeah," he says. "You know I'm getting to be pretty popular with these ladies with tape recorders."

Stanfield puts in to explain. "I bet you didn't know," he says, "that Daddy's got to be the oldest settler of Walnut Grove. Seems like the county historical society is after him all time about one thing or another."

"Of course, where they missed out," Hugh says, "was not getting started on all this soon enough. The Carliles and the Baileys was the oldest settlers of Walnut Grove, but they're all gone now. Frank Carlile was the one that could've told them everything. Or John, but of course he never did live here after he was a boy. They say he put something about Walnut Grove in a book he wrote, some kind of West Texas history."

"Nadine might know some things," Mother suggests.

"Oh well," Hugh says. "I know she must've heard lots of tales from her grandpa and grandma Bailey, and her Carlile folks, but most kids don't think stuff about old times is worth listening to."

"I hear Nadine is coming to Walnut Grove on a visit this summer," Tommye Jo says. "I saw her cousin Cora at the store at Herley today."

"I hope she might," Mother says. "I wrote her Gail might be coming to spend the summer. But I haven't heard from her."

Paul I think is really interested in the local and family history. "Are they going to publish some kind of county history, Hugh?" he asks. "What kind of material are they getting from you?"

"Well, to tell you the truth," Hugh says, "I don't know exactly what they are doing. They've already put out one book, with the history of every community in the county. That was when they come to me to get the account of the townsite opening, and all the first settlers. Now this lady the other day says they're working on some book they call *Early Social Customs,* or something like that."

"That sounds real interesting, Grandpa," Cyndi says. "What kind of customs was she asking about?"

"Seems like she had her mind on weddings and things that went along with them. Wanted to know about infares and shivarees."

"Well, I never heard of an infare," Tommye Jo says. "I do remember hearing Mother and Daddy talk about shivarees, I think."

"The infare," Hugh says, "was a big dinner for the couple at the bridegroom's house, best I remember, but I never did know of one in my day. Now I could tell 'em a thing or two about shivarees." He looks at Mother with a little teasing smile.

"Hugh, you didn't tell that woman about mine and Earl's!" Mother seems appalled at the idea.

"I didn't go into any detail," he says. "I concentrated on the time when they'as a little bit tamer than they got to be later on."

"Did they get pretty rough?" Stanfield asks.

"They got so rough they just had to quit having 'em. That un Laura's talking about I guess was the last shivaree at Walnut Grove."

"Hey," Paul says. "That sounds like a story. The Last Shivaree at Walnut Grove. Tell it to us, Hugh!"

I have sometimes suspected—or at least I have wanted to believe—that one thing Paul had in mind when he talked about being a farmer and living close to the land was experiences to write about. He had a fairly good story published in the college literary magazine.

"Yes, tell it, Hugh," I say. I am curious too. I would have thought the shivaree was a thing of the past long before my mother and father married.

"I could tell it," Hugh says. "But your mother might rather I didn't."

"No, it's all right," Mother says. "It's all just here in the family. It may sound like a story to me, too; it's been a long time since I thought about that shivaree."

"Well, I'll tell it the best I recollect," Hugh says. "If I get it wrong, you correct me."

II

"To tell the truth, Earl had been running around with kind of a wild bunch before he went off to East Texas to pick cotton that fall. When he come home around Christmas and started talking about a girl he had found down there, Mama was tickled to death, and I guess maybe all of us thought it would be a good thing if he married and settled down. He talked to Papa about working the place that year—the doctor had already told Papa he needed to give up farming, on account of his heart. And they worked it out that Earl would take over the farming (on the halves, I reckon—that was the usual arrangement when a feller didn't have his own team and equipment), and Papa would build a good little two-room house for him and his wife.

"You kids will think that sounds pretty bad, like what you might call poverty level or something, but you got to remember it was 1930 and the Depression was just beginning to hit us. A man might consider hisself lucky if he had a good tight two-room house; lots of young folks had to put off marrying because they didn't have anywhere to set up housekeeping. And then—well, it was just kind of a custom around here then: if a boy wanted to help his daddy farm, most times they'd build some kind of a little house for him on the place. Lots of folks used to call it the weanin' house. Well—like Stanfield and

Tommye Jo lived in, there on Mr. Stanfield's place when they first married.

"I reckon it suited Laura all right. Letters went back and forth, and pretty soon Earl told us he was going after her in May. They got the house built, and Mama helped him furnish it, mostly with stuff she could spare out of her house, and finally, one pretty Sunday in May, he brought her home. Everybody went to Mama's for dinner that day—Earl and Laura was spending the night on the way, and expected to get here by noon. Me and Estelle come on as soon as she got out of Church, and Buck and Uncle Nezer was here then. You know Uncle Nezer had taken one of his spells of thinking West Texas was God's country, and Buck had been laid off of his job in Fort Worth. They come out here and worked awhile that year, living that time, I believe, in the old house on the Carlile place. Yes, it must have been, because I believe that's about when Nadine got so struck on Buck. But no matter. That's not the story.

"Buck took me off soon as I got to Papa's house that day and told me something was up. He'd been somewhere—some café in town, I think—and heard Jap Carter talking. He didn't know Jap, except by sight, but he knew Jap was a ringleader of that bunch Earl had been running with. I don't remember now just what it was he overheard, but it give him the idea that Jap's bunch was planning to pay a little visit to Earl and Laura that first night in the new house. Buck felt like Earl ought to be warned, and I did too, but I didn't hardly know how to go about it. Earl had a way of flying off the handle when you said anything against any friend of his. Not that I blame him, or aim to run him down now, after he's been gone these many years. But Laura knows how he was as well as I do.

"Still, I made up my mind to come out with it, because, like I said, shivareeing had got pretty rough around Walnut Grove in them days. Just the winter before, they'd carried a boy off on his wedding night and left him tied to a tree out in a pasture somewhere. Course they didn't know it was go'n come up a norther that night and him without any sign of a coat. He took pneumonia and like to died. Course he was sickly anyway.

"Well, Earl and Laura come in pretty soon after we got there, and we had a fine dinner—and all took to Laura right away, I think. I know Estelle was tickled because she belonged to her Church. Mama never got over telling how Laura come in dressed in her wedding dress and put on a apron and made the gravy. I believe it was Mama's habit to hold back on making the gravy till everybody was what she called present and accounted for. And when Laura offered to help, Mama told her she could make the gravy—just to test her, I suspect, and sure enough she made it so good I don't think Mama ever served fried chicken again without saying 'Now, Laura, you can make the gravy.'

"Well, I get off the subject, but we had the dinner, and the womenfolks was in the kitchen awhile, and me and Buck got Earl off and told him what Buck had heard. Like I expected, he was fighting mad at first—he said Jap's bunch wouldn't do nothing to him. But then he got to thinking about it. 'I don't want Laura scared,' was what he said.

" 'Well, I just thought you ought to be prepared,' I told him.

" 'I just don't know what in the world to do,' he said. 'If they come up with the idea of taking me off somewhere, I don't know how I could stop 'em.'

"It was Buck that got us thinking along the lines we finally agreed on. 'If me and Hugh was there, we could all three stop 'em,' he said, or something like that. He said why didn't we go down to Earl's right after supper, and stay hid back out of sight, and then if anybody come we'd be there to help Earl handle 'em.

"Buck was the least one of us three, but he was kind of a amateur boxer and I think Earl liked the idea of him being there. But he had his doubts, seemed like. He said as soon as they got a glimpse of us they'd just go off and then come back some other time when he wasn't expecting them.

"Then somehow Buck got the idea that we finally worked out and tried. I don't know how he thought of it, or really why I agreed to it. It seems pretty silly now. What he wanted to do was dress up like a girl—like I said, he was fairly small for a man. Then when they come to the door they'd think he was Earl's wife and be put off guard. 'And then,' he said, 'I'll give 'em a taste of their own medicine, and I guarantee you they won't come back.'

"I asked him if he thought he could handle several grown men at one time, and he said he might, but he figgered on a little help from me and Earl.

"What we had in mind was that Laura wouldn't even be there. Her and Estelle would stay up at Mama's, was what we thought. But she always was a spunky little thing—said she wasn't about to be run out of her own house her first night in it. We finally agreed that she could be there if she would stay in the kitchen out of their sight through the door or window.

"Me and Buck went down there right after supper—he carried a bundle with him, but I didn't know what was in it. We all set down at the table to drink some coffee Laura had ready for us, and then in a little bit he went in the other room to fix up. He come back wearing some kind of a kimono—stuffed in front, you know, with cotton or something, and a cap like they used to call a dust cap over his head.

"Lord, we all laughed. Laura said if anybody in that bunch thought Buck was a bride, they'as dumber than they sounded.

"We finally agreed that if you couldn't see him too good he might look like a woman getting ready to go to bed.

"We locked the front and back doors—or really, just latched 'em with a thumb latch. I don't think they even had locks on 'em—nobody thought of locking doors in them days.

"We had to wait a good while, and'as getting kinda restless, before we heard a heavy knock at the front door. Our plan was not to open the door until they had knocked three times. We waited, but they didn't knock again. Somebody yelled, 'Open up—we know you're in there.' We didn't make any move, and he yelled out: 'Open up, or we're coming in!'

"And without another word of warning they done just that. Old Jap hit the door with his shoulder and about half fell in, and Buck danced out of the kitchen like a boxer in the ring. First thing I knew, Jap had landed about ten feet back in the front yard. 'That was a *woman* hit you,' somebody said like they couldn't believe their eyes, and Jap said, 'Cain't no woman hit like that.' Course he had a string of words in front of *woman*. You might hear 'em on some TV show, but I was always taught not to use words like that around ladies and children, so I won't say what they was.

"They started crowding back in then, and Buck picked up a cane-bottomed chair and commenced swinging at 'em. He said he would fight any two of 'em with his fists but blamed if he'd let the whole gang run over him. He was a tough little old character. I've always hoped maybe he went down swinging like that when they got him in Italy.

"I pulled him back, though, and stepped up to them. I wasn't aiming to fight, and didn't think we'd have to. I told 'em they'd better get out and stay out. I said we'd fight if they forced us to it, but we'd go to the law the next morning and swear out a complaint against 'em, for breaking into Earl's house. I told 'em that's what we'd do if they ever give us any more trouble.

"They left then, but threatening all kinds of things they said they'd do to us. One of 'em had a gun out; I saw it flash in the light from the lamp.

"Next day at Walnut Grove, somebody told Buck Jap was carrying a gun for him. But Buck left the country pretty soon after that—him and Uncle Nezer both; they never stayed anywhere very long at a time. Nothing ever come of it, but I admit I carried a gun myself for a while. I went back the next day and fixed Earl's door for him. There wasn't a blame thing we could do about that busted chair.

III

The kids are laughing and exclaiming. Stanfield really guffaws.

"Hey what a story!" Paul cries.

"I didn't know anything like that ever happened around Walnut Grove," Kevin says.

"What I didn't know," Mother says, as if inclined to worry over what might have happened forty-odd years ago, "was that you ever carried a gun, Hugh."

"Oh yes," he says. "Estelle knew it, and boy did she ever chew me out about it, too. But that Jap was about half crazy. There was no telling what he'd do. I tell you for sure, I couldn't sleep for a week, watching out for carlights turning down our lane in the night. I sure was glad when Buck and Nezer left that time."

"Why didn't you ever tell that before, Daddy?" Stanfield asks.

"Oh—a lot of reasons. It didn't seem as funny when it happened as it does to you now. It was pretty much of a scandal in the community, and it wasn't anything I wanted to talk about. I guess in a way I almost forgot it, till that woman come asking about shivarees."

It is growing late now, much later than I meant to stay anyway, and both Kevin and Hugh have been yawning. We take our leave, with some vague talk about Stanfield's family coming over to Mother's for supper pretty soon. It is the sort of plan that could be conveniently forgotten by everybody concerned, but I have a feeling this one won't be.

"Listen, Gail, we got to talk some more about old times," Stanfield says.

"It's sure good to see you again, Gail," says Tommye Jo.

She never cared about seeing me thirty years ago, but I think she really means it. For some reason that I still don't understand, we are going to be one big happy family.

We drive behind Hugh till he turns off at his lane.

"What a character," Paul says. "I never would've thought Hugh was mixed up in anything like that."

"What about me?" says Mother. "Did you think I was mixed up in anything like that?"

"It wasn't a very happy way to begin your married life," I say.

"I cried all night."

"Dear Grandma," Paul says. "I'm sorry I laughed. I ought to have thought about how it would be for you. How old were you, anyway?"

"Nineteen," she says, "and just about ready to go straight back where I come from."

"I guess Daddy consoled you," I say.

"No," she says slowly, as if just remembering. "I believe he thought it was funny too, after it was over."

FOUR

Sunday morning the raincrow is back. I awake to scissortail snippings, and then as I lie in bed watching elm-leaf shapes against the pale western sky, the raucous rain call comes. *Raucous* may not be exactly the right word for it, but it is not really a pleasant sound, and only the mystery of its origin, established in my childhood, could account for the old sense I had of its being a mystic summons. I can understand why some people consider it a bad luck sign. Apart from any effect it might have on the weather, there is something about it very like the raven's croak—the explanation, no doubt, of its odd name.

I would still like to know what the bird really is, but I am not now to be drawn out of my bed in a search for it. As I come full awake, the party at Stanfield's asserts itself in my mind. I hold it off as long as I can, for I know what it threatens: my own peculiar sort of hangover that follows a social high. I take a drink or two if drinks are offered, but it makes no difference in my morning-after: I always come awake reconstructing the evening, examining every word I can remember saying, fearful to realize what of myself I may in my loss of inhibition have laid bare, or what misapprehensions given rise to. As I think back now, I believe I must have been seized (as I sometimes am) to say what everyone wishes to hear. I wonder if I have given Tommye Jo and Stanfield (and for that matter, Mother and Hugh, Cyndi and Paul) the impression that as far as I'm concerned, whatever is is right. Or have I, rather, (perhaps with Stanfield in the master bedroom) betrayed my secret paradox: that I have come to Walnut Grove in order to flee from it.

There is only one remedy: get up, get busy, put last night out of my mind. Mother is going about her usual morning affairs now; I hear her as she goes to the bathroom, steps out on the back stoop, returns to the kitchen. I join her.

"It sure is a pretty morning," she says. "Did you hear the raincrow?"

"Oh yes, I heard it. Right over my head, it sounded like. I was tempted to go and spy it out, but I was lazy."

"No use," she says. I wonder if Mother really wants to know what the raincrow is.

"I thought we all had a good time last night," she says mildly, as she sets the coffeepot off the burner.

"Yes," I say cautiously, "but not the kind I'd want to repeat very often."

"They're really pretty good kids," she says.

I don't ask who. "Why don't we take our coffee out on the porch?" I suggest.

"I'm having a little more than coffee," she says.

"Well, I'll get the TV trays," I offer.

This is okay with her, and I set them up while she looks to the cooking of her over-easy egg. I take a small bowl of cereal myself: the country air makes me hungry in the mornings.

It is, as she says, a pretty morning. The sky is light and clear as a drop of dew and the birds are busy. "Them silly cuckoos," Mother says of the nesting pair in the honeysuckle. One is at the nest, and the other is singing a cluttered sort of song (matching the nest) in the mesquite tree near the corner of the yard.

As we are finishing second cups of coffee, Mother asks me what I want to do today.

Sitting on the porch would suit me fine.

"Sunday morning's a good time to go to the cemetery," she says. "There's not hardly ever anybody there then, and we could go while it's still cool."

Well, we are going sometime—an early-morning drive might be pleasant. "Yes. All right."

Our few dishes washed, a note left for Paul (though he'll probably still be in bed when we get back), and we are ready for our excursion. At least I assume so, but I see I have forgotten something that always was part of "running over to the cemetery a little bit." Mother still has to put on a bonnet and go around to the back yard after a hoe.

"I thought you said there's a caretaker now," I tell her.

"Oh yes," she says. "But everybody feels like they've got to give a little extra care to their own graves. Besides, there might be a snake."

This is a carry-over, I suppose, from the time of the cemetery working when women took dinner and everybody spent the day hoeing weeds, building up graves, and clearing away debris. Of course we never did go. But one day just before the time of the cemetery gathering, Mother and Mama would put on their bonnets and take their hoes and spend several hours doing their part. They would work over the family graves as well as others close by if they knew no one was left in the vicinity to care for them. They did this several times a year, and as a small child I would go along, to wander among the graves and study the tombstones. I liked the cemetery. Our family dead had never been part of my life; they belonged there peacefully sleeping beside a tangled yellow rosebush.

Not much grows in the Walnut Grove cemetery, which is a block of land at the foot of a little red hill known as Round Mountain, given for burying ground by an early-day rancher, in the beginning of settlement when Walnut Grove school was located nearby. I remember Mama telling me this tale. Here was where the walnut grove was first planted, excuse for the name of the school. In time Walnut Grove was moved to its site on the new railroad—even the trees were transported, not very successfully—but the graveyard had to stay where it was. And so it remains, several miles from the spot where Walnut Grove at last expired.

Not much grows there—a few dark old arborvitaes, a few scrubby bushes proved somehow drought-resistant, like the prickly rosebush Mama transplanted from her yard soon after Papa died. People try to carry water and keep some clumps of flowers alive, but they have not for the most part been very successful. Once I think an attempt was made to drill a well, but something went wrong—I believe Mama said it was causing some of the graves to cave in.

The cemetery is beautifully isolated. I remember some old houses in the vicinity, but they are gone now. A paved road runs by on the way to a small community in the next county, but not much traffic passes there.

This Sunday morning as we walk down an aisle through the graves, we can't even hear a car anywhere. A jet from an air base some fifty miles away leaves a trail overhead; otherwise, no sights or sounds suggest a living person anywhere except ourselves.

"I want to be buried here." This is the first time I have ever thought of caring where I'm buried, but I am suddenly certain of the place where I want to await eternity. I shall leave instructions to that effect.

"Why of course," Mother says. "I've had a curb run around the Messenger lot, with room for you and me—and Paul, too, if things turn out that way." Where else would I be buried?

"Oh look," I say, discovering a treasure. "A few yellow roses are still blooming." I love these little scalloped roses about as big around as a half dollar—the bush brought originally, I remember Mama saying, from her childhood home in northeast Texas.

It grows beside a large gray granite double tombstone with

MESSENGER across the top and "Mama" and "Papa" below that on either side. I examine the dates: it always comes as a surprise to me to realize she lived twenty years without him. Next to the big gray stone is a slender white column with the name Earl Messenger engraved upon it. This is all my father ever was to me.

Mother begins to cut a few weeds that are growing inside the cement curb. As she says, the place is well kept. There are few weeds and scarcely a blade of grass, except toward the back of the fenced enclosure, where graves have not yet made their way. I remember Hugh's reference to the grassless yards of my childhood—this ground, like them, is scraped clean, as though people begrudge wild things the right to live in this place they have claimed as their own.

There are two or three graves I remember especially, and I go looking for them while Mother finds something to do with her hoe. Here is a little white stone with the figure of a sleeping lamb; here is one of the earliest graves, that of the little girl who died of a rattlesnake bite. Oh, that was a scary tale of Mama's: the child "snake-bit" when she reached into a hen nest gathering eggs. Mama was one of the first neighbors to arrive; she watched her die. Whenever I thought of that little girl, I was scared enough of the Snake Den.

Near here, in the oldest part, is the first grave: Martha Elizabeth Carlile, 1833–96. She was the old lady who sent for the trees and gave the school the name of Walnut Grove—Nadine's great-grandmother. And here is the grave covered with sea shells, and here the one that bears a picture under glass of a lovely girl with thick brown hair and red cheeks. She committed suicide. These are my oldest and faithfulest Walnut Grove friends—as I was growing up, the only friends we visited. I am glad to see they are well taken care of.

I hear a bobwhite calling and follow half unknowingly toward the back of the cemetery. It probably has a nest there somewhere in the uncut weeds and grasses, among the white daisies and yellow tallow weed. I would like for my grave to be covered by wild flowers and grasses, but as long as the cemetery is well kept this never would happen. At least the flowers will bloom and the birds will call; I don't suppose anyone can stop them. I think if I should stay at Walnut Grove I would come back here often; I might even write an elegy but (unlike Gray) I would have no regret for the people who lived and died here in obscurity.

I come upon a large slab of sandstone, such as people once used for doorsteps. I have heard there was a church here once; perhaps this is a relic of it. I sit and lose myself in the diapason of birdcall and the delicate scent of grass and flowers. I turn to see Mother laying down her hoe, and I beckon. She comes and sits beside me.

"I could spend hours here," I say.

"It's a nice cemetery," Mother says.

"I remember when I brought Mama to Mrs. Bailey's funeral —it was freezing cold and a sandstorm was blowing. I always seem to think of it that way."

"It was winter when Mama was buried," Mother says, "but it looked just about like this when Earl died. Just about this time of year, after a rainy spring."

"And you brought me to the funeral."

"Mama wanted us to. She said you wouldn't remember, but in later years you'd like to know you had been at your daddy's burying."

"What was it like?" I idly ask.

"A crowd such as a young person would hardly ever attract," she says. "The church was overflowing, and nearly everybody come on here to see him buried."

"Was he so popular?" It occurs to me that I really know very little of my father. I don't think either Mother or Mama talked about him as much as they might have.

"He was likable enough, and an old Walnut Grove boy," she says, "but no—it wasn't that. It was the way he died."

"An automobile accident, wasn't it?"

"Not an ordinary accident, no," she says.

I feel that she is about to tell me something else I have lived all these years without hearing—like Hugh's story of the shivaree. "I think you ought to know," she says, as she sits down beside me on the stone.

II

"After being gone over a year, Buck and Uncle Nezer were near enough starving that they had to come back to Walnut Grove that fall and pick cotton. Me and Earl could have got the crop in without them—I always picked right along with him. (Of course people then generally took care of their own— or if they hired anybody it was neighbor women and children. That was years before folks got to using Mexicans.) Anyway, Papa wanted to hire them—he said the money could come out of his pocket, if necessary, he wasn't go'n let family go hungry. They lived over there in Frank Carlile's house again, and picked some for him.

"By that time I had found out Earl wasn't ever go'n be the kind of man that liked to set home with his wife every night of the world. Once in a while we used to go to the picture show— I remember one Saturday night right after we got out a bale of cotton, we got Buck and Nadine and all drove to town and got hamburgers and then went to the show. Seems like it was Rochelle Hudson. But it cost too much to run around like that very much, and besides, it didn't really satisfy Earl. While I was pregnant with you, he took up with Jap Carter and his bunch again. I thought after the shivaree turned out the way it did, he would have had enough of them, but seemed like there was something about Jap that drew him. After you'as born, I thought for a while he was through with them. He was so crazy about you, but then the novelty wore off a little, I guess, and maybe I let you take up more of my time than I should have. Anyway, he got to running with Jap and them again. I felt sorry for his mother and daddy. (I didn't start calling them Papa and Mama till after Earl died.) They didn't want me and the baby left by ourselves, but I hated to go and stay with them every time Earl went off and left me. And it was embarrassing to them to act like they just happened by the house to visit every time they heard his car drive off. Papa had a talk with Earl, but he was a stubborn kind of a boy.

"Still, when cotton picking time come round again, and he had to work hard all day and was so tired at night, he begun to stay at home again. And then a lot of times Buck and Uncle Nezer would come by on a Saturday night, and they would play dominoes, or maybe all four of us would set down together and play Forty-two. Sometimes, after a month or two of flying at Nadine—as we used to say—Buck would bring her to our house and we would play games or maybe just make coffee and talk.

"There was a lot of wet weather in the late fall, and we didn't get the cotton out till after Christmas. Buck and Nezer had to go without pay all the time it was too wet to pick, and although of course Papa wouldn't let them go hungry, he didn't have much to spare. Times was hard. It was the Depression of course, but I don't remember us using the word much. Times is hard, we would say. Anyway, it turned out that after the first of the year, when it got time to register cars, Buck just didn't have the money. A lot of folks didn't. They drove around on the dirt roads of the community with their old tags on. I guess it was against the law, but nobody ever bothered 'em. Once in a while, though, somebody felt like they needed to get to town pretty bad. Buck wanted to take Nadine to the show sometimes, and he got in the habit of borrowing Earl's license plates whenever he was aiming to drive on the highway. One night, though, he had a tire go down just while he was stopped at our house getting ready to change the plates. He was already late, and Earl said 'Take my car.'

"Jap Carter had been gone when Buck and Nezer first come back, but along in the spring of that year he come home. The boys was all restless them days, seems like—always going off somewhere to hunt a job, then coming home about half starved to live off of their folks and get what little work they could around Walnut Grove. Just about the first thing, Jap found out Buck was back and was going around saying he hadn't forgot about that shivaree, and he aimed to get Buck yet. I never did know for sure why he blamed Buck the most— only of course Buck was the one that tricked him and knocked him down. Jap wasn't one to let anybody get away with treating him like that.

"'Shoot, I'll stay away from him,' Buck said. 'I ain't goin' around lookin' for trouble.'

"He never did either, that I ever heard of. He was a scrappy fighter and not afraid of anybody, so he said, and so I believed. I think he really didn't feel like there was anything he had to prove.

"That night after Buck had drove off in our car, Earl said to me, 'I'm go'n fix Buck's flat and drive down to Bill Nix's a little bit.' Bill was a friend of Jap's that lived down in the Breaks a couple of miles, and I knew why Earl was going.

"'I wish you wouldn't,' I said.

"You'll remember it was not only the Depression—it was Prohibition times, too, and I heard folks say there was whiskey stills all through the Breaks. I never did know much about that, but I did know Bill Nix and his daddy made whiskey and I heard Earl say something to Buck about 'em running off a batch.

"'I won't be gone long,' he said. Earl never was hateful to me, and I don't know—maybe I got so I nagged him, made him want to get away, but he never was hateful. He just went.

"He didn't come back in a little bit. I went through the

stages you go through, waiting for anyone. I was impatient, and then a little mad at him, then worried, then mad again. I don't think I had really started to believe anything was the matter until a knock come at the door. Somehow I knew as soon as I heard that what it was going to be.

"Well, not exactly, of course. I couldn't have guessed at the way it had happened, but I knew something was wrong about Earl. Bill Nix and his daddy had found him, dead at the wheel of Buck's car in the bottom of a creek below the narrow road that used to run around the edge of Round Mountain— you can see the place from here. They come after Papa first, and then all three of 'em come to tell me.

"It come out right away that Jap Carter had caused that wreck that killed Earl. He recognized Buck's car in the moonlight, but he couldn't tell Buck wasn't the one driving it, and he deliberately run it off of the road. Another one of that bunch was with Jap—Carl Headstream, and he was the one that told. He never would have told it in court though, and I don't reckon there was anyone at Walnut Grove that wanted it to go to court. After rumors had been going around awhile, Papa went to Carl and asked him to tell the truth. Jap had left the country long before that, right after Earl died. And Carl told Papa, and then come and told me that Jap sent word he was sorry.

"And that was the outcome of the last shivaree at Walnut Grove, that everybody thought was so funny. Unless Papa dying four months later was the outcome. He had a bad heart all along, but they said this might have hastened the end. Or maybe the final outcome hasn't happened yet."

III

We walk slowly and silently back through grass and flowers to the populated part of the cemetery. I am tempted to ask Mother why she has told me about the manner of my father's

83

death after so many years. Maybe it was Hugh's story of the shivaree that reminded her. Or maybe she simply thinks I should know more about my background. Now that she's getting older, she thinks it's time to tell. And I believe I am glad to know. For so long I have lived in confusion about what manner of woman my mother really is—perhaps this will help me understand.

After all what I say is, "Thank you for telling me."

She says, "Thank you for listening. You mustn't think I am saying anything was his fault, you know."

"No, I didn't think so," I say.

Back at the Messenger plot, Mother picks up her hoe and we stand looking down at the graves:

> Earl Messenger, 1906–1932
> Andrew Messenger, 1870–1932
> Fannie Messenger, 1876–1952

It suddenly occurs to me that these are not all of the Messengers in the Walnut Grove cemetery.

"Mother," I say, "where is Estelle buried?"

"Why, over yonder with the Stanfields. Where else?"

"Of course," I say.

"Do you want to see her grave?"

Why ever would I? "No," I say.

Driving home, Mother remembers a little story.

"You asking about where Estelle was buried makes me think of something that happened one time at Mr. Bailey's store, probably the first summer after me and Earl married. I was at the store with Estelle one morning, and there was some woman there from up the other side of Herley—I don't remember who she was, somebody not acquainted in the Walnut Grove community. Miz Bailey was at the store, making a kind of a social gathering of the folks there buying groceries or waiting for the mail, and she introduced us. And this Herley woman said to

Estelle, 'Didn't you use to be a Stanfield.' And Estelle said, 'I *am* a Stanfield.'"

"And so she still is," I say.

"Always," Mother says. "I believe she thought Hugh taking the Stanfield land ought to've made him a Stanfield too."

"Hugh didn't marry her for the land, did he?" I wonder.

"Of course not," she says rather sharply, but then goes on, more in the explanatory tone she adopted for the story of Earl's accident. "It was just one of them mistaken marriages, I reckon. I remember Miz Bailey told me one time Estelle worked on his sympathy by pretending she was sick—pining away, you know. Mama thought she tricked him: made him think she was—you know—expecting. I couldn't hardly believe that, her family being so prominent in the Church, and all. I don't believe it of Hugh, either. No, I think more likely Miz Bailey was right, if either one was."

"I thought you didn't like Mrs. Bailey," I say.

"Oh no, I liked her well enough, and she took a kind of a fancy to me, when I first come to Walnut Grove. I have to admit I was a little bit afraid of her. Some people said she was the biggest gossip around, but that wasn't quite it. She knew everything that went on at Walnut Grove, and she didn't hesitate to make known what she knew of people's wrongdoings. She kind of kept Walnut Grove in line that way. The boys used to call her Queen Anne—her name was Annie, you know—and said she thought she owned Walnut Grove. I remember she said to me pretty soon after the shivaree: 'We just don't have goings-on like that at Walnut Grove; we've got a decent community here.' I don't know but what she might've had something to do with Jap leaving when he did, though of course he had to come back, and get into meanness again."

"I wish I had looked at her grave," I say.

"We'll go back sometime," Mother says.

I rather think we will. I would like to take Paul, too. If he plans to live here, he should become acquainted with the enduring part of the community. It occurs to me that if it doesn't get too uncomfortably hot, we might even go this afternoon. I would like to show him the earliest graves, let him learn what Walnut Grove once was, talk to him of the Messenger family, see him experience the peace that came to me this morning.

IV

Paul is up, has shaved and dressed, and is having a bowl of bran flakes while he reads *Newsweek*.

"Don't you miss the Sunday paper?" I ask.

"Not really," he says. "I used to drive to Herley to buy one, but then I decided there wasn't that much urgency about seeing anything that was in it. It comes with the mail on Monday, and I read it all week."

I put the kettle on for a cup of instant coffee. "May I join you?" I inquire.

I may, and presently do, while Mother makes her morning round of the garden and the chicken house.

"How was the cemetery?" he asks.

"Lovely," I say. "Have you been there?"

"Not since you took me, a long time ago. Is it a special point of interest?"

"It really is," I say, "for a lot of reasons. It's all there is left of Walnut Grove, you know, and really sort of sums up its history. Besides, it's so pleasant and peaceful—you'd be surprised."

"Well, I may go sometime."

"I was wondering about this afternoon."

"I have a date this afternoon."

"A date?"

"Oh well, not really a date. Just a bunch of kids going to the lake to water ski."

"What lake?"

"Lake Sloan City. I think it's been built since you lived here. As a fishing lake it's just so-so, but Stanfield fishes there once in a while. I may go with him sometime."

"You really like Stanfield, don't you?" I ask.

"Oh sure. He's great—a real redneck, you know. Mother, do you know he actually says *sombitch*—just like in the books? Not in front of *wimmen*, of course."

"You're not making fun of him?"

"No—really not. I do like him—he doesn't seem to have any pretensions."

"He's one of those *real* people you were expecting to find at Walnut Grove?"

"I think so."

"In spite of his Astroturf lawn and his plastic house plants?"

"Well, I expect those were Tommye Jo's idea. But yes. He doesn't pretend about them; he's proud because they *are* plastic. He likes being able to buy them. He works hard, and he makes money: it doesn't occur to him that there could be any other reason for working."

"Do you know that some of this sounds an awful lot like what you couldn't stand about your father and his business?"

"Oh, I suppose it does. The thing is, I like farming—for my own reasons. Nobody wants me to be like Stanfield—Stanfield least of all. He can be himself, and I can be myself—for instance, I think I'd really like to go fishing with him but I could care less about hunting. And that's all right with him."

"Well, but then—he's not your father."

"Maybe that is part of it. I had to break away, find my own path to follow you know."

"I don't know why it had to lead to Walnut Grove."

"I don't know why you never wanted me to come here—your old home, your own mother—and you always said you didn't care what line of work I chose."

"I don't know," I say, trying to explain without giving much away, "that Walnut Grove ever really was my home. I mean we never had many links with the community. It was this house, and my walks in the pasture, and the books I read that made up my home."

He has still been glancing at the magazine from time to time, throughout our conversation, but now he sits up straight and looks at me directly, as though he studies me.

"It's really not something new with you, is it?" he says.

"Not new?"

"I always thought it had to do with Dad—you know, the divorce and everything."

"What did, Paul?" I think I know what he means—I don't think I quite like him analyzing me this way.

"I think you know—shutting yourself away from everybody —all that."

"I guess I've always been shy."

He looks at me still, narrowing his eyes, shaking his head. "I bet you didn't even leave word with old Mr. and Mrs. Zimmerman where you were going to be this summer."

"Why, Paul, we hardly ever speak to each other. They have their lives, I have mine. They'd probably have been embarrassed if I'd gone barging in saying, 'Hey, I'm going to Texas this summer.'"

"They might have been glad if you'd left the door open in the wall, so they could come in and sit by the fountain. I bet Mr. Zimmerman would like to look after your side of the yard for you—he doesn't have much to do."

"You know I don't know them that well, Paul."

He shakes his head again. "I bet you didn't even tell Keith Wilson where you were going."

"He mightn't care. He's living with Olivia Salazar now."

"Oh. Well, it's probably your fault if he is."

"Look, he wasn't interested in me that way. The only thing we ever had to say to each other was out of some eighteenth century book."

"There are some pretty lively things in eighteenth century books, I believe."

"You know what I mean. For heaven's sake, I didn't come to Walnut Grove for lectures on how to live my life."

"I didn't come for that sort of thing either," he reminds me.

"I'm sorry, Paul." I really am sorry; I never wanted to be that kind of mother, and I don't think I very often am. "But I had other plans for us this afternoon."

"It's okay, Mother. You only want the best for me."

He is teasing, of course; but no matter how often I've said it, it's the truth. "Dear Paul," I say lightly—disguise for a voice near tears. I rinse my coffee mug at the sink, kiss him on top of the head as I depart. "If Mother asks, I'll be in my room awhile," I tell him.

Soon after dinner, Paul drives off in his battered Renault to join the party. Mother and I sit on the porch, watching him go.

"I hope he can get him a new car this fall," Mother says.

"That's not quite the thing for the promising young Walnut Grove farmer," I admit, "but I'm surprised if he wants a new car."

"Well, I expect he'll get a secondhand one."

As the dust of his alien little car disappears I sigh and say, "Well, this isn't exactly what I pictured when I thought of Paul living with you at Walnut Grove, or when I thought of spending the summer here with the two of you."

"Has he changed?" Mother asks.

"I suppose not. It's just that my picture was wrong. I kept thinking of those old days when you and Mama and I were here together, and I guess I thought it would still be that way: the three of us now like the three of us then."

"I've wondered how you thought of it," Mother says. "Does it seem to you now like we had a good time?"

"Sometimes it seems like the only good time of my life. There are a lot of happy things to remember, but mostly just the three of us loving each other."

"It was like that, wasn't it?" she says. "And yet I think you got restless sometimes, especially after you got along in high school. And of course I know there was one time at least—even before that—when you got pretty unhappy with me. I don't know but what Mama did too."

"When Nezer and Rosabella left? Well, I didn't understand that very well, and as you say I was just a little kid. Anyway I never dwelled on it. You ask how I remember my childhood— and what I remember most is a deep contentment."

"You don't know how glad I am to hear that, Gail."

It must be something she has wanted to hear for years, and I am sorry I didn't say it long ago. I don't have to add that perhaps if the contentment in that little world of mine had been less complete and absorbing the impingement of those other worlds to come might not have been so sharp.

v

The raincrow's prophecy finally comes true. We watch thunderheads rising in the south as we sit through the afternoon. Mother is crocheting afghan squares, and I am holding a book in my lap: *Red Plush*, an old favorite from the days when— having read all the readable books in the high school library (all, that is, except the ancient yellowed textbooks)—I finally persuaded Mother to let me join the Book-of-the-Month Club. It is a pleasant book to read, not too absorbing, for I remember it well. From time to time I put it down to listen to Mother, or just to look toward the sky and the towering clouds.

They grow higher, move closer.

"I'm kind of worried about them kids, off on the lake," Mother says.

I am too, but I say, "Oh, they'll have sense enough to come in if they see a cloud coming up. We can't tell what the weather's like there, anyway." The lake is some twenty-five miles away.

"I believe I'll just go turn on the TV and see if there's any kind of a weather watch on," Mother says.

She comes back to say, "Severe thunderstorm warning. I guess that's not too bad, after we lived with a tornado watch all spring. But they oughtn't to be out on that lake."

"They won't be," I assure her.

We sit on the porch as the clouds move close, turn dark, spawn winds that rake the elm trees. Then we go in and close up the house, turn on the TV for news of the storm, and worry silently. At last the phone rings, two longs, and Mother says, "You answer it."

"Mother?" Paul says. "I'm over here at Stanfield's. I just wanted you to know we got in all right, ahead of the storm."

"Is it raining there?" I ask.

"Yes, and hailing a little. About pea-size hail." He pauses to listen to somebody talking in the room where he is. "Stanfield says tell you that's *black-eyed* peas," he says. For some reason, this is a joke.

"Is Stanfield worried about the crops?" I ask.

"He says not. I really don't believe it's going to get any worse now—how is it there?"

Mother has just come in to say it is starting to rain.

"Raining," I say. "No hail that I know of."

"Well, I'm going to stay over here and eat supper and then they're going to Church, and I'll come on home. Okay?"

I want him home now, but I don't suppose it would make much sense to tell him to come on into the thick of the storm. "Be careful when you get on this caliche road," I say.

"Okay, Mother. I've driven on it in wet weather before now."

"Just being motherly," I say. "Okay?"

He laughs. "I'll see you in a little bit."

I pass the message on to Mother, and we look at each other with smiles that perhaps mean different things. "I suppose they go to Church," I say, "come hail or high water."

She offers an unamused laugh, and I can see her drawing into herself. I want to ask her why, after having left that Church so many years ago, she is still so uptight about it. But I don't.

We eat a bite, and watch a little television, and listen for Paul's car on the road. He comes in at last, wet and happy, singing "Singing in the Rain." He is a pretty good singer and has a repertoire of old songs, always one to suit the occasion.

"You must have had a good time," I say.

"Yeah, we really did," he says. "We didn't get to ski much, but we had a good time."

He goes singing about the house, getting ready for bed, and cuts down to a hum as he comes into the living room, where we are still watching TV, to choose a book for bedtime reading.

He sits and watches the end of the show with us, but he is restless. He starts for the kitchen. "Y'all want a Coke?" he asks.

Mother says she is going to bed.

"I'll have one," I say, and he brings it. We turn off the television and can hear rain falling gently on the roof.

"Just a good rain," I say, "no damage."

"Stanfield says we can use the rain, but it'll keep us out of the fields a few days. I may sleep late in the morning."

"Might as well. I think I will too—maybe the scissortails will sleep late if it's cloudy."

He starts to his room with his book and his Coke, then turns back to me. "Mother, why didn't you ever tell me about our cousins at Walnut Grove?" he asks.

"I hadn't seen Stanfield in so long," I say, "I guess I just didn't happen to think."

"Well, I'm kind of glad I found them," he says.

"Me too, then," I say. But I feel an apprehension that it will prove not to be the storm that I should have been worrying about.

FIVE

One day after the rains have passed and Paul is plowing again, Mother and I sit once more on the front porch. Mother is crocheting. My whole attention is on the heat waves chasing each other around the edge of the earth, until we hear a car coming from the west and I turn to see a cloud of white dust boiling up, traveling as the sound travels.

"Somebody in a hurry," Mother says.

"Not stopping with us, I guess."

But I am wrong. The car slows suddenly, wheels in at our drive, and stops in front of the gate.

"Why I know that car," Mother says. "I believe it belongs to Johnny Carlile.

"Nadine's brother?" I ask, guessing the identity of the attractive lady with blue-rinsed hair, getting out from under the steering wheel of the light green LTD.

"Why it's Nadine!" Mother cries, jumping up. "She always did drive like that."

I get up, too, and we go to meet her.

We hug and kiss each other, and say each other's names, and what a long time it has been.

"You don't know how tickled I was when I heard you were here," Nadine tells me more than once. "And they say Paul is here, working the place."

Yes, and what about her kids? All three are married, and she has five grandchildren. She also has their pictures, and we look at them, and they are cute. When did she get here? Day before yesterday. She flew to Dallas-Fort Worth, and Johnny met her there. Of course it would be a shorter drive for Johnny if she flew to Lubbock, but his oldest son is living in Arlington now and he's glad of an excuse to make the trip. Yes, she still lives in Wisconsin, and Ralph still works in the same department store, where he got his old job back after the war. . . . Yes, I still teach at the little college in California, only it is not so little now.

And how is Hugh? Mother tells about Hugh's heart attack and the diet he is supposed to stay on. Nadine guesses it's hard for a man cooking for himself to keep on a diet like that.

But Laura is all right, and Nadine is all right, and I am fine. Yes, Nadine's husband—Ralph—is fine too. I never saw Ralph, but Mother did. She said he was a good, solid-looking man, and so, I gather, he proved to be. He never comes to Walnut Grove any more. They feel like it's too expensive for both of them to fly, and a trip by automobile seems so tiring these days, takes up so much time.

Such is our conversation, on this, our first meeting in more than thirty years. I don't know—yes, I do know, exactly—the last time I saw Nadine.

A few months after Nadine came back to Walnut Grove to wait for him, Buck came home on a furlough. Uncle Nezer was living in the little house on our place then, helping Mother with the farm work. Nadine was at our house a lot, and at Uncle Nezer's, ironing and mending his clothes, bringing him something she'd baked. As Mama said, she made no bones about it: she'd come home to marry Buck. They were both along in their thirties then, and although I liked Nadine and thought her attractive, I was amazed when Buck came home and they began acting like two people in love. Why they were almost the age of my mother. I was really a little embarrassed.

One day a telegram came. A man had to drive out from town with it, because in those days we didn't have telephones at Walnut Grove. Earlier, there had been a line out this way from the exchange at Herley, but it hadn't been kept up in years and finally people had given up trying to have phones. The telegram cut short Buck's leave and ordered him to report to a camp in California. He drove right on over to Nadine's, and she packed her bag and left with him.

It was several years before she went back home again because of the stand her mother, Mary Carlile, and her grandmother, "Queen Anne" Bailey, took against her going with Buck. I think my mother was almost as shocked. I remember her face when they told her.

"Go without getting married first?" she said.

We were all in the living room—Uncle Nezer and Mama and all of us, on a summer morning. Buck and Nadine were standing together in the middle of the room, holding hands. I remember Nadine's red cheeks and her dark eyes glistening—with tears, I think, or maybe simply joy.

"We'll get married when we get there," she said. "We don't have time now."

I know Uncle Nezer had tears in his eyes—they were streaming down his face. He loved Nadine like a daughter, and he had hoped for many years that Buck would marry someone like her. Mama was happy, too. Nadine kissed us all around, and Buck shook hands, and we watched them drive away in Nadine's little black Ford. None of us ever saw Buck again. And I never saw Nadine again until now.

Her eyes are still dark and sparkling, and her curly hair springs from her head in just the same eager way. Perhaps she is not beautiful (perhaps she never was), but a youthful vibrancy seems as much a part of her as ever.

"Come and spend the day, Nadine," I say, "the way you used to do."

"Nadine always spends a day with me," Mother says.

"I can come Wednesday," Nadine says. I think she already has it planned. "I have to go now—got to get Johnny's car back to him."

"I'll come after you Wednesday morning," I say, "so you can stay as long as you want to."

When she is gone I say to Mother, "I guess you forgave Nadine a long time ago?"

"Forgave her? For going off with Buck? With all the kinds of forgiving I've needed in my life, I couldn't hardly imagine that was any kind of a transgression against me."

"How long did they actually have together?"

"About three months, I think. Nobody could ever begrudge them that."

After Nadine went to California with Buck, she used to write to me. Hers were the first letters I ever got. She lived in a bedroom in a house near the camp and took long walks to keep from going crazy, as she wrote me, on the days when she didn't get to see him. She would write me descriptions of those walks: the palms like big feather dusters, the pepper trees that reminded her of enormous tall mesquites, rows of eucalyptus smelling like Mentholatum, red geraniums growing wild as weeds, birds that spoke a strange language. "There are these little doves in the palm trees," she wrote. "They say the same thing over and over, and I keep trying to figure out what it is." (We had always liked telling each other what the birds said: the mockingbird that kept calling, "Nadine! Nadine! Nadine! Hurry, hurry, hurry!")

Seven years later, when I got to Southern California with my first husband, it all seemed familiar. I looked at the same trees and heard the same birds, and sometimes I almost believed I could find Nadine there too. But Buck lay dead in a far country, and she had married another soldier, who lived to return to her and take her away before my time there came.

"Do you like California, Gail?" she asks me this Wednesday morning as we drive away from her brother Johnny's house.

"I seldom think whether I do or not," I say. "Did you like it?"

"I like wherever I am," she says, "but yes, I liked it. I was excited about being there, both times. Of course the idea of Hollywood so near had something to do with it; everything seemed like something out of a picture show or a story."

"Do you remember writing to me about the little doves in the palm trees?"

"Oh yes," she says. "I hadn't thought of them in years, but I do remember. Did you ever figure out what they were saying?"

"No," I say. "It has been a long time since I remembered to try, or even noticed them. But I was thinking about them the other day when we heard the raincrow. They both used to seem mysterious to me, as though they were making some promise or sending some message I couldn't decipher."

"I remember the raincrow," she says. "It was crying the day Buck and I left Walnut Grove."

"I didn't remember that," I say, "and yet I know there were those who said it was a bird of ill omen."

"We had a wonderful time together, Gail."

"I always knew that, and was glad. Later on, when I was so miserable out there, I used to think how happy you had been. And even then I was glad, and didn't envy you."

"I wish I could have had any idea what was happening to you," she says. "It was years before I knew why you left Walnut Grove when you did."

"I tried sometimes to write you," I say. "When I first left home, and then again after I was married, I used to think it might help if I could talk to you. But whenever I started to put anything on paper I would literally get sick. I couldn't look at it. I'm not sure I could even now."

"But you've done all right, I know. You're over it now?"

"Over that—I think so. I don't know if you'd say I've done all right—I haven't been much good as a wife, evidently."

"But in your job—"

97

"Oh, well enough. Not as well as Mother probably makes it sound in her letters. You know after my last divorce I went back to school. I meant just to get my master's, and go back to library work; but I did so well in my English courses—well, you know I always liked to study and read, and when they suggested I stay on and work on a Ph.D. it seemed like the easiest thing. I just drifted into teaching."

"Well, I know you're a good teacher," she says. "And you have a fine son—and you and Laura get along all right now, don't you?"

"Oh yes."

"But you still don't really talk—about things."

"No, we never could. And yet—I don't know. She hasn't exactly talked about it this summer, since I've been here, but she's told me things, brought up things, that we haven't mentioned in years. Some of them I never heard before. Do you know, I never knew the real story of my father's accident, and then the other day in the cemetery she sat down on a rock beside me and told the whole thing?"

"I used to tell her you needed to know everything, and she always said she would tell you when the time came."

"I really think she meant to tell me after I had graduated from high school, before I left home. But then she waited just a little too long."

"I'm so sorry," Nadine says after a pause, and we are both silent a moment, being sorry.

We are on the point of turning in at Mother's house when she speaks again, suddenly, hastily, as if this is something she has put off but must say: "Gail, why didn't they ever marry?"

I shake my head. "I don't know," I say, "I just don't know."

Mother has dinner cooking and is ready to sit on the porch and visit. We settle down for a session of happy talk—not much of old times. We hear all about the affairs of Nadine's children and grandchildren. Since she never had a child until her third marriage, her youngest is not much older than Paul. He has finished college, with a degree in business administration, and gone to work for the store where his father has worked all his life.

"We thought Paul was going to do just about that same thing," I say, "and then Mother wrote him about coming here to farm, and it seemed to be the thing he'd been hoping for all his life."

"He really likes it?"

"Oh yes," Mother says. "I've watched him since January. He's a born farmer. [She likes saying that.] I never was—I never minded hard work, and I knew what had to be done, but I never had the feeling for it that he does. And his granddaddy sure never did. Earl hated farming, really—he believed if he could have got a job as a mechanic and lived in town, his whole life would have been more worth while. And I don't know but what it would've. The Depression put an end to his ideas about that, and changed our lives I guess—no telling how much."

"It changed a lot of lives," Nadine says. "I've sometimes thought if Buck could have had a settled job, instead of roaming the country like he did so long—if we could've married and settled down when we first knew we loved each other—how different everything would have been. Almost for sure he never would have joined the Army—and at his age he wouldn't have been drafted." She sighs. "But I try not to think that way. I have had a good life."

It is probably a good thing that Hugh and Stanfield drive up in Stanfield's pickup at just this time, or we should turn into three women summing up the sadness of their lives.

"Who in the world is this?" cries Stanfield, with a warmth that says he knows very well who it is and can't think of anybody he'd rather be surprised by.

"Nadine!" Hugh exclaims with pleasure.

99

Nadine jumps up and hugs them both. They talk about how long it has been since they've seen each other.

"I know I didn't see you the last time you'as here," Hugh says; they can't think how many years it has been since Nadine and Stanfield last met.

"You-all set down," Mother says.

Stanfield keeps standing, however. "Say, is Paul about through plowing?" he asks.

"I think so," Mother says.

"Well, listen, what I really come for was to tell him I know where we can get us some hoe hands. I think I'll go over yonder and talk to him awhile."

"You saw the tractor?" Mother says.

"Yeah, I know where he's at." He turns to go.

"Wait," Mother says. "Is Tommye Jo looking for you home to dinner?"

"Why no. Her and her mama and the kids went to town, and aimed to eat with Tommye Jo's sister. I'm kinda baching."

"Then you-all eat with us," Mother commands.

Stanfield pretends to study a minute, then says, "Shoot, I don't know why not, do you, Daddy?"

"I'd like to," Hugh says, "if Laura's got any of that mess I have to eat."

"I can fix something," Mother says.

"Real good," Stanfield says. "I'll see y'all after while."

It is a good old-timey dinner, except for Hugh's greaseless peas and pale chicken, and he says the company is so good it makes what he has to eat taste better. We linger a long time at the table, and at last, when no one can eat another bite, keep drinking iced tea, as we used to do, out of Mama's big old goblets.

Even Paul seems to be enjoying this re-creation of the good old days. "I ought to be back at work," he says.

"Aw, you haven't got a full evenin's work left, have you?" Stanfield says.

I usually have to stop and remember, when someone at Walnut Grove says *evenin'*, that what is meant is *afternoon*. Paul seems to be onto it, though, and responds without hesitation: "No, just a couple of hours, I reckon." He takes another glass of tea.

"Paul, I hear you need hoe hands," Nadine says.

He is a bit puzzled. "Well, I think Stanfield has got us fixed up now."

"Too bad," she says. "I was thinking about asking you for a job. I think I could get a recommendation from your grandmother."

"She's a pretty good hand with the hoe all right," Mother says.

"Well, I declare I'd forgot that, Nadine," Hugh says. "You hoed with Uncle Nezer that summer before Buck come home."

"I sure did, Hugh."

"Gosh, the fields was weedy that year," Hugh remembers.

"Hey, I remember that," Stanfield says. "Seems like everybody was hoeing that summer. I think even Gail went to the field."

"I did, some," I say. Mother never wanted me to work in the field much, but that year I was determined to hoe with Nadine.

"Seemed like we never would get through," Hugh says. "Do you remember that scheme Uncle Nezer got up about hoeing at night? Lord, that was crazy."

I remember it myself. It was one of those jokes Uncle Nezer was prone to, the kind that made Mother draw in and wear a strained smile when everybody else was laughing. Later she would explain to me that although we loved Uncle Nezer I had to understand that it wasn't really nice to talk that way.

"How it come up," Hugh recalls, "is that somebody in the community—probably Claud Stanfield; yes, I think it was Claud—somebody in the community had got a hold of a tractor with headlights. One of the first around here. Everybody was kind of laughing about it. I know Mama couldn't think

what in the world anybody would want to put lights on a tractor for—her idea being that if God had meant for men to plow
at night, He would have lit up the fields. But then some took
up for it, and said there was times when there just wasn't
enough daylight to get through plowing in time, and then
Uncle Nezer come up with this scheme for putting a light on
the hoe handle so we could hoe all night too."

Nadine laughs. "I remember," she says.

"Well, tell it, Hugh," Paul says. "Maybe we could work
something out."

"Well, I'll see if I can get it straight," Hugh says. "I believe
somebody—might have been me—said of course we'd have to
have a battery on the hoe some way, and it would have to be so
little, the problem would be keeping it charged. You'll remember we still didn't have electricity here then, and nearly
everybody had a Wincharger and a six-volt battery to run a
radio and maybe one or two low-watt light bulbs. So Uncle
Nezer, he said why we'd have to have a Wincharger of course,
a little Wincharger fixed on the hoe handle. And then he really
got carried away. Course, now, he said, there might be a problem in still weather. And then it come to him, and he started
laughing till he couldn't hardly tell it. We'll just get Fannie to
cook us a big pot of beans for dinner every day, he finally said,
and then we'll be sure to always have plenty of wind."

Mother draws in, but she manages to laugh a little while almost everyone else enjoys the joke a lot. (I don't know whether
anyone notices I don't work up a laugh either; my mother
trained me very well, I guess. But I remember how the plan
evolved that first time, and got funnier and funnier, with everyone contributing a little until at last Uncle Nezer came up
with the climax. I think I might have laughed that day.)

"Uncle Nezer never did get through making jokes about
beans," Mother says. "I remember the first time I saw him, he
wanted to know if I knew how to get the rocks out of the
beans—and he went on from there. It always did embarrass

me, I couldn't help it. And of course there was plenty of opportunity for bean jokes, because looking back now it seems to me like we lived on pinto beans and corn bread all through the Depression and pretty well on through the war."

"Seems like nearly everything Uncle Nezer said was joking or teasing," Stanfield recalls.

"Except," Hugh says, "when he got to talking about Rosabella."

"And of course we always joked about Rosabella," Stanfield says. "Remember, Gail, how he'd start out—'I bet you never heard tell of anybody getting married, sitting up on top of the Ferris wheel at the carnival?' he'd say. Then I'd get behind him and wink at you, and you couldn't keep from giggling to save your life."

"We ought to have been ashamed of ourselves," I say, "because he really was so pitiful about her. She was Buck's mother, Paul"—I interrupt myself to explain—"and for some reason I never did know went off and left the two of them when Buck was just a baby."

"Did they really get married on a Ferris wheel?" Paul asks.

"Yes, they really did," Hugh tells him. "Nezer went off with a carnival when he was just a young kid, and found Rosabella. She was a dancer, I think, or maybe a fortuneteller or both, I'm not sure now. She had long gold hair, so he told us. Many a time I heard him end his tale: 'and she was the prettiest thing.' For years he would go off hunting her and be gone for months at a time. He'd hear from somebody that thought they'd seen her, and off he'd go. You know, I think that's why him and Buck went to El Paso that time right after Earl and Laura's shivaree."

"Well, let's don't talk about that any more," Mother says. Nezer-and-Rosabella is one of the things that Mother and I have never discussed together.

"Save the good stories," Paul says. "I've got to get back to work."

Stanfield and Hugh have to go, too, they say. "Wait while I get Hugh some squash out of the garden," Mother says. "Now you can eat squash," Mother tells him, "and I know you never do plant any."

They all go out, and Nadine and I begin preparing to wash dishes.

"Mother never has wanted to talk about that," I say. "I don't much like thinking about it myself."

"It's sad to think of," Nadine agrees.

"I couldn't understand then why Mother acted the way she did. I always thought my mother was about perfect, I guess; it was the first time in my life I ever dreamed she could do anything to hurt anyone."

Nadine's dark eyes go grave, and she frowns a slight frown. "Listen, Gail, I never blamed her."

II

We were worried about Uncle Nezer after Buck was killed. He went around with his eyes red from weeping. Mother said he would start to do some job around the place and then break off in the middle of it and just stand staring into space. It seemed there was just one thing that might have helped him through his grief. "If only his mother could know," he said again and again.

"I want to tell him hush about that," Mama said. "She don't care whether Buck's dead or alive, or she wouldn't have run off and left him when he was a baby."

It wasn't like Mama to make that kind of judgment, but of course she didn't know Rosabella then. There was only one person I ever heard of whose actions she couldn't excuse by saying, "It's just their way."

"She might be dead," Mother said.

"I don't believe Nezer's ever even thought of that," Mama

said. "I believe he still thinks he'll find her someday." Mother and Mama began to be afraid he might go off and start looking for her again.

"In his shape, he'd never come back alive," Mother said.

One day Mother had a letter from Nadine. This was unusual. She wrote to Uncle Nezer at least once a week, and now and then still sent me her sunny little letters about things she saw on the way to work or odd people she waited on in the restaurant where she had found a job when Buck was sent overseas.

"I wonder," Mother said, standing with the letter in her hands after I brought it in from the mailbox.

"Open it," I said.

She opened it and read—and Mama and I heard her read—with amazement: "You never in a million years are going to believe this, but I have found Nezer's Rosabella."

Actually, Rosabella had come to Nadine. She had been waiting on the doorstep one afternoon when Nadine came home from work: a fat old woman with bleached hair like straw and thick pancake make-up. You could have dug it out of her wrinkles with a spoon, Nadine wrote. "Are you Mrs. Frederick Kelso?" the woman asked, using Buck's legal name that probably no one in the family had ever heard spoken before. "It scared me that she should know that," Nadine said, "but I admitted it." And the woman said, "Then I'm your mother-in-law."

It was indeed Rosabella, and she had seen Buck's name in a list of war casualties, along with the local address of his widow. She told Nadine she had been looking for her husband and son for more than thirty years. When Nezer married her, his home was back in East Texas, and she had sent letters to the town he had told her the name of. But Mama said the family had lived in the country, and although their home was near that town, they had a different address. The whole family was gone by that time anyway, but Mama thought if she had had the right address word might finally have reached Nezer.

"What I'd like to know is why she went off and left Buck and Nezer in the first place," Mama said. We never did know that.

The point of Nadine's letter was that Rosabella wanted to come and live with Nezer, and she wanted Nadine to find out for her whether she would be welcome now. "I think you ought to break it to him slowly," Nadine wrote to Mother. "Make sure he knows what she looks like, because he can't be remembering anybody that looks anything like she does now. Maybe you can tell whether it would be better for her to come, or for him to keep remembering her the way she's been to him all these years." Nadine had told her all about Walnut Grove and the kind of house Nezer lived in, but Rosabella insisted that nothing mattered to her now but finding the father of her son. Nadine said the woman had enough money for a ticket. She didn't know what she did for a living, and wasn't sure she wanted to know.

"If she's good to Nezer," Mama said, "I don't care what she does or what she looks like."

"Do you think it might be better not to tell him?" Mother asked.

Mama looked at her as if she couldn't believe she'd heard right. "After all these lonesome years?" she said.

Mother sent me down to Uncle Nezer's to tell him we wanted him to come for dinner that day. He walked so slow coming back with me that I had trouble staying beside him. While we were still at the table after finishing our meal, Mother and Mama began to prepare him, asking him how long it had been since he saw Rosabella. And what he thought she would look like now. She might have gained weight, they said, or gone gray.

Nezer grew impatient with them. "Of course she'd turn gray," he said. "I don't see what y'all want to go on this way for. I might as well keep thinking of her the way she was to me, hadn't I? She was always the prettiest thing."

Suddenly Mother seemed to realize they were teasing him. "Uncle Nezer," she said rather sharply. "What if you could see her? What if you could see her but you knew she'd changed—a lot?"

He turned pale and gripped the edge of the table to steady his trembling hands. "Tell me," he said, and they did.

He insisted on sending a telegram to Nadine, with money for Rosabella to come on. He never even went home, but started for town as soon as he got up from the table. Mother let him have gasoline out of the tractor barrel, because he had used up his ration stamps.

Four days later we went with him to meet her at the Walnut Grove depot. In those days the trains were always late, and we waited for two or three hours. Uncle Nezer would keep putting his ear to the rails, and sometimes say "She's a-coming!" But two freights went by before the train we were waiting for. You never could tell where a train would actually stop. People said engineers hated having to stop at Walnut Grove; anyway it was true that they sometimes carried a passenger nearly half a mile past the crossing just below the depot. The train didn't go that far this day, but the door opened some fifty feet down the track from where we were waiting. Nezer ran, and I ran with him— then suddenly stood back as a fat woman in a bright shiny blue dress let herself down the steps. I turned away as she and Nezer came together. Mother and Mama both looked on with tears streaming down their faces, but I was too horrified to watch. I thought it would have been like a scene from the funny paper.

As I turned back, he was leading her toward us. "Girls," he said, "here's Rosabella and she looks just the same."

That night Hugh and Stanfield came to our house for supper. Nezer happily refused an invitation, saying that on this first night he intended to cook for his bride. He said if Rosabella wasn't too tired, though, he'd like for all of us to come and visit with them after supper. Rosabella laughed and said she wasn't tired, she was dying to meet her bridegroom's family.

"Well, tell us about her," Hugh said, as we sat down to eat.

"Do you want to tell them, Mama?" Mother asked.

"No, you'd better," Mama said, smiling with her eyes. "All I could see was a pretty little slim thing with rosy cheeks and golden hair."

Hugh had read Nadine's letter, and Stanfield had heard enough to guess this wasn't true.

"Oh, Grandma, you're joking," he said.

"In a way she's not, Stanfield," Mother said. "What Mama means is that this is the way she used to look when Uncle Nezer married her, and even when he sees her looking old and fat she still seems like the same girl to him."

I knew exactly what Mother meant. I knew that in spite of her tears of sympathy she had drawn a little away from Rosabella, but she was going to do her best to treat her well for Uncle Nezer's sake.

I wanted to like Rosabella and be good to her too, but somehow—no doubt because Stanfield was there—I giggled. "He even called her his bride," I said.

Mother frowned. "You kids just remember that she's Uncle Nezer's wife and we respect her because of that."

When we walked up to Nezer's house, the door was open and in the lamplight we could see the couple sitting together on the bed. Rosabella, in a garment like a cretonne tent, lay back against a pile of pillows and munched a Baby Ruth. Uncle Nezer sat with a hand on her thigh.

He jumped up immediately when he heard us and opened the screen door. "Howdy, howdy, come in," he said.

"So this is Hugh and Stanfield," Rosabella said, without moving from her position. "And now here's Fred's family all around us." I knew that Frederick was part of Uncle Nezer's name, but we had never heard anyone call him Fred before.

Stanfield and I looked at each other, but kept from giggling. "Except our dear daughter," she went on, "and she sent her love to all of you." She said this rather as if she had practiced it. Then she looked with a wink at Hugh and said, "And Fred calls me his bride—how do you like that?" She roared with laughter.

Stanfield and I took the opportunity to giggle.

We didn't really see Rosabella very often. I think she stayed in bed most of the time.

One time I heard Hugh say to Mother, "I reckon she's still all right, as long as she's good to Nezer?"

"That's what Mama says," Mother said, "but we may have to change it and say as long as she lets Nezer be good to her."

I knew what she meant. One time I went down to see them —down the pasture trail that led to the back door, the way I usually took to Nezer's house, and met him carrying out the slop jar. "Rosabella's not used to having to go outdoors to the toilet," he said. In the front room I found her, dressed in her cretonne tent, propped up in bed eating a Baby Ruth and reading *True Story*. "He's the sweetest thing," she said. "I'm happier than I've ever been in my life."

If she had been satisfied to lie in bed and let him wait on her, we would all have been happier. But she began to be bored because, as she explained, she was used to bright lights and jolly company. The nearest she could come to this turned out to be Mr. Bailey's store at mail time. She had begun by driving to the store to buy candy, any time of the day she happened to feel like it, without remembering the scarcity of gasoline or Uncle Nezer's threadbare tires. Then she discovered that the rural mail carrier stopped at Walnut Grove post office about ten o'clock every day, and that was the time when you could depend on finding a good handful of people gathered there. So she began to fix herself up and go, nearly every day. "You ought to talk to her about it, Brother," Mama said. "She just don't understand how folks do at Walnut Grove." But Nezer said the poor little thing didn't have much pleasure; it was hard for her to live at a place so far away from anything like she was used to.

In those days Stanfield and I were always arguing. No matter what I said, it seemed, Stanfield made fun of me. Sometimes I would tell him something Nadine wrote in her letters, like how the mountains against the evening sky looked like blue-black ink spilled across pink blotting paper.

"That's silly," he would say. One time he went on about it. "Nadine is silly," he said. "Mother says she's silly, or she would have known better than to send Rosabella to Walnut Grove."

"Well, she's Uncle Nezer's wife," I said. "And after he's looked for her all these years—it's like the end of a story."

"I bet it's not the end of the story," he said. "I don't think most people believe she *is* Nezer's wife. You want me to tell you what the men are calling her?"

I didn't answer. I suspected it wouldn't be nice, but I was curious. I knew he would tell me if I waited.

"Nezer's big ol' whore," he said.

"I don't believe it," I said automatically. I really didn't know exactly what a whore was, but I was twelve years old and had looked it up in the dictionary.

One Saturday morning Mother and I were out in the front yard and heard Nezer's Model A rattling by. We looked up, and Rosabella waved to us, on her way to the store in the tight blue rayon dress that seemed to be her dressiest garment. "I wish she wouldn't wear that to the store," Mother said.

Not much later I was sweeping off the porch and I heard a car on the road again, rattling as though it would fall apart, so fast it was going. "Boy, there's somebody in a hurry," I thought, looking up to watch it go by. But it didn't go by, and I gasped as it swerved into our drive and stopped with a screeching of brakes and a grinding of tires.

"Poor Nezer," Mother said at the door, having come to see what the racket was. "He won't have any tires left."

While we watched, Rosabella slid out of the car without

even stepping on the running board and came trotting up to the gate and onto the porch steps, with her breasts and buttocks bouncing like shiny blue basketballs. When she saw Mother she began to spew out language that "not nice" wouldn't even start to describe. Mother stood paralyzed by it.

"That heifer! That old bitch!" she panted, the words half lost in her asthmatic breathing. "Where's Fred? He's got to go tell that old sow where she can stuff her high and mighty respectable place."

"Run on, Gail," Mother said, so shocked she couldn't think where to tell me to run to.

I lingered, fascinated by the babble of filth and barnyard metaphor that was like nothing I had ever heard or imagined.

"Go on to your room," Mother said then, "and shut the door, and don't come out till I call you."

"Why that old brood sow accused me of *soliciting*," was the last thing I heard Rosabella say.

In my room I looked up *solicit* but was not enlightened.

After a while Mother did call me and sent me to find Uncle Nezer. By the time he came, Mama was there, and the four of them (Nezer, Rosabella, Mother, and Mama) sat down together in the living room. Mother sent me out of the house, but a lot of what Rosabella said still reached me through the open window.

"That old heifer going on about this dress, like it was some kind of a burly-q outfit. Fred's got to go and tell her a few things."

A pause, while someone spoke.

"And that's another thing," Rosabella screamed. "That goddamned nigger-pay so-called job he's got. . . ."

I heard Mother then, in a voice of cold fury that came through the air like a slap. "Shut up, Rosabella!"

I heard very little more, and the conference soon ended. Mama was inclined to talk about it, though, and I learned through listening to her and Mother that Rosabella had demanded an apology of Mother. She had been trying to talk

Uncle Nezer into leaving, anyway—going to the Gulf Coast where she thought he could get work in the shipyards. She said if Mother didn't apologize she was leaving whether he did or not.

A few days passed. I scarcely knew what the real trouble was, but I kept hearing the word *apologize*.

"Maybe I should," Mother said. "I'd hate to see Uncle Nezer have to go off to the Coast—he's just not able to work the way she wants him to."

"Do what you feel like you have to," Mama said.

One day when the three of us were sitting on the porch we saw them walking up the road.

"It will be the showdown," Mother said. "Gail, you'd better go."

"Let me stay, Mother. You can't keep me from knowing something sometime."

"Let her stay," Mama said.

Mother sighed and shook her head. "Oh—well," she said. I knew she was worried in those days, and now perhaps she had little mind for anything but Rosabella, marching up the road with her great bosom thrust forward like a challenge.

"We may be leaving," Uncle Nezer said when they had seated themselves. Rosabella hadn't said a word.

"Where would you go, Nezer?" Mama said.

"Beaumont or Port Arthur, maybe. I used to like that country."

"Brother, you're not able to do the kind of work you're thinking about getting down there," Mama said.

"Oh, I ain't a old man, Fannie," Nezer said.

Mother was sitting stiffly with her hands in her lap, one gripped in the other. "Is there any way you'd stay?" she asked at last, tonelessly, not speaking Rosabella's name, hardly looking at her.

"Apologize," said Rosabella hoarsely. "I don't want to stay in this Godforsaken place, but I might if I was treated right."

Apologize. Mother looked at me. I didn't know why. I didn't know exactly what Rosabella wanted Mother to apologize for, but I had heard Mother say to Mama that if it wasn't for Gail she guessed she could put up with the woman.

No one was saying anything. We heard a car approaching from the east, a noisy car, and we all looked toward it. It was an old, open car, full of boys I knew to be Walnut Grove high school students. I could have called some of them by name. As it came even with the house it slowed down, and they all craned their necks to stare at us. Then the boy on the side next to the house hit the door of the car with the flat of his hand and yelled "Whoop! Nezer's whore!" It came clear in the evening air as if he had yelled through a megaphone. Jeering laughter burst from the car as it sped away.

Rosabella was already packed and ready to go. They left the next morning, and Nezer's little old house was the emptiest thing in the world.

"I wish it would burn," I said once, and Mother and Mama scolded me. I remembered that years later when Mother wrote me that it had indeed caught fire, no one knew how, and burned to the ground. I wasn't sorry to hear it.

Uncle Nezer wrote a few scrawled, almost illiterate letters. He did not find work in a shipyard; he discovered he didn't have quite strength enough for that. But there was plenty of work for anybody willing to undertake it. The trouble was, there was no place to live. He and Rosabella were able to rent a room, at last, but it was a dining room and they had to get their own cots and set them up. People passed through it on their way from the other bedrooms to the bathroom, but Rosabella put up a curtain. They were doing just fine; no one was to worry.

We all cried then, and Mother said, "Mama, I'll write him to come home."

"With Rosabella?" Mama said.

"She'd never come back here," Mother said.

Mama shook her head. "I don't know. I'm afraid it's too late," she said.

After this letter we didn't hear anything for a long time. We all wrote to him, but I never knew whether Mother asked him to come back or not. Finally a letter came saying he was not able to work. He was an older man than he thought, he said. He had collapsed on the job. We never even knew what the job was but guessed it was some kind of day labor. Rosabella was making a little money, he didn't say at what, and he hoped to be better and back at work soon.

Mother sent him fifty dollars soon after that, but she never heard whether he got it or not. A few weeks later Mama had a letter from Rosabella saying Nezer was dead. "Whatever you may think," she said, "I loved him, and he was happy with me here. I guess I'll go back to California."

He was already buried when we heard the news of his death, and we never did know where. "If only we could have had him at Walnut Grove," Mama said.

Mother cried in her arms. "Will you ever forgive me, Mama?" she asked, and Mama said, "Hush, honey, there's nothing to forgive. We must only be glad that he found her, and had her with him at the end."

I used to imagine we would find Rosabella once more, as Uncle Nezer had found her. Sometimes I used to see someone like her on some California street, but when I came close I would know she wasn't Uncle Nezer's prettiest thing.

This was the only sad thing that happened in my memory up till then, and I wondered and wondered how much to blame my mother was.

III

"Listen: I never blamed her," Nadine says.
"Rosabella never got in touch with you?" I ask.
"Never."

"None of us ever heard from her again. I wonder what she expected when she came to Walnut Grove."

"I'd rather not even guess," Nadine says. "I'd rather just think how lucky Nezer was: not many of us can dedicate our lives so completely to one hope and have it fulfilled in the end." She laughed at her own high-flown language—a thing she wouldn't once have done. "Actually, I expect she was all the worst things Grandma Bailey ever imagined about her."

"Are you talking about Nezer and Rosabella?" We haven't heard Mother coming in through the living room, back from seeing Hugh and Stanfield off.

"I was saying no matter what she was, I hope Nezer was happy with her at last," Nadine says.

"I have always tried to keep them out of my mind," Mother says. "I'm afraid I wronged them."

"I don't know what else you could have done," Nadine says. "Rosabella never belonged at Walnut Grove—I knew that the minute I saw her on my doorstep. I know Grandma Bailey thought you did right."

"If I was right," Mother says, "I'm afraid it was for the wrong reasons. If I had been better myself, or braver, I needn't have sent Uncle Nezer off to die."

"It's no good thinking that way, Laura," Nadine says.

"Sometimes you have to face yourself," Mother says.

Now I feel that I am the one who does not want to talk about Nezer and Rosabella: I am the one who must change the subject, in defense against this disturbing new tendency in my mother.

"Mother," I say, "wasn't there some old milk pitcher of Mama's that you wanted Nadine to have?"

"Why yes, and I was about to forget it," she says.

She gets the kitchen stool and starts rummaging in the top of the old corner cupboard. There are a lot of old things there to exclaim over: even a Gold Plume coffee can.

"Laura, you've got a fortune there!" exclaims Nadine, who is a collector of what she calls collectibles.

"It's mostly junk," Mother says. "I should have cleared out that cupboard a long time ago. It's no good keeping old stuff stuck out of sight somewhere, just because it's old. I ought to make a trip to the dump ground."

This seems to me another change in my mother, for she has always wanted to keep all of Mama's things, as well as odds and ends belonging to the brief period of her own marriage. She has known for years that Nadine wanted that pitcher, but only this summer made up her mind to give it to her.

It is a blue pitcher, glazed pottery, with a cow's head embossed upon it. We used it on the table in the years when milk didn't come in a box from the store.

"Gail, don't you want this?" Nadine asks, as Mother puts it into her hands. "I oughtn't to take it."

I really don't. I think I should, but I don't. "There's no place for it in my apartment," I say. "You've always liked it so much. I think Mama would be glad for you to have it."

"You can have any of this stuff you want," Mother says. "I know Gail don't want it."

"Paul might," Nadine says. "And if not you ought to sell these things."

"What could I get for them?" Mother asks. "A dollar or two."

"You'd be surprised. Why look at those pink bowls: perfect specimens of Depression glass."

"We got 'em with oats," Mother says. "Do you want them, Nadine?"

"I think you'd better offer them to Paul or Stanfield's wife and daughter. They ought to stay in the family, after you've kept them so long."

"Let's just leave everything out," I say. "Paul can look at it when he comes in, if he's interested."

At least we have become sufficiently removed from topics it is best not to speak of. We finish putting up the washed dishes and go to our chairs on the porch for our afternoon of visiting.

Mother and Nadine can talk, it seems, of Mother's earliest days at Walnut Grove: the first time they saw each other, at Mother's bridal shower.

"I remember Grandma Bailey was really impressed with you," Nadine says.

"And I was flattered when she paid attention to me. I remember she was the one that got me started going to the home demonstration club."

"You went with Mama and me the first time. I couldn't imagine how you could get so interested in that demonstration on canning with a pressure cooker."

"I thought maybe me and Earl's mama could go in together and get us one, but somehow we never did."

"Mama was always holding you up as an example to me. She said I'd never get married if I didn't take more interest in cooking and canning and all that."

"Did you ever reach the point where you preferred housekeeping to walking in the pasture?" I ask Nadine.

"I haven't walked in pastures much," she says, smiling her old gay smile, "but I've never needed much of an excuse to walk out and leave the housework undone."

"You ought to come with me once, Nadine, down to the big mesquite."

"Gee, I'd love to, Gail, but seems like the family always have so many plans for me now. And I never can stay long enough to get everything in. Like tomorrow night, Johnny and Christine are going to play Forty-two at the Community Center. They say a lot of folks I used to know come to these gatherings —it'll be kind of a reunion, and I feel like I've got to go. But listen, why don't you come too? I bet you'd see a lot of people you haven't seen in years."

"I never learned to play Forty-two, Nadine."

"Well, I expect they're pretty uptown at Walnut Grove now. I believe I heard somebody say they play bridge, too."

"I never learned to play bridge either."

That's not quite true. I learned the rules of the game, but I was so bad, and Ted used to get so mad at me, that I stopped admitting I could play at all. I suspect Nadine knows, anyway, that what I mean is I never had any friends at Walnut Grove to be united with.

It is around five o'clock when she begins to talk of my driving her home.

"Why you'll stay for supper," Mother says. "There's plenty left."

"We're expecting kinfolks," Nadine says. "My cousin Cora and her bunch, and I told Christine I'd be back in time to help her fix supper."

Just as we are about to leave, Paul comes in, unexpectedly to me, although I remember now that he told Stanfield he would finish work early.

"What's all that on the kitchen table?" he asks, having come through the house from the back door to find us on the porch.

Mother explains what it is, and why it has been left. "I don't suppose you would want any of it," she says, "but Nadine thought you might."

"Hey, I bet Cyndi would like to see it," Paul says. "She collects old kitchen stuff."

"She does?" I exclaim. I remember the ice cream freezer, but I keep fitting Cyndi into Tommye Jo's house.

"Oh sure, she's one of these back-to-basics girls, you know. Bakes bread, cans fruit—all that sort of thing. And she likes all this preautomatic kitchen stuff."

"Well, you'd better let Cyndi have a chance at it then, Laura," Nadine says.

"Say, maybe I could bring her by while we're out tonight," Paul says.

"Sure, do that," Mother says. I don't say anything. I didn't know he had a date. I didn't know he would know what Cyndi collects.

Nadine gets up to go and picks up her pitcher, which she has set on the floor with her purse. "Your grandmother gave me this," she tells Paul.

"Hey, a cow!" he says, taking it in his hands. "That's nice."

"I feel a little guilty about taking it," Nadine says.

"I've meant to give it to her for years," Mother says.

"Oh, sure. That's fine." But we all suspect he is thinking how much Cyndi would like it.

"Will you come with us, Mother?" I ask as Nadine and I start down the porch steps; but she says no, Paul will be wanting supper soon, and she'll be putting it on the table.

She wouldn't go in any case, I suppose. I have never known of her going to any house in the community, even to sit in the car while someone else goes in.

"No, she wouldn't," Nadine says after we've started. I suppose she knows what I am thinking. "And yet you know, I believe she'd be welcome anywhere at Walnut Grove."

I don't respond; I am still thinking of Cyndi as a back-to-basics girl.

Nadine seems good at guessing my thoughts. "Cyndi's Stanfield's daughter, isn't she?" she says.

"Yes, about Paul's age. They seem to be getting along rather well this summer."

"And you don't much like it?"

"Well—they say she's all but engaged to a boy she met at college. I guess I shouldn't mind if the kids have some summer fun together."

"But you worry a little."

"Well—okay; yes, I do."

"Something happened between you and Stanfield, didn't it?"

I have felt comfortable all day with Nadine, as if I could tell her anything—I won't have to worry later about what of myself I've revealed. "Something," I say. "I hardly remember now what it was." This is not a lie; I doubt I could re-create the incident if I tried. I taught myself long ago not to try.

"Well, I can see several reasons why the families might not

be too happy if they got to liking each other too much," Nadine says, passing it off. "But of course it's what you say—just a little summer fun for them."

"At least Stanfield and Tommye Jo don't seem to be concerned about them. And they know Cyndi, and have seen them together more than I have. The night we had supper with them, they were treating Paul just like one of the family."

"But not like they wanted him in their immediate family? I mean, you know how a girl's mother can court a boy. Tommye Jo wasn't like that?"

"Oh no. She had her mind on something else altogether, I think." I pause to let Nadine's words register; they bring up an image I had not recalled since that night. "Oh," I say, really to myself.

"Oh what?"

"Tommye Jo *was* acting like that. But she wasn't thinking about Paul and Cyndi. I guess I was dense, but it was the farthest thing from my mind, and it's just now got through to me."

"What, for heaven's sake?"

"Nadine, they want Mother and Hugh to marry."

"Surely not."

"They do. I don't know why, but they do."

With this we have reached Johnny Carlile's house, and she gets out of the car. We'll see each other, we say.

"And don't worry, Gail," she says at the last. "It will all straighten out, you'll see."

When I get home, Paul is going through the collectibles, having moved them to a table in the back hall. I suppose he is figuring out which ones Cyndi might want.

He drives off immediately after supper, like a boy looking forward to seeing a girl he likes very much.

"He likes her," I say to Mother.

"Of course," she says.

In a little while he calls to say they have decided to go to town to a movie and won't have time to come by and see the things, but Cyndi is really excited about them. She wants to come soon.

"Why don't we ask them all to supper Saturday night?" Mother says. "After all, we've got to sometime, and they could all look over this stuff and take what they want. Then I can clean out the cupboard and put it to some better use."

"Well, why not?" After all, as she says, we have to do it sometime.

SIX

Paul is pleased at our plan for a family supper. I am resigned to it. Mother, after the first excitement has lasted through a phone call to Tommye Jo, is suddenly scared.

"There haven't been so many people around this table since the first year I was married," she says. "Whatever made me think I could manage a meal like this?"

"We can do it together," I say. "The first thing is to plan a menu of good but simple food. Things that won't all have to be fixed at the last minute."

She looks relieved. I must sound very confident, when the truth is I haven't had more than four people at my table since I was married to Ted Stoneman. And as I remember, every dinner party Ted and I gave was a disaster that ended with our quarreling far into the night.

"Well, I think everybody's tired of fried chicken anyway," Mother says, "and Hugh can't eat it. How about a nice beef roast?"

We are off and planning. There isn't a big enough roast in the freezer, so we shall have to go to town. Anyway, it turns out there are about two dozen other grocery items we will have to have, besides other unexpected articles Mother keeps thinking of.

"I wonder if there is a cloth anywhere big enough for the

table since we put the extra leaves in," she says suddenly, when we are on the verge of starting for town. We rummage through two old trunks and a quilt box, where we finally discover a heavy linen cloth that is big enough but so yellowed with age that it looks like a hopeless task to make it presentable.

"You had better offer it to Cyndi," I say. "It looks old enough, and laundering that linen would surely be basic enough."

"I'll buy a cloth," Mother says. "If I never use it again, at least I'll know I've got one."

On the way to town she also decides that she will buy a dress, since she hasn't had a new one for ten years and it strikes her that a pants suit isn't the thing for this party.

"Will we go to Seibels'?" I ask.

"It's called Bakers' now," Mother says. "But it's still the best store. Yes, I might as well go there."

I am thinking—both of us have to be thinking—of another time (the only other time) we went to Seibels' to buy a dress for Mother. But it is not a happy old memory to bring forth and fondly examine. I do not think we will speak of that.

Then, "This reminds me of the time we bought the dress for your graduation," Mother says.

"Yes," I say, "I suppose it does."

"Many a time I've wished I'd stayed at home that night," she says.

"There are more things than that to wish different," I say. "Starting a lot farther back."

"You never have got over it, have you, Gail? Never could forgive me?"

"As you said about Nadine—if there was anything to forgive!" I am not exactly lying; I just don't know the truth. "I only meant—I guess—what the psychologists say: what happens in your early childhood has a lot to do with what you become later on."

"Don't you like what you are, Gail?" Mother says softly.

"Does anyone?" I say lightly. "Anyway, Mother, I do admire you—for being brave enough to live your life the way you wanted to." I want to say I don't blame her—that I have been grown a long time now and can be whatever I want to be. But I can't say that.

"Thank you," she says. We don't pursue that subject.

After a busy day in town, we arrive home to find a note from Paul saying Cyndi called and he has gone with her to a party in Herley.

"I don't like it," I say.

"Oh, Gail, those two are not thinking about getting married," Mother says. "You're just hunting up something to worry about."

"There's always been more than enough," I say, "without hunting."

"You're not worried about me now?" she asks.

"I don't think so. Wondering, maybe, but not worried."

It is some time before she responds to this remark; but when we have put the most perishable groceries away and seated ourselves for the snack that will be our supper, she asks, "What are you wondering?"

"What's all this visiting in the family for?" I say. "And Hugh—in past years sometimes I wouldn't see him at all, and I don't think I would ever see him more than once during my whole visit."

"Oh, naturally Hugh stayed away, knowing how you felt about him. When you weren't here he came as often as he always did."

Of course. I don't know why I ever imagined their relationship had changed. "But Stanfield and Tommye Jo—you haven't been seeing them before."

"It really seems to be their idea—this visiting," Mother says.

"I don't know, Mother," I say. "I think you've changed."

"I've changed," she says, as if entertaining the idea for the first time. "Yes, I believe it's true that I have. I think it's just barely possible that I may be about to be happy for the first time since I was ten years old."

I open my mouth, but she says, "No, don't ask. You will know when the time comes. I haven't quite made my decision yet."

If she is planning to marry Hugh, I can't imagine why she should be coming to her decision now, fifteen years after Estelle died. She wasn't fifty years old then; Hugh was a vigorous sixty. That would have been the time; but if they weren't sure then, how can they come to an understanding after all these years?

I won't ask that. But I will ask something else: "Weren't you really ever happy, Mother, all those years of my childhood when I thought we had such good times together?"

"Oh yes," she says. "I was. I put it wrong. Sometimes I'd really forget for a little while, and be happy."

"But weren't you happy when you married Daddy, at first at least? I can understand that he must not have made a very good husband"—surely she has been wanting to let me know that—"but you must have been happy when you were looking forward to getting married."

"I suppose I was. But it was such a little while, and even then I was upset all the time because my brothers and sisters were against us marrying. Earl wasn't in the Church, you know. And I was worried about that. You see, as long as I lived with Grandma she never let me go with anybody. Or she kept saying I had to wait till I was eighteen, and then when I was eighteen there just didn't happen to be the right kind of boys lined up waiting. Mama and Papa never were that strict; if they had lived, everything would have been different. Then the year after Grandma died, Earl come to pick cotton for one of our neighbors. And he didn't know all about me, how queer I was because I was eighteen and never had gone with a boy. And he asked me for a date, and I went. And I guess he loved me. Right away he said he did, and I thought I loved him. I didn't

125

know anything about what love might be; probably I was just excited because a boy was paying attention to me. Then my brothers and sisters got after me, and preached against him so hard that I made up my mind they couldn't stop us getting married if he wanted to. And pretty soon he said he did. Like I said, I was worried because he wasn't in the Church. I used to pray every night after he brought me home that he would obey the Gospel and come into the Church. And of course all the time I was tore up about breaking with my family."

"Didn't you ever hear from them again?"

"I let them know when Earl died, and they sent word there wasn't any of them able to come to the funeral. And then you may remember I had a letter during the war telling me one of my nephews had been killed. He was my favorite when I lived among them, and I wrote to my sister that I appreciated her letting me know, but I never heard from them again."

"They didn't treat you very well."

"I never thought they did. But they saw things different, of course."

"Do you think Stanfield and Tommye Jo would feel that way if one of their children wanted to marry out of the Church?"

"I think that's one reason why you don't have to worry about Cyndi and Paul. Cyndi's not like I was: she's got somebody else, somebody her folks approve of."

"And approval means a lot to Cyndi."

"That's what I think."

"Then all I have to worry about is Paul falling in love with her and getting his heart broken."

"Don't reach, Gail. Like you say, there's always been enough to worry about."

On the next day we get our supper ready, and it seems bountiful and good. We call it supper because we are having it at night and dinner comes at noon. Of course if you are somewhat advanced socially you may call your noon meal lunch, but even then it is an affectation to refer to the third meal of the day as dinner. It is seven o'clock and broad daylight now as we begin looking for our guests, but we have announced our party for Saturday night because of course the time between midday dinner and about six o'clock is evening. Again, some of the more sophisticated members of the community may speak of that time of day as afternoon; but to apply the term *evening* to suppertime or later would be pretentious and misleading.

Such is the transitional state of language at Walnut Grove, which I am explaining to Mother and Paul until I notice that neither is paying any attention to me. What they are doing is admiring each other's appearance, and I suddenly realize that both of them have gone to rather unusual lengths in dressing themselves up for the occasion. Paul's freshly washed hair falls into a lightly waved pageboy, as it will when he dries it carefully with his styler-drier. He has on a shirt new to me, a pretty brown print open at the throat to show a silver necklace with a turquoise pendant. (It is the sort of thing that looks suspiciously like a gift from a girl, but I keep from asking questions.) I wonder if his months of tractor driving have broadened his shoulders and filled out his chest. Or maybe this seeming change results from some new way he feels about himself—a new posture. Whatever the reason, he looks to me tonight almost frighteningly handsome.

Mother has just combed out her pinned-up hair, which fluffs out flatteringly around her face and makes her eyes look dark and sparkling behind the bifocals in their flesh-tinted plastic frames. Her new dress, a rose-print voile, is fashioned with a well-fitting waist and flaring skirt, enhancing her good figure, which tonight looks almost girlish.

"Grandma, you'll be the prettiest girl here," Paul says, looking her over carefully. "Hey," he says suddenly, "haven't you got any lipstick?"

"I think so," she says, "but I don't expect the color's quite what the girls are wearing now."

"Mother, you've got something—something pinkish, not very dark. Loan it to Grandma."

We follow Paul's instructions—the lipstick lights up her face, adds another stroke of youthfulness.

"You are both incredibly good-looking," is my judgment. "Now don't tell me I look nice too," I hastily warn them. I know what I look like: a good haircut so I can wear my hair straight with no bother; large glasses (rather stylish) with tortoise-shell frames; a decent blue cotton dress that readily reveals I am about ten pounds plumper than my mother. I look all right, but I don't look as though I have dressed and polished myself tonight for the admiration of someone who cares especially what I look like. I suppose I project the image of the old-fashioned type of serious-minded lady professor.

"There's not another thing to do till they come," Mother says. "Let's set on the porch and wait."

We wait, each in his or her own way. Mother and Paul are impatient; they chatter at each other—about the cuckoo that sits calmly on its untidy nest, the moths at the sage, the promise that the sun will set clear.

I am not impatient; I could wait and wait. This is not what I expected of a summer at Walnut Grove: family dinner parties, lovers on every hand, the departure of silence from my mother's house where it dwelled so long I thought I could depend on it to stay.

We are looking for them all to arrive at the same time, but when we hear the first car it turns out to be Hugh's, and he has come alone.

Mother stands to greet him. She is lit by the rays of the sun streaming in under the porch roof. He comes to her. I can't tell whether he even sees Paul and me. He comes to her, and he lifts his arms to embrace her, and she moves toward him. "Laura!" he says. The embrace is not quite an embrace—one arm encircles her shoulders; one hand clasps her hand. It is the warmth in the word that he says (*Laura*, in happy recognition of her dressing up for him, with joy, with affection—with love) that streams with the sunrays back into my early childhood where I see the same scene and hear the same warmth in Hugh's voice and know only now (for what could a little child know?) the love that has lived an eternity between them. I never quite believed in it before.

Paul has seen, too, or felt the warmth. I look at him and see in the sunlight the trembling of his lips, a glisten of tears in his eyes.

They do not stand very long looking into each other's faces bathed in yellow light. It is long enough.

And now we must talk again about how the cuckoo sits on its nest, and the moths hover over the sage, and the sun sets clear. (There is no sign of rain.)

And then the rest arrive, in a burst of greetings and a flutter. "Hey, Laura, you've got a bird on this nest," Kevin calls; and going up to look at it scares it off into a tree where it begins to make tripping, sputtering sounds, just as though it belongs to this noisy big happy family that we have gathered together.

"That's my cuckoo, Kevin," Mother says.

"Cuckoo, cuckoo," he says like a clock, going into spasms of laughter.

Everybody chuckles mildly, to show that we are all going to get along beautifully together, even if Kevin does scare Mother's bird, and we go in to the dining table.

Mother doesn't have to worry about the supper. She is as good a cook as Mama was, and everybody enjoys it. Hugh brags on the roast beef. "I ought to fix me something like this at home," he says. "This is all right, ain't it, Tommye Jo?"

Tommye Jo says yes, she believes his diet allows meat like this, as long as he doesn't put gravy on it.

When the weather, the condition of the crops, and the effectiveness of the new hoe hands have all been discussed, Mother says, "Nadine thought you girls might be interested in some of the junk I cleaned out of the old cupboard."

"Paul told me about it," Cyndi says. "I can't wait to see it."

"You can look it over after supper then," Mother says. "I don't know whether it's anything anybody would want or not, but Nadine seems to think there's people that collect stuff like that."

"Not me," says Tommye Jo. "I had enough to do with oil lamps and dishes out of cereal and old black wash pots when I was growing up."

"Oh, Mother," says Cyndi.

"I feel the same way about some of these things," says Hugh. "I never could understand why these rag rugs got to be so popular. You'd see them in nearly every living room here a few years back, and all I could think of was my mother trying to braid every scrap of material she could find into something to cover our old splintery floors."

"Mama?" I say.

"That was when we lived back in East Texas," Hugh says. "Papa prospered a little better out here, but we still had a lot of making do. I guess I have to agree with Tommye Jo: I'd rather buy something good and new, if I can afford it."

Cyndi wouldn't try to argue with her grandfather—she just looks at Paul and smiles. They can't expect old people to understand, she seems to be saying.

"Our preacher's wife collects Depression glass, though," Tommye Jo says. "If there's any of that . . ."

"I think that's what Nadine called them pink bowls," Mother says.

"Say," Stanfield interrupts, "why don't we bring Kay and Cecil down here to look at Laura's things? He's just as interested as she is."

Is this the preacher Stanfield is talking about? I look for Mother's reaction.

She smiles and shakes her head. "You all just take the dishes," she says. "Or let's find out if Cyndi wants them first. Then you're welcome to take them, but I don't know how long it's been since I had a preacher in my house, and I don't believe I'm ready to invite one just yet."

"You ought to come back to Church, though, Laura," Stanfield says. This is a little forced—there is no way he can pretend it is spontaneous and casual. "Everybody would be glad to have you."

"Do you think so, Stanfield?"

"I *know* so," says Tommye Jo. It is clear to me that she and Stanfield have been discussing this move. I wonder if Mother's coming back to Church will be presented as a condition for their approval of a marriage. But I know pretty well now that they want the marriage anyway, and I wouldn't be surprised if Mother does too.

"Well, it would be good to think so," Mother says, with a smile. (I wouldn't be that tactful in her place; I would let them know about the chances of my ever coming back to that Church, if I were she.)

"What church do you go to, Gail?" asks Stanfield.

"Presbyterian," I say. I don't know whether it is quite true to say I "go" to the Presbyterian church. Once in a few months I attend a service at the largest church in town, where no one will notice I'm a stranger. I don't know whether I am attempting to propitiate God, or prove to myself that I do not really live cut off from the rest of humanity.

"But you're not a Presbyterian, are you, Paul?" Tommye Jo's question sounds more like an accusation, and I am sure she already knows about his religious status: that he was confirmed a Catholic, but has left the Church.

I remember Mother telling me once that the only thing worse than her marrying a boy like my father, who didn't belong to a church, would have been for him to be a Catholic.

"No, ma'am," is all Paul says. It seems to put an end to the interrogation.

"I believe it is time to get the pie, Gail," Mother says.

"Let me help," says Tommye Jo.

We have two kinds, lemon and chocolate. We all talk a great deal about which kind each person prefers and why, and how big a piece each one can eat. Mother has made Hugh a bowl of rice pudding, which we confer about. After hearing all the ingredients, Tommye Jo agrees that it is probably all right.

We get through the meal.

"Now, Cyndi," Mother says. "I put all that stuff out there in the back entryway. Paul knows where."

Discussing the prospects of Saturday night television, the men and Kevin head for the living room.

"You go on with them, Laura," Tommye Jo says. "Gail and I will clean up this kitchen."

Mother looks doubtful about being put out of her kitchen, but I insist too. I suppose Tommye Jo has some reason.

Presently we are achieving the confidential relationship of two women alone together in a kitchen, or at least Tommye Jo is working at it.

"Laura sure looks pretty tonight," she says.

"She bought a new dress for tonight," I admit. "You look awfully nice yourself," I feel I must say.

As a matter of fact, she does look nice—and different, somehow, from the way she looked at the supper at her house. I turn to look at her more closely. It's her hair—a different style, and it almost seems to me a different shade, lighter and brassier. I suppose she has had a new color job.

"Your hair looks pretty," I say.

She puts her hand to it. "Did you really think it's my hair?" she says. "I guess you don't remember how my hair was—mouse-colored, and so frizzy and fine I never could do anything with it. Now I buy wigs just like I do dresses, and never have to worry about what my hair looks like."

"Just like the lawn," I say.

She laughs. "Well, I never thought of that, but I guess so. I'm like Hugh—I like these modern conveniences that save work and bother." She pauses, and I feel she is about to say something else as soon as she can think of just the right way to put it. "Of course Hugh needs to save hisself," she goes on at last. "He's not as well as he might be, you know."

"He seems pretty well to me," I say.

"But you don't know how hard it is to see after him. I sure appreciate the way Laura fixed for him tonight."

"She gave a lot of thought to what he could eat," I say.

"That's just it," she says. "I declare I don't know what I'm go'n do about Hugh. I go down there about every day to try to see if he's got the right things to eat, but he won't fix hisself anything that takes any extra trouble. Hugh, I say, you know you're supposed to cut off the fat and just broil this meat. And he says he can't hardly get around to doing that, and besides he don't see how you can eat meat without a little fat on it."

"I can understand how he feels," I say.

"Yes, but the doctor's talked and talked to him and told him how much depends on him eating the right thing. And Stanfield and I feel like we've got to try to see to it that he does. It's like trying to take care of a little kid sometimes."

"Hugh doesn't seem senile though," I say.

"Oh no. He's not really childish. Except he just wants to have things his way. And then I think maybe he's getting to where he can't see too good. You ought to see his house. Cyndi and I go in and clean it up once in a while, but of course Cyndi's gone a lot now and will be more and more I'm sure. And I've got just about all I can do to keep my house now that we've built the new one."

"It must take a lot of time," I agree.

Now Tommye Jo moves in a little closer to the target. "It's a shame they can't just look after each other."

"You mean Mother and Hugh?" I say innocently. "Well, I think it is in a way, but of course Mother has Paul with her."

"Aw, he won't stay, will he?" Paul clearly doesn't belong at Walnut Grove, she seems to say.

"I don't know," I say. "I believe he thinks he will."

"Is that what you want for him?"

"It is not what I ever imagined for him," I confess. I think he has a potential that will never be realized in the repressive, anti-intellectual atmosphere of Walnut Grove. In our warm kitcheny confidence I almost find myself saying this, and I don't suppose it would offend Tommye Jo if I did.

"Anyway, he won't be satisfied to live with an old woman very long," Tommye Jo says. "Gail, do you ever think what will happen to your mother?"

"I have thought of it," I say. "But she seems well able to take care of herself now, so I don't know what decision I could make."

"She's nearly sixty-five," Tommye Jo says.

"She's likely to outlive Hugh by a good many years, if that's what you're thinking about," I say. For it is clear to me now that Tommye Jo has indeed decided that Hugh and Mother ought to marry, and that whatever reasons there may have been against it in former times, there is a very good reason for the marriage now. Tommye Jo and Stanfield don't want to take care of Hugh in these last years of his life.

"They could be a lot of comfort to each other," she says.

"Yes, comfort." Again I see them come together in the flow of the sinking sun and I know that none of us can tell what they might be to each other. But *comfort* is a good enough word.

"I thought maybe they might be getting around to deciding something."

"I wouldn't be surprised," I say.

"She hasn't told you anything?"

I shake my head. "Nothing." But of course I have known that I am being prepared for something—something is going to be revealed. Suddenly I wonder: Mother's bright eyes and pink cheeks—the affectionate greeting so oblivious to lookers-on. This night. Could it be time for the announcement Mother hinted at? What a happy surprise for Tommye Jo! But if it's to be a surprise, let it be a complete one.

"I guess we'll just have to wait and see," I say. "I have to admit I don't know for sure how I feel about it—but I suppose it's the same as with Paul. They'll both do as they please. I don't think I can control my child or my mother, either one."

Tommye Jo laughs. "Well, I guess that is a problem," she says. Not hers though, one supposes.

All except Paul and Cyndi are in the living room watching the Carol Burnett show, and we join the party as a commercial begins.

"Where's Cyndi and Paul?" Tommye Jo asks.

"On the porch," Mother says. "They said they'd seen this."

"Did Cyndi find anything she wanted?" I ask.

"She liked just about everything," Mother says.

"Well, I hope she won't take too many things," Tommye Jo says. "I expect she'll get over this old junk craze, and then when she gets married and leaves I'll have it all at my house to dispose of."

"What are you having, Laura?" Stanfield asks lazily from the sofa where he is reclining. "Some kind of a belated spring house cleaning?"

"Oh I don't know," Mother says. "I've just made up my mind to quit holding onto old things that don't have anything to do with the way I live now."

"Just tie you down to the past," Hugh says.

"That's exactly it," Mother says. They look at each other with little nods of understanding, and Tommye Jo looks at me.

"Does anyone want to watch anything else?" Mother asks suddenly, getting up.

"Yeah!" Kevin yells, but Stanfield and Tommye Jo shake their heads at him and say No.

"Turn that thing off," Stanfield says. "We can watch TV any time—we come to visit."

I don't know whom he thinks Kevin can visit. I am not quite

135

sure I like Kevin, but I feel sorry for him now. "I think I still have some old books in my room that I read when I was Kevin's age," I say. "Maybe Kevin would like to look at them."

"Wouldn't that be nice, Kevin?" Tommye Jo says falsely.

"No," he says, and lies down in the middle of the floor to look at the ceiling.

The television off, Mother has gone to stand rather tentatively by Hugh's chair. I wonder if she has been waiting for everything to quiet down before she tells us what we've been expecting to hear. I see Tommye Jo and Stanfield look at each other; I look away from them. "Here it comes," I say to myself. I don't know whether I am ready for it or not. I wonder why she doesn't wait for Cyndi and Paul to come in.

But all at once here they do come: the screen door is flung open and the two youngsters burst in from the porch.

Both of them are laughing and rosy. Tommye Jo clears her throat, and I expect her to quiet them down for the announcement we are all anticipating. But they ignore her as they move into the room hand in hand.

"Guess what!" cries Cyndi, trying a little too hard for a joyful ingenuousness. "Paul and I have decided to get married!"

Mother sinks down onto the arm of Hugh's chair. Kevin jumps up and then, looking around at the grownups' faces, sits down on the floor again. No one else moves. No one says anything.

I know now I haven't really believed this would happen. Certainly not soon. Not now. Sometime in the months ahead, maybe, if they went on seeing each other—but then Cyndi would go back to college, and the totally appropriate Bob would be there. Cyndi's life would follow its proper, ordered fashion, and Paul would find himself. He must find himself before he marries: this is the important thing, not the age (though twenty is so young), but that he should know who he is—discover the talent within him, integrate Paul the farmer (if indeed farming is more than a passing fad) with Paul the scholar of life.

Paul and Cyndi still stand in the middle of the room. "Well, gee, thanks for your congratulations," Cyndi says.

"We never expected you-all to be this thrilled about it," Paul says.

What is to be said, I wonder. I am not sure I could speak if I knew what to say. I feel as though my heart has just begun to beat again after having stopped for some unmeasured time. It is pounding now. My mouth is dry. The symptoms I feel, it occurs to me, are those of fear. I wish I were just a doting mother afraid my son is about to marry some ordinary little country girl unable to appreciate his virtues. Perhaps I am that, too. But if it were only that, I could speak.

Stanfield is the one who speaks at last. "We'll talk about this in the morning," he says.

He gets up. Tommye Jo gets up and reaches out to take Kevin's hand. Paul and Cyndi keep standing, waiting.

"Why can't we talk about it now?" Paul says. "We're going to get married."

"We weren't prepared for that announcement," I manage to say. "Give us a chance to sleep on it."

Cyndi's smile and rosy glow have faded, but she still stands with her hand in Paul's. Paul is looking puzzled. I think Cyndi is a good deal less surprised than he is by everyone's reaction.

Stanfield and his family begin moving toward the door. Tommye Jo beckons to Cyndi, who kisses Paul, saying brightly —to him, and perhaps to anyone who may be concerned— "Good-by, then; see you in the morning."

She stops at her grandfather's chair and bends to kiss him. "Good-by, Laura; good-by, Gail," she says and with another look at Paul she is gone.

Hugh must go too, he says, making no comment on the scene just past. Mother goes with him out onto the porch. Paul hasn't moved. "I don't understand this," he says. "You are *all* against us."

"We simply couldn't have expected it," I say.

"I don't know why not. I would have thought it was fairly evident that we enjoy each other's company."

"But you're cousins." This is a ridiculous thing to say.

"Some kind of cousins. Who could care about that?"

"It matters more than you know."

"I don't see why. There's no hereditary disease or anything like that, is there?"

Mother comes back in as we hear Hugh's car leaving. "Oh no," she says, "there's nothing like that."

"Grandma," Paul says rather pitifully, "are you against us too?"

Mother goes to him and puts her arm around him. "I'm not," she says, "but I know why it's going to be hard. They will have to tell you." She goes on into the kitchen, thinking, I suppose, that it will be tactful to leave us alone. I don't believe it will help.

"Mother?" Paul says.

"Not tonight, Paul," I say. "I suppose you will do as you please, but you will have to be told. We will talk in the morning."

"Well then. Good night."

I have hurt him. He is angry and puzzled, but he is mostly hurt, as when he was scolded as a little boy for doing something he thought I would praise him for. I would rather he stormed out of the room and slammed the door. I say good night rather shortly, for I must keep back the tears until I am alone.

Mother calls from the kitchen, "Cyndi forgot to take her things."

"Oh," Paul says, going to the door to talk to her, "we both like it all, and we thought we'd keep it, at least until we get a house and see what we can use in it. I told her I'd just keep them all here for the time being."

They didn't decide on the spur of the moment, alone on the front porch. I wonder how long they have had their understanding. But I don't ask. Paul goes on into his bedroom, and I go to mine. I cannot collapse on the bed and weep, as I would like to do, for I know without doubt that Mother will come to me. Shortly, she does.

"Tell him everything, Gail."

"Mother, I can't."

"Must I, then? I suppose it is nothing but right that I should."

"No, where Paul's concerned I think it's my place. It's just my part in the whole long sad tale that makes it impossible for me to think of Paul marrying Cyndi."

"It's Stanfield and Tommye Jo that will stop them," Mother says. "It's up to us to tell the truth and let it go."

"How much of the truth, Mother?" I say.

"Don't punish yourself, Gail," she says. "The punishment belongs to me, and is my right—alone."

"We've each had our share," I say, "whatever you may want to believe about the right of the matter."

"We'll tell him together, in the morning," Mother says.

"All right, Mother. Together."

"Good night, Gail," she says, and comes and kisses me. As long ago, when I lay here a child, I want to cling to her and cry; but I let her go as I did then, bravely silent when she blew out the light.

For through this night I must be examining years that I have tried to keep closed up in the darkness at the back of my mind.

SEVEN

At the beginning of my senior year, I reluctantly began to look for ways to leave off being a child. I had as happy a childhood as anyone could wish. Since I was often inclined to look at life in terms of books I had read—to get outside myself and view myself as a character—I was quite conscious of the fact that I had a happy childhood. I lived, as it were, in a little nest with two people who loved me dearly and made me the center of their lives—Mama and Mother, really two aspects of mothering in my life. Mama kept house and cooked and made my clothes and doctored me when I was sick. Mother went to the field and did the work of the farm, but there were numerous free and companionate times when we sang or read together, or packed a picnic lunch and went off to eat on the grass beneath the old mesquite. Uncle Nezer perched on the edge of the nest and looked in now and then with a special gift or message. Hugh and Stanfield were our only visitors from outside—all we needed to add a little variety to our lives without, however, spoiling the gentle, steady rhythm that we lived by.

Until the affair of Nezer and Rosabella, I had never imagined that my mother could be anything less than perfect in her understanding and treatment of any human being. I think I was vaguely aware of her disapproval when Nadine and Buck went away unmarried, but she never spoke of it and it had no effect on our lives. I was profoundly disturbed by the expulsion of Rosabella, and I couldn't altogether understand it, but in time I almost forgot it. The little world with me as its center hadn't changed, after all.

I liked school. It was entirely separate from the rest of my life, and I preferred it that way. I rarely saw any of my schoolmates anywhere away from school; they belonged there and—as far as I was concerned—had no existence anywhere else. In the first year or two, the big kids on the school bus used to tease me. They would accuse me of having garments on my back, or hesitating on the doorstep; but, contrary to their expectations, I knew the meanings of their words, so I never gave them much satisfaction. I knew they were teasing me, but I accepted teasing as part of the price I had to pay for going to school—the generally uncomfortable feeling I experienced outside the nest. Later, when they used words I really didn't understand—words like *bitch* and *bastard*—I gave them the same smile and looked out the window. They didn't bother me much, after the first few months. "Ask your mother what a bitch is, Gail," they said insinuatingly to me; but guessing from their tone that it was not a nice word, I thought I could predict Mother's answer and so I never asked.

As the years passed, I grew to like most of my schoolmates fairly well—in their place—and I thought they liked me all right, or at least recognized the position I held and accepted it. I was always head of the class: out of the fifteen members of my senior class, I confidently expected to be valedictorian, and as far as I knew no one expected anything else or cared. As valedictorian I would get free tuition for the freshman year at any state college (amounting to about seventy-five dollars, as I recall); and as I was the only one in the class with any notion of going to college, no one begrudged me this help. From the beginning of my school days, Mother had talked of the time when I would go to college and study to become a teacher. The small state scholarship would be a significant addition to the amount she had doggedly saved for this purpose.

I spent my days at school as a spectator. As far as the other kids were concerned, I knew I was a freak: I kept my nose in a book all the time, never had dates, never went out for basketball. All this was more or less true. I was strange. Sometimes I cherished my strangeness. There were other adolescent times when I wished I did go with boys or even imagined I might become a basketball player. I actually believed I could do these things if I happened to care enough to give up a way of life that had suited me very well for many years. I knew this incredibly private and happy life I led would have to change when I went to college. I was scared of going to college, but it never occurred to me that I would do anything else. And I assumed that with this change would come all others. In the last year I had begun to create fantasies about the romantic meeting I would have at college with the man of my life (some older man, with rugged features, of stern but gentle heart). I had a most satisfying novel, called *Nancy of Paradise Cottage*, about a seventeen-year-old girl who loved and married a man of thirty-five.

I never indulged in fantasies about any boy I knew—except, very rarely, one. Nothing would ever come of that. I didn't want anything to come of that. In a way—through those last years of high school—I didn't especially like him, for he became more and more like all those others who lived outside my life. I didn't see him as often at home—he began to have something he'd rather do than come with Hugh to our house for Sunday dinner—and when I did, he in his new identity was likely to taunt me for being different from him and the rest of the kids at Walnut Grove school. Besides, first cousins don't marry. Our affairs always ended with a kiss and an embrace. That was all there ever could be, of course. Only a sweet, sweet sadness. Sweet sadness was what I liked in those days. I can't imagine now why my fantasies involved Stanfield Messenger. I suppose it was because he was the only boy I had ever really known—the only boy who had ever touched me. But in those days I don't believe I ever remembered the puzzling reach of Stanfield's hand, on the sand rock roof of the Snake Den. And besides, he was in love with Patsy Wilkerson.

Some of the boys would flirt with me a little at school. They knew they were safe. I knew I was safe. I liked two or three of the older boys and used to have long conversations with them during study hall periods when I kept the library. Boys would lean through the big window opening between the two rooms and talk half the period with whatever girl was serving as librarian. None of the teachers at Walnut Grove bothered much with discipline in that last year of the school.

Or sometimes it would be a bunch of girls who would gather at the library window to talk. There was a rule that no more than two people could be at the library at once, but it had evidently been forgotten.

It was at the library window that I first heard about Stanfield's broken heart. "Stanfield and Patsy's broke up," somebody said. They were never talking to me, but to each other.

"Stanfield and Patsy's broke up."

"How come?"

"Their folks."

"His mama."

"Her Church."

"I heard his mama went to see her folks and said they had to quit going together if Patsy didn't join their Church."

"Stanfield don't even belong, does he?"

"No, but he goes. He wouldn't dare go anywhere else."

"He went to church with Patsy some."

"His mama put a stop to that."

"I heard Wilkersons said they'd let her join if she wanted to, but she joined the Baptist last summer. She said she wouldn't."

"He cares more than she does, I bet."

"Well, they've broke up. Patsy told Billie Sue all about it."

"Who wants Stanfield?"

"Who does?"

"Who'd have him?"

"His mama done had him. She can keep him."

Giggles. End of scene.

I was sorry to hear about Stanfield and Patsy. They were in love, I had believed; but I never did think Patsy cared as much as he did. At home I told Mother and Mama about it. "Their folks belong to different churches," I said. "They say that's what the trouble is."

I rarely mentioned the Church to Mother. I never had known exactly what caused her to leave the Church; I just thought it was what appeared to me to be their strict, unreasonable doctrine. It was what had caused the split between our family and Estelle. I had stopped asking questions about the exact nature of my mother's difference with her Church a long time ago. I think I had forgotten by that time that I really didn't know what it was.

"Well, that's too bad," Mama said. "He was aiming to bring her to eat dinner with us. I wish I could have seen her just one time."

"He'll have to marry in Estelle's Church," Mother said. "It's just as well he's found that out."

Stanfield never said a word to me about Patsy; he never had, and he didn't now. I hardly ever talked with him at school about anything, so the fact that he didn't speak to me didn't mean much. I did notice, though, that he went around with a glum look on his face and didn't seem to be speaking to anybody else either.

Then one afternoon as I started to my bus I noticed him, heading more or less in the direction of the bus he rode but loitering, perhaps waiting for me to catch up with him. This was rare but not unheard of; sometimes he waited to tell me he wanted to come over that night and get me to help him with his lessons. This hadn't happened since he had been going with Patsy, because she could give him all the help he needed, but the year before I had done his geometry for him nearly all the time.

"Hey," he said, as I came up to him. He had always a partly intimate, partly shy way of speaking—a manner that you might expect would be accompanied by a wink, but it never was, with Stanfield.

"Hey, let's me and you go to the show Saturday night," he said.

For a moment I was afraid I would be petrified and unable to speak. I had heard the same words before, in my head, alone, in the dark of the night. I had never expected to hear them aloud in broad daylight, standing on the dusty school ground while kids eddied around us, saying their good-bys to each other, making their dates, then moving on toward one of the four big yellow buses lined up in front of the schoolhouse.

I never thought to say "What's showing?" I don't suppose he knew anyway, or thought it mattered.

"Well, I might," I said, "if Mother doesn't care."

"Aw, you don't have to ask your mother."

I didn't, actually. She wouldn't have stopped me. But I had to know what she thought. What she and Mama thought. I wanted them to say yes, it's all right, a good idea, you and Stanfield have fun. I wanted this because I felt instinctively that there was something wrong about it. Was it just that we were first cousins? I remembered Mama's talk about first cousins marrying, from way back, but I knew for sure that I would never want to marry Stanfield. It was probably just my silly fantasies that made me uneasy. I had guessed all along that they might prove unwise, but never dreamed of being put to any real test. But then I laughed at myself and put my misgivings aside, for of course in Stanfield's presence—in real life —I knew he was just the same boy cousin who had teased me and tormented me and ignored me, as I supposed any boy cousin was likely to do.

Still I wanted Mother and Mama to say it would be okay to go.

Mama said yes, why not? I ought to get to go and have a good time, like other girls.

"We can go to the show, if you want to, and take Stanfield," Mother said.

"I don't think he'd want to do that," I said. "If you don't want me to go, just say so."

"Maybe I ought to talk to Hugh," Mother said.

"Don't talk to Hugh," I said. "It's just between me and Stanfield, and if it's got to be made a big family deal I'd rather just forget it."

"Well—" Mother said.

I went. But I wished Mother had taken a more doubt-dispelling stand.

Still, as I had known he would be, Stanfield was just his same old everyday self. We went to the show and afterward to a drive-in for hamburgers. There were a lot of high school kids there but no one from Walnut Grove. I half imagined I was like any other high school girl out on a date.

It was nearly my birthday. I would be seventeen. I had looked forward to this as the landmark age—the time when I would graduate from high school and go away to college, would at last and forever renounce my childhood. Sixteen had seemed the magic age for most girls. I had known of one or two who weren't allowed to date until that age, and even those who had been dating since they were twelve or thirteen seemed to think of it as a threshold of some sort to be crossed in their relationships with the opposite sex.

On any girl's sixteenth birthday (except mine), everyone around her would be chanting:

> Sweet sixteen and mama's pet,
> Ain't been kissed by the right boy yet.

When would I be kissed?

Stanfield had not come to my birthday gathering for the past two years at least, but this year he told me in advance that he would be there. "I've got you a present," he said.

As always, I had a new dress—as always, made by Mama. It was pink—a pale, brownish pink, all right with my ruddy complexion. I had read enough magazine articles to know that the favorite color of my childhood wasn't an easy one for me to wear; but I felt quite confident about this shade—in a shantung bought at J. C. Penney's. I had learned something about color, but I still had a lot to learn about style and fit. I never knew a dress was supposed to fit until I left home. Mama's only rule was that it shouldn't be too tight in the bodice or too low in the neck.

We had the same birthday routine we always had. The pink frosted cake that Mama baked. The blowing out of the candles. What wish? At seventeen I didn't dare to make a wish, but no one knew. Then I had my presents. Stanfield had got me a bottle of cologne. From the drugstore, not Woolworth's. Not Blue Waltz. Shalimar. None of us knew any better. I daubed it in the hollow of my throat and along the underside of my arms. I loved it.

It was not the following Saturday that he took me to the show again, but in two or three weeks he did. I wore that dress and that cologne. Coming home, he turned off the highway at Herley, taking a way that led along dirt roads. It was no farther, really closer, than the way we usually came, keeping to the paved highway as long as we could, but it took longer. The heavy moist leaves of the mesquite trees hung like blossoms in the bright moonlight, as he drew up and parked in a clearing by an unused pasture gate.

"Have you ever let a boy kiss you, Gail?" he asked.

"You know I haven't, Stanfield," I said. "I've never even gone with a boy, and you know it."

"Yes, you have," he said.

"Oh well. You."

"Me. I'm a boy, you're a girl. You do know that, don't you?"

I didn't say anything. I wasn't sure I did know what his low voice insinuated.

"Listen, let me kiss you," he said. "I'll show you what it's like, that's all. Then when you start going with boys you'll know what to expect."

That made sense. Or struck a weak spot—my fear of being thought ignorant and inexperienced for a girl of my age. "All right."

He took my glasses off and laid them on the dashboard. "That's how you let a boy know you want him to kiss you," he said.

He put his arms around me, pulled me around facing him, dropped his wet mouth on my apprehensive lips. I felt nothing except wetness.

He pulled away. "You're supposed to kiss back," he said. "Let's try it again."

We did it again. I pressed back with my lips. He held me tight. It was pleasant, even somewhat exciting. I thought, "So this is the way it is."

In a little while he pulled away again. "You oughtn't to let a boy hold you this long," he said, rather severely.

"Okay," I said. "I'm glad to know." I was a little embarrassed, but not very. He knew I lacked experience; I didn't have to pretend, with Stanfield. And I was relieved. Whatever might have happened beyond the point where my fantasy ended, in real life nothing did. Not with Stanfield, my cousin Stanfield. That was going to be all right.

I didn't tell Mother or Mama about the kiss, though. I knew it was all right; they might not have understood. Mother especially, I thought, for she still seemed doubtful about my new kind of friendship with Stanfield, and when I told of things we had done together she drew in and her voice lost its resonance.

Toward the end of school Stanfield began to talk about

going to a dance at Altheim schoolhouse. He had met some boys from Herley that had been to one of the dances and it sounded like a lot of fun. I knew about the Altheim dances. The school, which had originally served a small German community, had long ago consolidated with Herley; but for years the schoolhouse had been used mainly for community dances. I had heard scandalized gossip about them from my place by the library window. Germans believed in dancing and beer drinking and went to the Catholic church. In the Walnut Grove community most people knew all three of these things were sins.

"Let's go sometime," Stanfield said.

I was shocked. I "believed in" dancing, having long ago decided through my reading to reject false puritanical values; but my far-spreading ignorance enveloped that sin like so many others. I couldn't dance and was surprised to learn that Stanfield with his Church background had any interest in dancing.

"Do you know how to dance?" I said.

"A little," he said. "Patsy showed me how."

"I don't know," I said. "I'll think about it."

I did think about it and decided that if he mentioned it again—if he really wanted us to go—I would; but I would not tell Mama and Mother. I doubted that Mama would care because I knew she had gone to dances herself, as a girl, but Mother—I didn't like to believe this because of what I had always considered her bold stand about the Church, but in many ways Mother was downright puritanical.

Then we were preparing for graduation and I didn't think about the German dance at all. I wanted Mother and Mama to go to the commencement exercises. Never in all my school life had either of them gone to any program at Walnut Grove. I had never thought much about their not going—lots of parents didn't go to school events, or so I supposed, not actually having much experience of them myself. They just didn't care for such things and I couldn't blame them. Often, I suspected, school programs really were pretty silly.

But silly or not, commencement was important to me. I was valedictorian and had written my own speech, a sentimental double farewell based on the fact that this was the end of our school days as well as the end of the school itself.

"Mother, you just have to go," I pleaded.

Mama, who had grown fat and arthritic by that time, said she would like to go if her knees would let her. Her only two grandchildren would be graduating from high school—the first members of her family ever to achieve that academic height.

"Laura," she said, "I think you had better make an exception in this case. Gail never will forget it if you don't go to her high school graduation."

"Estelle will be there," Mother said.

"Which is more important," Mama asked, "this love or that hate?"

They didn't talk about commencement any more in my hearing, until one night at supper Mother said, "Well, I'll have to get something to wear."

Saturday of that week, the week before graduation, we went to town. Mama declared that she would have to save her knees for the night of the program and she wouldn't know how to buy a new dress anyway. She would wear the same good navy blue that she had kept hanging in her closet ever since I could remember.

In preparation for the shopping trip Mother and I studied the catalogues and the women's magazines. I looked at my mother as I hadn't in years—or more likely, never had. She was thirty-seven then. Nearly forty. Old—well, like anybody's mother. My mother was different in that she always worked in the fields and rarely put on a dress, never wore make-up except for a little lipstick when she went to town or sometimes on Sundays when we had company for dinner. She was a little taller than average, taller than I was, long-limbed and slender.

Perhaps because of Mama's continual preoccupation with long sleeves and bonnets, she had protected her skin more than most women did in those days. Her face, though faintly lined, was soft and clear. Her hair, a lighter brown than mine, was short and fluffy—the style she had always worn, cut at home with Uncle Nezer's old barber scissors. Her eyes, which often seemed to change color with her mood, were dancing with gold-brown lights as I solemnly compared her to a model in the *Ladies Home Journal.*

"Mother, you're beautiful," I said.

She laughed happily. Neither of us fully believed what I said.

What I really thought was that she could be quite attractive, nice-looking as anybody's mother at Walnut Grove. "Listen," I said, "let's get you a ready-made dress. You won't really have time to make one anyway, and it will have more style."

"Why, I can't afford—"

"Mother, you know you can."

On the way to town I said, "We'll go to Seibels'."

"Why I can't go in there in this old print dress," she said.

"I don't think you have to have on a fine dress just to get in the store," I said. "Besides, that brown-and-white check looks good for an everyday dress."

She had made it in the spring; it was the only dress she had with the long sweeping skirt they were calling the New Look.

"Just a cotton dress," she said.

"Cotton's fashionable now," I said. I was pretending to know a great deal about fashion, and Mother was pretending to believe I did. I had read the magazines.

"Well, all right," she finally said. "We'll look there. I expect I'll buy my dress at Penney's."

Then as we started into the store, she stopped and clutched my arm. "I can't, Gail," she said in sudden panic. "My underwear!"

"Mother, they don't care what your underwear looks like. They want to sell clothes," I said, affecting a superiority I didn't feel. I had never been in Seibels' in my life and was afraid of clerks anyway.

Once in the store, Mother put on an air of certainty, too. I suppose we bolstered each other. We walked to the back of the store where we could see the dresses on racks, and Mother asked for something suitable for her daughter's graduation. She told me later it was the first time since she bought her wedding dress that she had even looked at anything ready-made in a store. She didn't know her size—she was accustomed to buying a size twelve pattern, but it turned out she wore a ten in the dresses we were looking at.

I had pictured her in something beige or brown that I thought would go with her eyes and hair, but she chose a soft clear blue with a full flared skirt and a collar that opened low in front and stood up at the back of her neck, framing her face. It brought out the rosiness of her complexion and deepened the golden highlights in her brown eyes.

She bought the dress, and then the underwear she thought she needed, and then shoes and gloves and a purse—"You'll want white accessories," the ready-to-wear lady said.

Then, to my amazement, and without my having even thought of such a thing, Mother decided I should have a ready-made dress too. It had been understood that I would wear my birthday dress for graduation, the one made by Mama; it was what I thought I wanted to do, an appropriate thing. But now I was excited, too; we were like two young girls carried away on a shopping spree. We discovered that my best fit was a junior size eleven, and I found an apricot-colored dress with a brown-stitched, buttoned bodice that, while fitting snugly, still managed to make me look as if I had more bosom than I did.

Having bought our own things, both of us said—almost at the same time—"We have to take Mama something!" Not sure of her dress size, we decided on a white purse and gloves.

"At least she will have new accessories," Mother said, "even if she don't know she needs them."

"Or even what they are," I said, laughing. We laughed a lot that day.

The evening of commencement we couldn't eat. Mother and I couldn't eat. "Let's just have a bite of cold corn bread and milk," Mama said.

At last we got ready, after two hours of running from room to room looking at each other, zipping or buttoning, combing back hair. "Wait till I get my accessories," Mama said, laughing as she picked up her new purse and gloves. It tickled her to think she had had accessories all her life and didn't know it.

Then when at last we stood together in the living room, and all of us had our accessories, and I had my cap and gown in a box under my arm, Mother said, "I can't go."

"Oh, Mother," I cried, but Mama simply took her arm, and hobbling along on her arthritic old legs, propelled her daughter-in-law to the car, already parked in front of the house.

Mother drove in complete silence. I sat in the back seat and could see the stiffness, the tension, in her silken blue shoulders. I knew it wasn't the old disapproving stiffness, but I was so excited I hardly thought what it was. I was saying my speech to myself as we went along.

We were early. The graduating seniors were supposed to be early. I saw Hugh's pickup and said, "Stanfield's here. He was coming in the pickup, and his folks are coming later in the car."

"Oh," Mother said. "They're not here then."

Mama said, "I'm kindly anxious to see her. Hugh says she's got fat."

I said I had to go on in the schoolhouse, to the study hall. We had to put on our caps and gowns there and march into the gymnasium together, through a side door.

"Well, come in with us a minute, can't you?" Mother said. "Mama and me never have been in this gymnasium, you know." It had been built by the WPA, the year I started to school.

"Mother, I can't," I said. "I can see through the window, they're all there, already putting on their caps and gowns."

Mother turned to me, started to speak, then didn't. God forgive me, I turned away from her. And those two in their terrible loneliness walked at Mama's slow hobbling gait across the caliche-surfaced ground, but I didn't even wait to watch them.

I saw them again when we walked into the gym, to Mrs. Martin's thumping rendition on the old upright piano of the "Soldiers' Chorus." They had found their way—or I suppose been guided by one of the junior girls acting as ushers—to the group of folding chairs set up on the playing floor of the gym, several feet behind the row of chairs where the senior class would sit. They were in the second row of parents' chairs, between a big red-faced man in a khaki shirt and a faded-looking woman wearing an incongruously bright pink dress. I suppose they were parents of some of my classmates, but I had never seen them before. At the end of the first row I glimpsed Hugh, with a woman beside him who had to be Estelle. With the impression only that she was grotesquely fat, I hastily looked another way.

In my chair on the front row, I sat pleating my hectographed program while I waited for the time of the valedictory address. When it came I pulled my graduation gown around me like a cloak of invisibility (almost believed that it was) and mounted to the stage. Facing the audience, with the footlights glittering in my glasses, I saw no one (not gross Estelle, or Hugh, or my proud and anxious Mother and Mama); and deliberately lifting my eyes above all the anonymous heads for fear I should see someone, I recited my memorized words to the shadowed roof trusses and sat down. Afterward, a few people told me I made a good speech, but I never really believed anyone heard it.

At last all the songs were sung, the speeches said, and the honors distributed. To the thumping of "Onward Christian Soldiers," we marched out of the old rock gym. I wasn't able to go to Mother and Mama until we had gone back to the schoolhouse and removed our caps and gowns and packed them in their boxes to be sent back to wherever they had come from. We were all filled with a nervous excitement that had become hilarity. Girls hugged each other. Boys kissed girls. Even I was kissed and hugged in the study hall that night. As I was leaving, hurrying back to Mama and Mother, Stanfield came up to me.

"Listen," he said. He seemed to start most of his sentences that way, as if he thought it emphasized his earnestness. "Listen, let's go out here and talk a minute."

I followed him down the hall and out the schoolhouse door, into the dark May night. A band of stars (big liquid stars with wide black spaces between them) stretched overhead as we stood on the concrete walk that led to the side door of the gym. "Listen," he said. "You remember I'as telling you about them German dances."

I remembered.

"Well say, listen. They're having one tonight. They don't, usually, in the middle of the week, but the Herley seniors get through with their exams today and they're having this dance in honor of them. It's just a regular community dance, like they always have, and everybody's welcome. Why don't we go?"

"Oh, I don't think I could," I said. "Mother and Mama . . ."

"Well, heck, Laura can drive home, can't she? I'll bring you home—early. We won't stay late, I promise you we won't stay late."

As we talked there under the stars, I thought I never wanted that night to end. I didn't want to go home, have it over. I wanted to be graduating for the rest of my life. And so I made up my mind.

"I'll ask," I said.

"We won't stay late," he said. "Now you tell Laura we won't stay late."

He had to talk to somebody while I was gone, he said, and I should come back and meet him at the pickup. He said if I wasn't there in about fifteen minutes, he would go on without me and that would be all right.

I said I would probably meet him. I went on into the gym. Several of the seniors were already back inside, being congratulated, talking to parents and friends. There was a crowd near the door that I had to push my way through.

A fragment of somebody's conversation came to me out of the chatter and buzz. "They're both here, I seen 'em." "You can see why he prefers the one he does." Giggle. "Shhh!"

I didn't even wonder who was meant, but later I remembered the words.

Some of the parents were still standing near the chairs they had sat in, while friends swarmed around them. I saw Hugh and Estelle standing a little way back from the last row of chairs. No one was near them. Mother and Mama were walking toward the door, separate, too, from the groups of chattering friends. I started toward them.

Hugh moved into my path and stopped me. "Congratulations, Gail," he said. "You made a good speech."

"Thank you," I said, trying to move on.

"I want Estelle to see you," he said, taking my arm.

I could hardly break away, though I wanted to refuse to speak to her. I had kept from looking at her all evening, except for that one glance. In all my life I had never really seen her; once or twice in town I had glimpsed her at a distance, but I had never been close to her or spoken to her. I didn't know why, I didn't try to say why, but I never wanted to come close enough to speak to her. I felt no hatred toward her (how could I?); what I felt was more of a revulsion, a desire to stay right away from her, the way I felt about rattlesnakes. Some people evidently felt a keen hatred for the snakes; it was a kind of code of our country that you never passed by a rattlesnake without stopping to kill it. I never tried to kill one, but

Stanfield did sometimes when we used to walk together in the pastures. If I was walking alone, and a bush seemed to buzz at me, I simply gave it a wide berth and walked on.

So I would have preferred to do with Estelle. But Hugh stopped me, and of course she was Stanfield's mother—and so I went and stood before her and tried to be polite. She wore a tent dress that concealed her shape but exaggerated her size. Her bare arms lay like pale hams against the dark cotton cloth. At last I looked her in the face. Yellow and deep-lined, it ballooned out (like sagging, leaking balloons) below her tightly waved, faintly yellowish, pale brown hair.

Hugh introduced us as if we were two strangers who wanted to meet each other. I think I said "Hello."

"So this is Gail," she said, and laughed: "Tuh-huh-huh!" There was no way of knowing what she meant. There was a kind of irony in the tone of voice when she spoke as well as in the humorless laugh that puzzled me: I couldn't tell whether she was saying "What a disappointment" or "Just about what I expected" or "Who cares?"

"Yes," I said, and tried to smile. "I have to hurry and catch up with my mother."

I left them standing there. I think she was waiting for friends to come and speak to her. I never knew whether they came. Mother and Mama were almost at the front door of the gym when I caught up with them. I still had my diploma and the several certificates I had received (the state scholarship, the subscription to *Reader's Digest*, some private-school scholarships I couldn't afford to accept), and I gave them to her.

"We were so proud of you," Mother said.

I hardly listened. "Stanfield wants me to go somewhere with him," I said.

"Tonight?" Mother said.

"Oh, Mother, it's just nine-thirty," I said. I knew very well she wasn't talking about the time. Thoughtless as I was, and necessarily ignorant of what her real feelings must be—what an ordeal it had been for her to come to my graduation—I really knew my place that night was with those two.

"Where is he going?" Mother asked. The hurt, the disappointment, was out of her voice; it was the flattened, give-nothing-away tone that I had always understood to mean she disapproved of something I had done or said. It made me argumentative.

"A dance at the Altheim schoolhouse," I said defiantly.

We had walked outside, out into the soft dark in front of the gym. Cars were leaving, one by one. Sometimes headlights caught us in their beams as we stood talking, and I would feel Mother draw herself in.

"I don't think I want you going there," Mother said. "What do you want to go for? You don't know how to dance."

"Just to see what it's like, really," I said. "At college I may go to dances."

"I never danced," Mother said. "Besides, I've heard there's drinking goes on there."

"Mama used to dance," I said.

Mama said, "I expect that was a different kind of dancing."

"Oh, we're not going to drink any beer," I said.

"No, I don't think Stanfield would do that," Mama said.

"We won't stay late," I said. "We'll be home by twelve for sure."

"Twelve is late," Mother said.

"On my *graduation* night?"

By that time I was sorry, really sorry. I didn't even want to go. I would rather have been at home with Mother and Mama on my graduation night, looking back over the long years that had led up to that, drawing close to them because in only a few months I would be leaving that house where the three of us had had so many good times together. But Mother was making it necessary for me to go, whether I wanted to or not.

"Well, go," she said. That was all.

With tears coming close, I watched them walk away. I almost ran after them calling, "Wait! I want to go home." But I let them go, and hurried to where I supposed Stanfield might be waiting in the pickup. He wasn't there yet, so I climbed into the cab. Soon he came ambling along. He never wanted anybody to think he would get in a sweat about anything. When he climbed into the seat beside me he was singing an old Bob Wills song that we had heard on the jukebox at the drive-in in Sloan City. He had a rather high, clear voice—not much range, not very sure of the pitch, but good for songs like that. He put a kind of a pout in his voice when he sang. "You don't love me but I'll always care."

He didn't even speak to me. That didn't surprise me. I had seen Patsy Wilkerson getting into a nearby car with Bruce Basham. Stanfield gunned the pickup as he turned around to head west toward Altheim.

"I'd just as soon you wouldn't turn this thing over," I said.

He didn't answer me. He drove too fast all the way, about three miles. He didn't even stop before crossing the main highway.

Windows of the little square frame structure blazed with light. Men were standing around on the front porch and moving among the cars. I guessed there might not be room for everyone who came to dance at one time.

The big room (originally two classrooms—you could see where the partition had been) was really full of dancers. There were benches around the walls where a few people sat, mostly older people. I guessed the young people not dancing would be outside somewhere, courting in a car or drinking beer. We stood at the entrance a minute, looking for someone Stanfield knew. I recognized a few people who had gone to school at Walnut Grove, married couples now, some of them. There were all ages among the Altheimers, as I presumed most of those present to be: families with small children, middle-aged couples, some who were undoubtedly grandparents. Stanfield bent and said low in my ear: "Look at them squareheads."

I knew no one could hear him, but I blushed at his crassness.

The band—two guitars, a violin, a mandolin, and an accordion—was playing the last strains of the "Wednesday Night Waltz" when we came in. There was a great milling around when they finished, and the musicians picked up cans of beer from the floor and refreshed themselves. Some boys came up on the porch then and spoke to Stanfield—they were the Herley boys Stanfield knew, I assumed, though I saw Cotton Holt from Walnut Grove among them.

"Come out here a little bit," they invited.

"Listen, Gail," Stanfield said, "why don't you set down in here and wait for me. I'll be right back."

I found a place on a bench and watched while the band struck up "The Beer Barrel Polka" and the next dance formed. This one appeared to be popular with the older people—I had never seen dancing except in the movies, but I guessed they were doing a real polka now. They were having a good time. Stanfield didn't come at the end of that dance, and I wondered a little, but I didn't really care. It was fun to watch. Then a boy—short, blond, and stocky, with a pleasant smile (undoubtedly one of Stanfield's squareheads)—came up and asked me if I would like to dance with him.

"I can't dance," I said. "I just came with my cousin, to watch."

The band was playing a tune I knew. "Aw come on," he said. "It's 'Put Your Little Foot.' You can dance that, can't you?"

Actually, I could, a little. Once or twice at school, in the gym at the lunch hour, somebody had sat down at the tinny old piano and played that. Some of the kids really knew how to dance to it, and a good many others would try. One girl showed me the steps, and we danced together. Then some of the parents heard there was dancing going on at school, and the trustees called a special meeting to put a stop to that.

"Come on," he said. He told me his name was Leo Schneider.

I told him my name. "But I can't dance," I repeated.

He reached out his hand. "Come on and try. What difference does it make if you can or can't?"

"I'll feel silly," I said. "Look at all these little kids dancing like they've been doing it all their lives."

"They have," he said, "and you haven't."

I got up shyly and we took our positions, waiting for the right place in the music to begin. He guided me through the first movement, and although I was stiff and uncertain I began to think I might be able to get through it without making a complete fool of myself. I even thought: if I meet a boy as nice as Leo when I get to college, maybe I won't have to be afraid. Then as we came around near the door I saw Stanfield. He was standing in the doorway apart from anyone else. He had a hard, strange look on his face. I thought he looked pale, and then I thought perhaps it was only the way the light fell on his face. "Come here," he said. I could see him mouth it. He beckoned with his finger.

"I'm sorry, I have to go," I said to Leo. "My cousin is calling me."

"I'm sorry, too," he said. "Maybe we can dance the next dance."

"I don't think so," I said. "I think we'll be going home. I think something must be wrong."

"Well, thank you for the dance," he said, leading me to the door where Stanfield stood. I would have introduced them, but Stanfield wheeled around and strode toward the pickup, leaving me to follow him. I never saw Leo Schneider again.

I ran after Stanfield. He had the pickup started before I got in, and then, grinding the gears, drove off. He didn't explain anything. There was an odor that I knew was beer on his breath, though I had never smelled it before.

"Stanfield, what's wrong?" I asked.

He didn't say anything.

"Stanfield, have you been drinking beer?" I asked.

"Four," he said.

"Isn't that a lot?" I asked. "Are you sure you can drive all right?"

"Don't be a damn fool, Gail," he said.

He seemed to be driving all right, too fast but otherwise all right. I didn't know anything about beer, but if he wasn't drunk then I couldn't think what might be wrong. I had never heard him say damn before; I wondered if he had ever drunk beer before. But I didn't say anything else.

When we reached the highway he turned in the direction of the road we had taken coming home from the show. It was not the best way home. I still didn't ask any questions, but I wondered. Could he possibly be heading for the place where we had parked? I didn't think he was in the mood to kiss me this time.

Hardly slowing down, he turned off the highway on the road we had taken. At the old pasture gate he pulled off and braked to a stop. The mesquite leaves that had hung like blossoms in the moonlight were dark blobs against the starlit sky.

He turned to me. "C'mere!" he said gruffly. I didn't move or speak.

He moved a little toward me. "I said come here," he said.

"Stanfield, let's go home," I said.

He threw one arm around me hard, pulling me against him. "Take off them glasses," he said.

I couldn't move. He took them off and laid them on the dashboard. He bent to kiss me. But if that first time he had kissed me, then this was something else. Just his mouth hard against mine. I tried to move. He lifted his head and I said once again, "Let's go home," but now with the arm that was around me, hurting me, he began unbuttoning my bodice. He fumbled, then grew impatient, tore it open with both hands. At the same time, in a way that seemed unaccountably familiar, he was reaching up under my skirt, pulling at my underpants.

Several times he said, "What's the matter with you? Can't you do it like your mother does it?"

For years this has been all I can remember, the most I have been physically able to remember. It has been as though I fainted in the midst of Stanfield's reaching, and yet I know I didn't. For years if I thought of the incident I had to draw a curtain over it in my mind or become sick at my stomach. Tonight I have made myself come this far. I tell myself it is far enough. If I decide this is part of the story that Paul must hear; it will surely be enough to make him see what kind of father-in-law he is insisting upon for himself.

It is not the worst part of the story.

The worst part begins with what I remember next—myself pressed against the cold metal door of the pickup, sobbing, tears streaming. I am not sure now what I was crying about. In a way, it seems that it was the ruination of my cherished new graduation dress. Stanfield was at the other side of the car, a motionless shadow behind the steering wheel.

At last he said, "You don't know anything about it either, do you? They've kept you ignorant, too."

I had no idea what he meant. I didn't answer.

"My daddy and your mother have been—they've been—hell, they've been sleeping together. Just about all our lives. Now what do you think about that?"

I scarcely understood what he was saying, I simply knew it couldn't be true. "I don't believe it," I said. "I don't think you do either."

"It's the truth," he said. "I heard it tonight."

"If anybody told you that seriously, they were lying," I said. "I don't believe anybody did."

"All right," he said, "but you listen. You listen, and you'll believe it too."

He had heard it a long time ago, as surely I would have myself if I had not lived in a kind of magic circle of silence. He had heard it long ago—not so long but that he knew what it meant, but he had thought it was just lying gossip. It seemed so clearly impossible to him that he was able literally to put it out of his mind. He hadn't thought about it for years, until this night. At Walnut Grove, in the gym, he had heard something about like what I had: "Did you see them two women? No wonder Hugh likes his sister-in-law better."

It bothered him a little, but then he tried to talk to Patsy and they had a row and her boy friend wanted to fight him. It really was that upsetting him when we left the gym to go to Altheim. Then at the dance he was out at Cotton Holt's pickup drinking beer when a man came up—a man Stanfield knew. He used to go to their Church—the Stanfields' Church —till he married a squarehead and took up squarehead ways. He had a niece graduating at Walnut Grove that night (Nita Fay Lineberry) and had been to the program, as several had, before coming to the Altheim dance.

He came up to the boys around the pickup and, singling out Stanfield, said, "Say, I seen your pa and his old lady at the graduation exercises."

He had been drinking a lot, Stanfield said. He knew that and didn't pay much attention to what the man said. He answered, "Yeah, my folks was there all right."

"I don't mean your mama," Lineberry said. "That other'n— his brother's widder, can't recall her name right now. Say, she's better looking than she was about twenty years ago when they throwed her out of y'all's Church."

"That's a lie," Stanfield said. "We don't throw people out of our Church."

"Well, whatever you call it. It's the same thing. I was there the day they read 'er out. She walked down that aisle with her head in the air, and that's the last time I ever seen her till to-night."

Stanfield told me almost word for word what was said. Gradually I ceased crying and, listening, almost forgot the prelude to this revelation. Not quite recognized in my mind was the growing certainty that the man's story accounted for the sometimes puzzling way our lives were lived.

"You didn't know it, did you?" Stanfield said to me when he had finished.

"No, and I don't believe it now," I said. That was true, in a way. I was still too stunned to be sure I believed anything.

"I know now where he goes late at night," Stanfield said.

"He doesn't come to our house," I said.

"You don't know."

"Yes, I know that," I said thoughtfully. I did, because for years I had been staying up later than anybody else in our house. I would have known if Mother had had company. But I knew there were other times—plenty of times when I wasn't around. And I remembered Mama's habit of leaving Mother and Hugh alone for a little while on every visit. But such a little while!

(Then I remembered the girls at the library window and their talk one day about a girl whose parents wouldn't let her sit out in the car more than ten minutes when her boy friend brought her home at night. "You can do anything in ten minutes," one said, and they all grabbed each other and giggled, till even the teacher at the study hall desk looked up and cleared his throat.)

"There ain't nothing else," Stanfield went on, "to account for the way things are in our family. Daddy going to your house so much. Mother never going there. Laura never going to Church. It all adds up."

I didn't say anything. It was beginning to seem possible to me. It explained a lot of things I had wondered about. It answered a lot of questions that my mother had skillfully parried through the years.

My mother had lied to me.

What would she have to say to me when I came in with my torn dress? And then what would I say to her? What comparisons would I make?

"Did you think it was my fault?" I said at last.

"I don't know what you mean," he said.

"You know what you did to me."

"I don't know, Gail, I swear I don't," he said. He was beginning to whine a little, a way he had when he started feeling sorry for himself. I had heard it when the geometry lesson seemed too long. "I guess I was a little bit drunk, and it seemed like to me if we done the same thing they did it would be getting even with them somehow."

It was crazy enough to be true, maybe, but it didn't help me. "Take me home, Stanfield," I said. "I hope I never see you again as long as I live."

He took me home. We didn't speak again. He let me out at the front gate and roared off before I had time to slam the door.

Mother stood on the porch waiting. As I came into the light from the doorway, I realized what I looked like and slowed down.

"Oh, dear Lord!" Mother cried. "What happened?"

I didn't know how late it was, I didn't think. I didn't even remember any longer how worried she must be.

"Nothing happened, Mother."

"Oh, Gail." She threw the screen door back waiting for me to go in.

I walked in slowly, filled as I looked at my mother with a sense of angry betrayal.

"Tell me," she demanded. "Did Stanfield Messenger do that?"

"Stanfield did it," I said, "but it's not the worst thing that happened to me tonight."

"What on earth do you mean?" Mother cried. "Tell me everything that happened."

"Mother," I said wearily, "I don't have to tell you anything, ever again. I found out tonight what you have been keeping from me all my life. I guess I don't have anything else to say."

She stood as if paralyzed. I walked on through the room, through the kitchen. As I came to the door of my room, she called—she screamed—"Gail! Come back!"

It nearly killed me. But I had already thought what I would do. I quickly shut my door, which had never had a lock or needed one, and wedged a chair under it.

"Gail, let me in!" Mother cried at the door, and I threw myself across the bed and cried. She soon stopped pleading. I knew she didn't want to wake Mama up. I knew she would soon go away. What I didn't know was whether I could let her go, could keep away from her through the night, while I decided what to do in the morning. I didn't know whether or not my heart might really burst, with the anguish of loving her and hating her.

By morning I knew what I had to do. I slept late, having lain awake so many hours; and when I walked into the kitchen, Mother and Mama sat at the table still drinking coffee. They both were silent and pale.

I stood before them without a good morning, and I said to them: "Now this is what I want to do. I can never live in this house again, after you have both betrayed me. I could never live at Walnut Grove again—I would be ashamed to show my face, as I see now *you* always were. [I couldn't pronounce the name of Mother; I thought I never could again.] Oh, I understand my whole life now," I said bitterly.

Neither of them spoke. I went on to tell what I intended to do. We had planned for me to start college in the fall. I wanted to go then, the very next day. I could start in the summer term, if Mother wanted to give me enough money for that. I told her I'd try to find a job and work my way through because I didn't like the idea of using her money. I suppose I knew then that refusing the college money that had been one of the main goals of her life—the one that gave her the reason to work and do without and save—would hurt her more than anything else I could do.

"Aren't you going to give me a chance to speak?" Mother asked at last.

"What could you say?" I demanded.

"That what you have heard is not true," Mother said, speaking low and tonelessly.

"It has to be true," I said. "It explains too many things. About the Church. About Estelle. It all adds up."

"Estelle accused us," Mother said. "It wasn't true."

I thought of what could only be Hugh's faithfulness to my mother all through the years, their evident friendship for each other. It was more than friendship, it had to be, I saw now. But it seemed unbearable to me to discuss it with my mother. I preferred not to hear her side. I preferred not to believe her.

"I'm going to pack my things," I said. "I want to go tomorrow."

I spent the day destroying the signs of my childhood. Looking in the old starch box that I had always kept under my bed, I remembered my stupid illusions—in what ignorance I had written all those pages. There was the silly raincrow poem: I never finished it, never did learn what the raincrow cried. There was the first draft of my valedictory speech—how silly and sentimental all that stuff about saying a double farewell. My wonderful senior year had been nothing much after all—I wanted to destroy every sign of it. I was glad it was the end of Walnut Grove school, the end of Gail Messenger's incredibly stupid childhood, the end—in a way—of the world.

About midmorning Hugh came. I heard his pickup (he drove it almost exclusively now, leaving the car for Estelle) and

I slipped out the back way before anyone had a chance to call me. I walked in the pasture a long time, among the birds and flowers of May—a May as beautiful as I can ever remember there, and as I returned to the house in late morning I thought I heard the raincrow cry.

"I wish you could have talked to Hugh," Mother said.

"I didn't want to," I said.

"You are going to have to tell me what Stanfield did," she said. "Hugh and I have a right to know that."

"Let him ask Stanfield," I said.

"Gail, you have to tell me," Mother said. "Otherwise, whatever you say, I cannot let you go."

"It was nothing," I said.

"Are you sure?"

"It was nothing." I don't believe I really knew what I was saying. I simply never wanted to hear his name again.

In the afternoon, while I was burning papers at the trash barrel, Mama came and tried to talk to me.

"They never have done anything wrong," she said.

It didn't seem to matter whether that was true or not. "She ought to have told me," I said.

Mama shook her head slowly and hobbled back into the house.

I packed all my summer clothes in the two suitcases we had bought for me to take to college. "Maybe you will send me the rest of my things later on," I said to Mother.

"You'll come back for them," she said.

"No," I said.

I kissed Mama good-by. She clung to me weeping, and I wept too, but I hardened my heart.

Mother took me to the bus stop at Herley, and they ran up the flag to stop the bus, and she waited with me till it came. And all that time I never spoke to her, and I didn't kiss her good-by.

EIGHT

Not every morning now does the cacophony of the scissortails arouse me, but on this Sunday morning I am readily awakened. This is an uneasiness about me that has not slept at all, though at first I don't remember the source of it. Then I lie awake, in the silence of the household, remembering. I see now that, although I was disturbed by Paul's interest in Cyndi, the real likelihood of an engagement hadn't even entered my mind. "Sometime—if this goes on . . ." my thoughts all began. I recall now the re-creation of past times that occupied me in the night, but I do not dwell on it. I sense it as a great dark wall that will stop this impossible marriage, perhaps without the children ever having to understand what comprises the obstacle. It appears so dark and solid to me that I imagine they will feel at once its implacability.

There is still no sound in the house as the top leaves of the elm trees begin to catch the rays of the rising sun. But there is a car on the road—or a truck: a heavy vehicle, roaring fast along the road. Somehow I am not surprised when it slows abruptly and stops in front of our house. I grab a robe and hurry on tiptoe through the house to prevent a knock at the door. If Mother and Paul are still sleeping, I don't want them to wake up. I don't know what we will say to each other when we meet today.

Through the front windows I can see Stanfield's big red International pickup in front of the gate. He is still sitting at the wheel, and I hurry to him before he can get out and slam a door.

I feel my throat close up as I approach him at the open window on his side, but I manage to say, "I'm the only one up." I want to have my talk with Paul before Stanfield sees him.

"Well, I didn't want to wake the whole house up," Stanfield says. "I was wondering if I could come to your window and get your attention. I'm on my way down yonder to that place I told you about to see about my cows. Why don't you get in and go with me?"

For a moment I have an impulse to laugh—I almost hear myself sending crazy laughter into the air like the cries of morning birds. What I let myself remember last night comes back to me unbidden: Stanfield and me in a pickup, parked on a lonely road. I search his face and see only the worried look that I remember from his earliest boyhood: a deep frown, a pouty look about the mouth. It is Cyndi he is thinking of, and I see for the first time the possibility that he has completely forgotten the incident that I have blamed for much of the trouble of my life.

"I figure me and you need to talk," he says.

I can't see how anything we can say might help, and yet if there is anything to be done before I talk to Paul I would like to do it.

"Wait till I dress," I say.

"Shoot, we won't see anybody. You look all right."

I look all right, but I am wearing my nightgown. If I had ever dreamed or imagined that I might go anywhere with Stanfield in a pickup again, it would not have been in my nightgown.

"It won't take long," I say.

If anyone wakes as I hurry silently through the house and back again, no sign is given. I climb into the pickup and wait until we are moving down the road to slam the door.

Stanfield's pasture, as he told me, is a couple of miles down the road, just into the Breaks. No one lives anywhere on this road now, but I have an idea this is the place where the people lived who had the moonshine still that brought my father down in the Breaks on the night he was killed. Stanfield may know, but it is not a thing I want to ask him.

Stanfield drives fast and doesn't speak until he has stopped at his locked pasture gate.

"Does everybody lock gates now?" I ask him.

"Just about," he says. "I got a tank over here stocked with bass—and of course there's hunting in the fall. I don't want nobody in here without me knowing it."

He points to a small herd of cows at some feeders nearby. "There they are," he says. "We won't go in. I just like to come down here and look at 'em on Sunday mornings. See that pretty little Charolais heifer yonder?"

It is pretty—a grayish-white, slender animal. I make a suitable comment, but we did not come to talk about cows. I wait to see what we did come to talk about.

"You don't think them kids would actually get married, do you?" he says at last.

"Kids do sometimes," I say, "when they make up their minds to it."

"Well, I just can't have it. Listen, Gail: it's not that I don't like Paul, you know that, but he just can't marry Cyndi."

It occurs to me for the first time that Stanfield doesn't have any notion that I might object to Cyndi as the wife for Paul. He has brought me here to tell me my son can't marry his daughter.

"Stanfield, if that's what you have to say, Paul is the one you need to be talking to."

"I thought you might make him see."

"There are several things I'd like to make him see," I say. "I don't know whether they're what you have in mind."

I don't think he even hears me. "They're just not the same kind of kids," he says. "It just won't do."

"Why are you telling me?" I wonder.

"Well, listen," he says, "I just don't know anything about Paul. I like him, he's really a likable kid, but I just don't know nothing about him. Has he ever smoked marijuana?"

"Has Cyndi?" I ask.

"What do you mean?"

"I ask you the same question you ask me."

"That's silly, and you know it. [Arguments from our childhood: "That's silly." "It's not either." "It is too."] That's too silly a question to even answer."

"That's what I thought."

"You know what I mean: you just wouldn't ask that about Cyndi. She goes to Church, she's a nice girl—why she just don't do nothing we don't know about."

"I am inclined to think Paul is a nice boy," I say, "but he may possibly do some things I don't know about. So I guess the thing to do is ask him."

"I don't think you're taking this very seriously."

"Taking it seriously! My God, Stanfield, I was awake all night taking it seriously, trying to think how much I would have to tell Paul to make him see that this marriage is out of the question."

Stanfield looks up frowning. "You mean you're against it too?"

"Did you ever imagine I would be for it?"

"Nobody could have anything against Cyndi."

"Of course not. She's a charming girl. But, Stanfield, do you mean to tell me the only reason you don't want them to marry is that Paul doesn't go to your Church?"

"It seems like a plenty good reason to me."

"And all the rest—everything between us, between our families—is nothing to you."

"Everybody's forgot that."

173

"I haven't. And you cared a lot once, I seem to remember."

"There was nothing to it. At least, I know they never did do anything wrong."

"Oh, you know that? How could you know that?"

"I won't tell you," he says, "but I do. You can believe it's the truth, all right."

"The night we graduated from high school you didn't believe it."

"I was pretty silly."

"You were extremely silly, if that's what you want to call it. Stanfield, can you imagine for a minute that I'd want my son to marry the daughter of a man that did that to me?"

He looks away. He mumbles. "I don't think I know what you're talking about," he seems to say.

"What if Paul did it to Cyndi?" I ask.

He wheels around with eyes blazing. "By God, I'd kill him," he says.

"Since I know you don't take the name of the Lord in vain, Stanfield," I say, "I can only assume that you do remember that night after the dance at Altheim schoolhouse."

"It wasn't anything. I didn't—" Again he is mumbling.

"But you do remember it."

"I was awful upset and a little bit drunk, but I know blame well I didn't do what you seem to be accusing me of."

"I don't know exactly why you didn't."

"Because I come to my senses, that's why." He looks at me with a rueful smile. "You brought me," he adds, "you might say."

"I did?"

"You fought me like a tiger, Gail. Don't you remember that?"

"Sort of," I say. The whole scene begins to come back to me, the part of the picture my mind had rejected.

"Listen, I was grateful to you," he says. "But you did me more damage than I done you."

I wish I had remembered this. I wish I had known years ago that I was in some sense the victor. I always knew of course he didn't rape me, but I never freed myself of a sense of debasement, as of a maid upon whom a man has been allowed to work his will. I wonder if this could make a difference to me now.

"I'm glad you told me that," I say. "I feel better about myself, at least."

"And you do understand what made me act that way?"

"Of course I understand. You wanted to punish my mother, and I was the one at hand. I understand, but I don't really like it any better than I did when I didn't understand so well."

"But it's all over a long time ago, Gail. You know I'm sorry. Can't we forget?"

"We can't forget what lay behind it all—and I don't suppose the community of Walnut Grove forgets either."

"Oh, there hasn't been anybody thought about that in years."

"Then why do you suppose my mother doesn't go to Church?"

"I don't know why. You heard me ask her to come back."

"I don't know what your rules are, but I would imagine it would take more than one member of the congregation to reinstate someone."

"She can come back if she wants to," he says.

"And if she does—then you think everyone wouldn't remember why she'd stayed away so long? You think the tales wouldn't be told in every house around Walnut Grove and Herley? I hope she won't ever go back."

"Well, of course you're not a Christian," he says.

By his definition I am not, since he means I'm not a member of his Church, and I don't protest.

"I didn't leave any message about where I was going," I say now. "If you've said what you had in mind, I ought to go home."

He starts the pickup. "Well, I reckon you don't want them to get married either," he says. "But what are you aiming to tell Paul?"

"The truth." He doesn't have the nerve to ask how much of the truth, and I am not yet sure myself.

"I don't see any use in that."

"However I may feel about his marrying Cyndi, it's the only valid reason I can see against the marriage. It may not look that way to Paul, but if I can't stop him I at least want him to know the family background. Especially if he plans to stay at Walnut Grove, I think it is something he has to be told."

"You ought to think about Daddy and Laura."

"I am thinking about them most of all," I say. "I believe Mother will tell Paul herself."

When he lets me out in front of the house he says, "I'll see you." I wonder if he will. I'm afraid the regeneration of the big happy family is doomed to failure. But who can say? Perhaps we'll see each other at the wedding.

Mother and Paul are at breakfast. As they both look up questioningly, I say, "I went for a ride with Stanfield."

"Well, did you decide my fate?" asks Paul. He tries to make it sound like a pleasant little joke.

I get my cup of coffee and join them, but I can't think what to say.

"You really can't stop us, you know," he says. "We've thought about it a long time. Cyndi thought her folks would be against it, because of the Church, and she wanted to tell them last night, when we were all together. I had no idea you would be against us."

"What makes you think I am?"

"I saw as soon as Cyndi made the announcement. I can always tell if you don't like anything by the way you turn all vertical and seem to draw yourself in."

"It was a shock," I say. (And something of a shock to hear myself described that way.)

"I don't see why."

"Paul, I think—Grandma and I want you to see why. It may not make any difference to you, but we want you to see."

"What has it got to do with Grandma?"

"I'll tell you, Paul," she says. "I don't believe it is going to make any difference to you, but your mother and I both feel like you need to know. It wouldn't be fair to you and Cyndi not to let you know. It's not an easy thing—"

"Grandma, don't tell it," Paul says. "It doesn't matter."

"It matters," she says. "I want to tell. It may take awhile for you to see all the reasons why we think you should know. But if you can be patient—"

"I'll listen," he solemnly says.

We keep sitting at the old oak table while my mother tells her story. Some of it is new to me, and I know she is telling it for the benefit of us both.

II

"My only excuse is that when I met Earl Messenger I had never been allowed to go with boys. He paid attention to me. I thought I loved him. I believe he really thought he loved me. My only family were brothers and sisters, all married, and they all opposed us because Earl wasn't in the Church. I said that didn't matter, but in my heart I believed that he would come into the Church with me sooner or later, because I believed he was a good man, and an intelligent man, and I didn't see how he could keep from seeing the truth. But I studied the Bible, and I knew it was all right for a woman to be married to an unbeliever. I took my stand, and left my sister's house to marry Earl, and never saw any of my family again.

"I wish I could make you understand how I felt about Earl's

family and the community. Since my grandmother died, I hadn't really belonged anywhere, and belonging meant a lot to me. I looked forward to having a real home—I was glad we would be living close to Earl's folks. I was anxious to meet Earl's sister-in-law, because she was in the Church; but I looked forward to the whole community. Well, you've heard about the shivaree—that part wasn't so good, but the women gave me a shower and I started making friends. Nadine was one of my first and best.

"I found out fairly soon that I didn't love Earl the way I had thought a wife ought to love her husband. What I guess you would call the romance was gone right away, and it may be he felt the same way because he left me pretty often to be with the bunch of boys he had run with before we married—the bunch that was responsible for the shivaree. One of them—as I told Gail lately—caused the accident that killed him. But even before that—long before he died—I found out I was in love with Hugh.

"I didn't know why, I don't know why now. It sounds like a silly thing to say, in a way, but I was in love with him. I don't know any other way to put it. Maybe it started the night of the shivaree, when Earl stayed back in the kitchen with me. Buck was the one that struck out with his fists, but Hugh was the one that handled the situation. But that was just what called him to my attention. If it hadn't been that, it would have been something else. I think we both knew it that night, when our hands touched while I was handing him a cup of coffee.

"But neither one of us was the kind to give in to that sort of thing. I was determined to be a good wife to Earl, and I didn't have any reason to think Hugh felt different about Estelle. We tried to keep from looking at each other, never touched each other, though we were fairly often visiting in Mama's house at the same time. But Estelle knew anyway, I think. Or everybody said she was just naturally jealous—of any woman Hugh ever looked at. I don't know what it was—maybe just my guilty conscience—but I got to where I felt like, whatever she said, she was hinting at some suspicion she had of Hugh and me.

"That first fall I was married I aimed to show everybody that Earl had got a worker for a wife, and I went to the field and picked cotton. Hugh and Earl had decided to trade work, and it happened that our field got ready to pick before Hugh's did, and so we started together—just the three of us. Of course Estelle didn't go to the field—Stanfield women never did. I knew I wasn't feeling too well, and I had a pretty good idea what the reason was, but I was determined to pick cotton anyway. And then one day when I was up in the wagon emptying my sack I fainted. Earl was at the other end of the field, but Hugh saw me sink down and he come a-running. I never did know exactly what had happened. I picked up my sack, and it seemed awful heavy, and next thing I knew I was laying down in the cotton. And Hugh was kissing me.

"We didn't say a word, just looked at each other, and then he was up hollering for Earl, and they took me to the house. Mama knew right off what the trouble was, but Earl took me to the doctor next day anyway. And of course what we found out was there was a baby on the way. I wanted a baby, and I tried to be thrilled, for Earl's sake. But nearly all I could think of was how I felt when my husband's brother kissed me. And all the time praying God to forgive me, 'cause I knew the way I felt was sin.

"You know, it's not easy to say that, to you two setting there, but I was living with sin from the first. Even while I was telling myself—even when later on I told Gail—we didn't do anything wrong, I was living with sin. And I wasn't lying either. Both was true, and you have to understand that or you can't understand what I'm trying to tell you now. I was sinful, but I wasn't lost, as long as we could keep apart.

"And we managed. I kept my mind on getting ready for the baby, and I kept away from Mama's house when I knew Hugh might be there. Of course Hugh and Estelle and Stanfield would be there for dinner one Sunday a month, and Mama expected Earl and me, too. But that was the only time we ever saw each other. It liked to killed me when we did.

"But we went on that way pretty well till after Earl was killed. Then I just couldn't tell what to do. I felt like I ought to leave, but I had my baby and I didn't know where to go. Maybe my own folks would have taken me back, but I hadn't heard from one of them since I left my sister's house, except to say they couldn't come to Earl's funeral. And Mama and Papa was begging me to stay with them. It was too easy to give in, and so I stayed.

"Then Papa died. I'll never forget the morning his team come in from the field without him. I grabbed you up stark naked, Gail, from where I'd just started to pin on a diaper, and Mama and me drove to the field where he had been plowing. Of course we'd been afraid of what we'd find—the doctor had warned him not to work in the field, but with Earl gone he thought he had to. I made up my mind then to take his place. I was a farm girl and had worked all my life. I knew I could do it, but I had to have help—or at least some advice—and Hugh was the only one I knew to turn to.

"Paul, all this hasn't got much to do with what I wanted you to know. Maybe I'm talking more to Gail because, you see, there's things she don't know either. I still believe that if Earl had lived I would have made him a good wife, somehow, but when I didn't have him any more seems like I just couldn't keep from depending on Hugh more and more. Not that we ever so much as touched one another, no matter what Estelle may have believed. And I don't, to this day, know for sure what she did believe.

"Nothing happened—nothing. But of course there was times when something could've. I guess I was trying so hard, and feeling so proud of myself—yes, I guess it was that. Proud because we never did anything wrong—not as much as to hold hands.

So I didn't even think how many times there got to be when we *could* have done something. Hugh would go to the field with me sometimes, to help me about something—Estelle stayed at home, she would hardly ever come to Mama's then, but she knew. Estelle I guess was jealous-hearted, like they said, but I see how we did give her cause. The thing is, she never said anything—not outright. She had this way of saying something with a twist to it, so you didn't know whether she meant what she said, or just the opposite, or maybe something else again.

"I know one time she said, with that funny laugh of hers ['Tuh-huh-huh!'], 'I believe the Bible says that a brother ought to take care of his dead brother's wife; I believe I ought to just tell Brother Files how righteous you-all have got to be.'

"I don't think it was long after that till Brother Files come to the house to see me one evening. Mama and me was setting on the porch, but when we saw who it was she got up and went in, saying she would probably go out and see about the chickens. I invited him to take a seat, pretending I thought he was there on an ordinary visit such as a preacher might make to a widow in his congregation, but knowing very well it wasn't. Except when Earl died, he had never come to our house before. 'Sister Messenger,' he said to me, 'I feel like you have come to a bad time in your life and maybe you think you haven't had all the help from the Church that you might have expected.' I protested, of course. 'Have you prayed?' he asked. He didn't say about what. 'Day and night,' I told him, and truthfully.

"Then he said he had heard things that made him wonder if maybe I might not be turning to someone who in the end would give me more trouble than help.

" 'You mean my brother-in-law,' I said, for I was determined not to pretend I didn't know what he was talking about. 'Hugh has been a big help to me about the farming,' I said, 'a comfort to his mother and me both.'

"Then he warned me about taking too much comfort from a man that was somebody else's husband. And I spoke up to him: I said I was fond of Hugh, but I was raised in the Church and knew the difference between right and wrong.

"I think he got mad then. He got up. And he said, 'Don't let your righteousness turn to anger against those who only wish you well, and remember—the Christian must avoid even the appearance of evil.'

"I am ashamed now of what I said to him, but it seemed to me then to be the truth that explained his presence there: 'Evil might be in the eye of the beholder sometimes, Brother Files.'

"He left then. I don't think he even stayed to ask me to pray with him before he left, the way the preachers always used to do.

"Mama come in right away, and I told her what he had come for. 'He thinks I take too much comfort from Hugh,' I said. 'Hugh needs to comfort *somebody*,' she said, and from that time on I knew she saw what was between him and me and sympathized with us.

"'Stanfields sent him,' she said. Then in a few days when I got the letter from the elders she said just about the same thing. I was summoned to appear before them in the Church house, on a Saturday afternoon, and Mama said, '*She's* behind that. I wouldn't go.' Hugh didn't want me to go either, but of course they didn't know our Church.

"There was three of them, all Stanfields or kin to Stanfields. I sat on the bench before them, and they charged me with breaking the Seventh Commandment. They said the charge was brought by one of the members, not naming her name, and I in my ignorant pride looked back at them and said, 'Sister Estelle is mistaken.'

"They got mad then—especially her brother Claud, and accused me of adding to my sins by calling her a liar. I knew then they hadn't called me to give me a chance to speak for myself. They were doing what we learned later on to call issuing an ultimatum. Estelle had accused us, and that was that. I had a choice, and they would give me six weeks of grace to make it. I could come before the Church and promise, as they said, to correct my fault, that way of course admitting to adultery. Or the Church would withdraw fellowship from me—what we used to call turning their backs on a member.

"And that started right away. The next day no one spoke to me at Church, not even Estelle. It was her day to come for dinner at Mama's, and she sent me a message by Hugh: 'First Corinthians 5:11.' I didn't have to look that verse up, I knew how it ended: 'with such a one, no not to eat.' Maybe I wasn't so much surprised at that. But when on the Monday I went with Mama to Walnut Grove store I got a surprise all right. Miz Bailey and her daughter—Mary Carlile—was there towards the back of the store, I think getting soda pop out of the box. They looked up and saw who had come in. 'Howdy, Miz Messenger,' Miz Bailey said. She was looking straight at Mama, keeping her eyes off of me. Mary didn't speak at all, to either one of us, and they turned their backs on us and walked out of the store. And of course they was Baptists.

"Not everybody in the community was like that, of course. But I felt like they was, and I didn't want to show my face anywhere. Still I went to worship service at the Church; I was that stubborn. I hadn't done what I was accused of, and I was not go'n act like I had. I went to Church for six weeks, and on the last Sunday Mama and Hugh begged me not to go. What good could it do, they said. And I said just this much—that I would know that never of my own volition had I stayed away from the worship of the Lord on a Sabbath.

"And so it all happened. They called me forward, and I would not correct my fault—for I had done nothing wrong. So I had already said to the elders, and so I still believe. For whatever was in my heart, it was not the same as the deed I had been accused of.

"So they read me out. I went home and marked the lines in

red in my Bible, and I can see them right now just as plain as if they were blazing before me:

"In the name of our Lord Jesus Christ, when ye are gathered together, and my spirit, with the power of our Lord Jesus Christ,

"To deliver such an one unto Satan for the destruction of the flesh, that the spirit may be saved in the day of the Lord Jesus."

III

Her head is bowed low. Paul and I stay silent, thinking perhaps that she is praying; or overwhelmed, it may be, by the same force that is overpowering her.

I never guessed what it was like before. I had despised the community for a lack of understanding or compassion, for condoning a pack of gossips that I imagined were to blame for Mother's plight. I never guessed at backs formally turned upon her, or dreamed of her standing like Hester on the scaffold, consigned to the devil in words that are burning her still.

I get up and start to put away the breakfast things, wash our few dishes, and presently she looks up and says (like Mama the time the preacher came) that she believes she will go out and see about the chickens.

Paul keeps sitting at the table, and presently I fix myself another cup of coffee and sit again, with him.

"Dear Grandma," he says, and I guess from his voice that he has been close to tears.

"I'm sorry in a way you had to hear it," I tell him. "I really didn't know what it would be."

"You didn't know all that before?"

"No, not all. Somehow I think I had overlooked what must have been the most painful part to her."

"Excommunication."

"You understand it better than I do, maybe. I had just never thought of it that way before. Delivered unto Satan."

"So it wasn't that, especially, that you wanted me to hear?"

"I had the family background in mind. But I see how this might give you a better understanding of the Church."

"It makes me wish Cyndi was out of it."

"She never will be, Paul."

"I can see that. Grandma isn't really, even now."

"There was something else—something personal with me." (I see now that's all it was—my problem with Stanfield is nothing to do with Cyndi and Paul.) "But it needn't concern you. What might make a difference, it seems to me, is the community attitude toward Mother and Hugh. Stanfield says people have forgotten—I don't think they have. Anything that brings the two families together will make them remember— bring out the old tales to be told. For the community—contrary to what I thought and what I told you—isn't really gone. It may be a bit amorphous, but it's here, and many of the same people are here that knew Mother when she first came to Walnut Grove."

"And you think this should matter to Cyndi and me?"

"Maybe not. But I thought you should know. And I think Cyndi should know."

"Don't you think Stanfield will tell her?"

"No," I say, "I think the Church is the only barrier Stanfield can see."

"Why didn't they marry, though—afterwards?" Paul asks, after a little while. "Hugh's wife died a long time ago, didn't she?"

"Fifteen years," I say. "They weren't young any longer."

"Maybe that was all," he says doubtfully, "but it seems to me they care a lot for each other now."

"How would you feel if your fiancée's grandfather married your grandmother?" I ask.

"I think it would be great," Paul says. "I think Cyndi would too. What could it do but bring us closer together?"

"Neither the past nor the future bothers you?"

"No, really not," he says. "But I can see why you wanted me to know."

Suddenly he gets up and comes around the table and kisses me. "It was hard on you, too, Mother," he guesses.

"It was."

IV

In the afternoon he goes to Stanfield's. He lets both Mother and me kiss him good-by, but none of us can think of any wish to voice.

As we sit on the porch in our accustomed places, we hear a car coming and watch its dust cloud moving down our road.

"Cars don't seem to sound as distinctive as they used to," I say.

"That's Hugh's," Mother says.

"Come and join us," she calls as he comes through the gate. The life that seemed drained out of her voice by the morning's storytelling is returning to it now.

He takes his place in the old rocking chair. "How's the cuckoo?" he says.

"Brooding," I say.

"Looks like the rain's about gone for a while," he says.

"We can do with a dry spell," Mother says.

But we are not going to be able to get very excited about birds and the weather today. I wonder if we are going to try to pretend that Paul and Cyndi never made their announcement.

Then after a small silence, Mother says, "I told Gail and Paul today about a lot of things that happened before Gail can remember."

"That's good," he says. "That's a good thing."

I feel they may expect me to say something, but I don't know what to say. I have never quite got over the awkwardness that came with believing he was my mother's lover; her story has brought it back.

"Did you tell Gail why we never did get married?" Hugh asks.

"Maybe I don't know myself," Mother says.

"Tell her sometime," he says, as though she hasn't spoken.

Mother doesn't answer that.

"Paul has gone to Stanfield's, I guess," he says.

"Poor boy," Mother says.

"He's in for a hard time," Hugh says.

Yes, we all know that. It occurs to me that I have letters to write. As I take leave of them I remember how Mama used to see that they were left alone for a while whenever Hugh came to our house. "Come on, Gail," she would say, "and we'll—" See about the chickens, bake some teacakes, or do whatever she could think of to do.

Of course it was Mama talking to me when she lay dying that ever made me think I could bear to look at Mother and Hugh together again. In my room, never having intended to write letters, I lie across the bed where the elm tree shadows fall and think of the way I came back.

When I left the day after graduation, I thought I would never return to the house of my mother and grandmother. I was angry with both of them. It is hard now to tell whether I was angrier about what I thought Mother had done or about their not telling me. I had read a lot of novels and was a very liberal-thinking girl. I had cried over *The Scarlet Letter* and in general derived from my reading the notion that love should conquer all. Where my own mother was concerned, my theories seemed rather badly shaken, and still I thought that at least if I had known the truth I would never have been sitting in a pickup with Stanfield by the side of the road on our graduation night.

I have always believed and still do that if I had grown up with the truth, instead of the sort of romantic isolation in which I enveloped myself, I would not have married before I was eighteen years old. I would certainly never have married Tony Crewe. But it was all predictable. The GI's were still in college, and the older man I had always dreamed of was there waiting. After my sudden decision to enter summer school, I couldn't get a room in the dormitory and so took a bedroom in an old house near the college. Six young men shared the house across the street. I suppose it was because his schedule matched mine and we began walking to class together that I fell in love with Tony. I'm not sure why he got interested in me—probably because he had never known anyone so naïve before. So pure, as he came to express it. He said he had never known a girl like me anywhere. He was disillusioned about women after going through the war, and he hadn't believed there were any more girls like me. When he graduated at the end of the summer term, we married and went to live in California. He said he wouldn't dream of touching me before we were married, and it turned out that he hardly touched me after we were married. In a few months he had discarded me as hopelessly frigid. I supposed I was, and it never occurred to me to wonder why I was or whether frigidity was an unchangeable state.

I was lonesome and scared and without any money at all. I never even thought about asking for money from Tony. Scared and inexperienced as I was, I couldn't let myself starve. I thought of the only kind of work I ever did in school and managed to gather enough courage to apply for a job at the public library. I was hired as a clerk at a salary that barely paid for room rent and two meals a day. I sent Mother my change of address, having sent her my new name and address when we first moved to California. I hadn't written anything about my marriage, and I told her nothing about my divorce. I only asked her not to write to me except in case of an emergency, and (whatever I might secretly have hoped she would do) she took me at my word.

In the fall, after I had been away for three years, I had a letter saying Mama had terminal cancer. I acted on Mother's suggestion that if I couldn't come twice, I might want to come immediately, instead of waiting for the funeral.

Mother met my train in Sloan City, for Walnut Grove by then was not even a flag stop. I saw her walking toward me as I came down the steps with my white Samsonite train case, part of the matched set of luggage that we had decided on for my graduation present. I think it was when she saw it that she began to cry. I cried, too, and we embraced, but we found very little to say to each other on the drive to Walnut Grove.

She told me about Mama: "Too far gone," the doctor said. "There's nothing he can do."

"Is she in much pain?"

"Not as much as I expected," Mother said. "It will come later, I guess. We may have to put her in the hospital then."

"I'm glad she's at home," I said. I hadn't even known that much.

"We'll go by Walnut Grove," she said. "I want you to see it."

Mr. Bailey's store and house were gone. The churches were still there then.

"I cried when they tore down the store," she said, "though I hadn't been there in so many years."

"I don't know how you could care," I said.

Within a mile of home, she said to me, "Hugh is there, at our house. He came to stay with Mama."

"All right," I said.

He met us at the door, shook my hand (I let him), and said, "Mama's awake. She had a little Cream of Wheat a few minutes ago."

"Does she know I'm coming?" I asked.

"I haven't told her," he said.

Mother said she would go and prepare her. She had been afraid to tell her I was coming, she said, for fear I would be delayed and Mama would be disappointed.

Hugh carried my bags into my old room, and I followed him there. It would have been easier to keep back the tears, I thought, if Mother had made some change in it.

Soon Mother came to tell me I could go to Mama. "Are you ready?" she asked.

"I don't know," I said, "but take me to her."

"Mama, here's Gail," she said, standing in the doorway between the living room and the room where Mama lay.

I went in. It was what I had come for.

There was the old brass bed, which had never in my memory been polished, standing in the spot from which I suppose it never had been moved since Mama came to live at Walnut Grove. It faced away from the living room door; she lay in it very still and did not see me until I had gone a few steps into the room and was standing at her bedside.

She was white and shrunken and very old. I saw that she had not been old, as I thought, when I left her. I had to speak. I said, "Mama, how are you?" Anything else would have sounded just as stupid.

She didn't answer me. I thought she had little breath for that, and was saving it. She tried to lift her hands, and I knelt and took them in mine. I thought I could keep from crying. That was one reason I had let myself go with Mother—I hoped I would use up my tears. But when I saw Mama's tears start to flow I knew my supply was endless and I buried my head in the sheet and let us cry together.

She went to sleep, and I got a chair and sat by the bed until she awoke, perhaps an hour later. She moved her head at last, opened her eyes, and looked at me—dark, burning little eyes, shaped like the isosceles triangle in the geometry book. Those eyes, I thought, would be a long time dying. All of the old Fannie Messenger looked at me; she was not gone, as I had feared.

"I thought you might bring your man," she said.

"Mama," I said, "I haven't got a man."

"You went off with one, from that college," she said. "You had another name."

"It didn't work out, Mama," I said. "We're divorced."

"Was he mean to you?" That would be the only reason Mama could think of.

"It seemed like it to me," I said, "but I guess what he thought was I wasn't very much of a wife."

"If he had known how to be nice to you, you would have been," she said. "I'm glad you left him."

[He left me. But let it go.]

"Stanfield married," she said.

"Yes, Mama, that's nice," I said. It was the first time I had heard that, but she was getting tired and I didn't want her to waste her strength talking about Stanfield.

"You and him ought to be friends," she said.

"I don't guess we ever will any more, Mama," I said.

Her eyes clouded over, I saw that before she closed them. "It was *her* fault," she said. "Everything was her fault."

She would go to sleep that way, sometimes in the middle of a sentence. I would go then and try to talk to Mother without saying anything. Or I prowled about the place, seeking and escaping. They were into the worst drought anyone could remember, and when I walked in the pasture, dry whitish grass crunched under my feet and sent up fogs of dust. The sun bore down out of a steely sky, sucking out the life it had nurtured. Who would embrace that dry and brittle earth? I wondered. And yet the chinaberries hung from their branches, clusters of amber beads in nature's old bazaar. But surely the raincrow had fled. I believe I hoped it had. Or would they have heard its silly cries in the spring of this dry, lost year?

I would never know: a contracting in my breast when I thought of the mythic bird made me know it was one of the things I would not mention to Mother. Why, I didn't wonder.

191

It was enough to keep moving through the days, tiptoeing over the thin and brittle crust that held us from the abyss of truth. I heeded all the warnings.

Mama seemed better for a while after I arrived, and she announced that she would get up and sit in a chair in the living room for a few minutes every afternoon. It was then I sat and talked to her the most—or listened to her talk, for then, after her morning rest and her dinner, she had the greatest strength for talking. I recall one day when Mother had gone to the store at Herley, and I sat with her.

"How long will you stay?" she asked me.

"I have a week," I said.

"But you've got nobody to go back to."

"I have a job, Mama."

"You don't need a job, you could stay with us."

"No, I never could, Mama. Not any more. I have to make my own way, be my own self."

"Is it a job that needs doing?" she asked in her old abrupt, challenging way.

"I think so, Mama," I said. "I work in a library, help people get books to read."

"Like you done in high school," she said.

"Just about like that, but it's not a school library. It's a public library in a nice little town, and everybody that lives there can come and take home books to read."

"I knowed they had such things," she said, "but I never did see one."

"No, we never did, here. But Mother says they're building a library in Sloan City now, one for the whole county."

"Seems like I heard that," she said. "Your grandpa would have liked that, in his day. If they had books by Zane Grey."

"Oh they will," I said. "Or anyway they would have in his time. I never knew Papa liked to read. You never did tell me much about him, really." I thought I might guide her into talking about him; maybe it would be a restful, pleasant topic for both of us. But that wasn't what she had in mind.

"Andrew's been dead nearly twenty years," she said. "He ain't what I aim to talk about. Your mother's here now—and your uncle Hugh—and I want you to understand about that, while you're here with me and I've got my mind."

"You don't have to talk about that, Mama. It's all right—it's really all right now, but I just don't want to hear about it any more."

"You've got to hear it, and hear it straight," she said. "You don't know the truth of it. Maybe if you did you wouldn't go back out yonder."

"No, Mama," I said, "you don't understand about that. I've got to go back. I never could live at Walnut Grove any more."

"Well, there's libraries in Texas. You could come and tell 'em how to run that new one at Sloan City. But that ain't it though. Whatever you do, wherever you go, you've got to know the truth."

And Mama told me her truth. I knew she wasn't lying to me, and I listened and began to understand a little of what my mother's life had been.

"They loved each other from the first," she said. "I believe from the first time they ever looked at each other."

"Didn't Mother love my father then?" I asked it, for I knew that she wanted to tell.

"She thought she did," Mama said authoritatively. "I know she thought she did, but she hadn't seen Hugh when she married Earl. I knowed that from the start—that she didn't really love him; but I tell you if he'd a lived he never would a knowed it. She would have been a wife to him, which was more than that Stanfield woman done for Hugh."

"And more than I did for Tony."

"That was different, I expect," Mama said. "But leastways you can see what I mean. A woman can marry a man in good faith, and then find out she never did love him. Estelle never even thought she loved Hugh, or I never seen any sign of it. She tricked him, was what I always thought."

"And so both your sons married women that didn't love them?"

"It was a grief to me, but it was so. Still, it's not very uncommon, you know. I learned to thank the Lord I had lived with a man I loved, and that loved me. But I can't keep from asking myself why He let us find each other in time, and kept Hugh and Laura apart."

"Kept them from marrying," I said.

"Kept them apart is what I said and what I mean. Folks has thought they was lovers, but I know better. You can't live with a person day in, day out, for nearly twenty years, without knowing that much about 'em. Your mother don't hardly know what it is to have a man. I reckon her inside's dried up like the pasture grass and the water holes."

That was when I first began to believe I might have condemned my mother too soon. I thought, "Mama knew her so well."

"And I'll tell you something else," she said. "Estelle knows it too—knows the truth and always did."

"Always did?"

"Always did. You find that hard to believe, but you don't know Estelle. They say she's ailing now."

"Serious?"

"I don't know. She'll die some day."

"Do you think Mother and Hugh would marry?"

"If it ain't too long a dry spell."

I knew Mama had talked enough, tired herself out, said all that needed to be said. I accepted all she told me, but I wanted one thing more. "But why did she stay?" I asked her.

Mama's tired little eyes widened, brightened. "Because she loved us. Me and Hugh. She loved us both."

She closed her eyes then and sank back in her old wicker chair. "I'll help you to bed now, Mama," I offered.

She shook her head. "I'll set here," she said, "till Laura gets back from Walnut Grove."

I needn't have said anything. It didn't matter. Time fooled her; she was clear on everything else.

"Walnut Grove is gone, Mama," I said. "Mother went to Herley."

"Of course," she said, angry with herself. "I keep forgetting they tore it all down—and it was go'n be such a fine town once. Do you remember when they had the townsite opening and Mr. Bailey sent up the balloon?"

"I remember," I said. It was twenty years before I was born, but it was as real to me as Walnut Grove had ever been.

She didn't get out of bed on the day I left. I don't think she ever really knew I was leaving. She was having pain, and we gave her the pills for it. I went and stood by her and said "Good-by, Mama."

"If you see Miz Bailey," she said, "tell her my beans is bearing and I'll send her a mess pretty soon."

I ran out of the room, out to the car, and cried most of the way to Sloan City.

"You and me didn't get to talk much," Mother said finally.

"We talked, Mother."

"You know what I mean though."

"Mother, it's all right," I said. "Mama told me how it all was —if it was all right with her, then surely it ought to be all right with me."

"But I ought to have told you. I've cried my heart out about the way you had to find out."

"You couldn't have known. I know you meant to tell me."

"Couldn't you come back—maybe go back to college, maybe someday live closer to home?"

I told her something of my plans then. I meant to enroll in the junior college in our town and keep working at the library while I completed my sophomore year. Then when I had saved enough I would go on and get a degree. I wasn't sure then whether I would teach, as she had always hoped I would, or go on with library work.

"Let me put you through college then," Mother said. "Out there, or wherever you want to go. I've got the money still."

"No, Mother," I said. "I thank you, but I'll make it on my own."

"It's not to punish me?"

"No, Mother. Really not. I don't know how to explain—the way we were going got changed. The thread we were following broke. I lost the way, and a lot of things happened. I picked up an entirely new thread, and now I have to follow it."

I don't know why I said things like that. I don't even know what I meant. But I still thought then there was hope for me if I escaped from Walnut Grove.

"Maybe I see," she said. "You'll come back again though? Some better time?"

"I'll come," I said. I wasn't really sure then I ever would. I wasn't sure how far back I could go, or wanted to go, but I was through being estranged from my mother.

"Will we write?" she asked.

"We'll write," I said. "I'll write to you as soon as I get home."

"Home" was the key word. I said it deliberately, telling myself where home was: my bedroom overlooking the quiet pepper tree street, where I lived alone, and kept a box of scribbled-on papers under my bed, and walked in the evenings into the foothills, toward the mountains that spread before me like blue-black ink spilled on pink blotting paper.

And then I left her alone in the dusty, shabby railroad yard, where no other passengers went or came. And I cried and cried, on into the sunset, and I didn't know where home was.

NINE

Paul is not home at suppertime.

"We'd better go ahead and eat," I say.

"Them kids might've gone somewhere together," Mother says.

"I wonder." I wonder if Stanfield won't succeed in breaking them up altogether—if they will ever go anywhere again. I wonder what Paul would do if Cyndi acceded so readily to the wishes of her parents. Would it break his heart—or simply change his feelings toward Cyndi? I know he has never cared much for the spirit of submission, nor would he expect it of a member of his own generation. As he has so often told me— and no doubt his father too—he is the one to decide what he will do with his own life.

I wonder if it has ever occurred to him that he might decide to be the husband of a girl who wouldn't or couldn't become his wife.

Mother and I have our bite of supper and then sit in the living room watching television, to provide ourselves with a way of not talking about Paul. When we go to bed after the ten o'clock news he has still not come in.

But I have not been asleep when I hear him. He goes through the house to the bathroom and then stops in the kitchen. The light goes on, as I can see under the closed door between us, and I hear him open the refrigerator door. I have a small debate with myself about whether to go in and see if he wants to talk. Should I? Probably not. I get up and slip on my robe, open the door, and look in at him.

"Can I help?" I say.

"Yeah," he says, straightening up from the refrigerator. "Help me find something to eat."

"There's some cold fried chicken," I say. "Would you like that?—or I could make you a chicken salad sandwich?"

"Make me a sandwich," he says.

Perhaps this simply means he wants my company. He sits at the table drinking a Coke while I strip off the brown-crumbed outside layer of a wishbone and thigh and cut up the meat to mix with mayonnaise, celery, and pickle.

"Is everything okay?" I ask.

"No," he says.

I set the sandwich before him and sit down myself, with a glass of milk.

"Didn't you have supper?" I ask.

"Oh yes," he says. "I ate at Stanfield's—before they went to Church."

"And then?"

"And then went to town. Not for any reason. But it was so early. You wouldn't believe how little there is to do in Sloan City on a Sunday evening. I just kept driving till it was dark enough for the drive-in movie to start."

"So you saw a movie."

"I think so. I may have slept through it mostly. I couldn't even tell you what it was."

"Paul, tell me," I say at last.

"I don't know, I told you."

"You know I don't mean the movie. Tell me what happened at Stanfield's."

He doesn't answer for a while. "Yes," he says finally, chewing the last bite of his sandwich. "You know, once I thought if you

198

loved a girl and she loved you, what you did about it was up to the two of you."

"Not at Walnut Grove," I say.

"No," he says. "Not in the Messenger family anyway. I didn't think getting married had been like this since the Middle Ages."

"Your father's family were pretty concerned about his marrying out of their church, too," I tell him.

"All right, maybe that's partly what I mean. I didn't think Protestant churches were like this. You know what he said to me—what Stanfield said?"

I shook my head.

"We were all sitting together in the family room or whatever they call it."

"Kevin too?"

"Oh no. They sent him visiting somewhere, I believe. But we were sitting there, Cyndi and I on that love seat in front of the fireplace, and Stanfield and Tommye Jo in the chairs on each side, you know. 'So y'all are aiming to get married,' Stanfield said, and of course we said we were. And he said, 'Now I want you to understand one thing, Paul. I want you to be absolutely sure you know what you're doing, because we don't tolerate divorce.'

"I didn't know whether he meant him and Tommye Jo or the Church. I told him we were sure. And he said, 'Well, of course you would think that,' and Cyndi said, 'No, Daddy, we really are.' It was the sort of thing that could go on for quite a while, but Stanfield got enough of it right away and went on to the nitty-gritty."

"The Church."

Mother comes in quietly and joins us at the table. "Yes, you will have to understand the Church," she says.

"Maybe you can help me, Gran," Paul says. "You know, you'll think I'm pretty dense but I really hadn't believed until

Stanfield made it so clear to me this afternoon that they think they have the only way to salvation."

"It is the only Church because it is the Church that Christ founded," she says. "This is what we believe."

What we believe. And they turned their backs on her those forty years ago.

"You see, Paul?" I say.

I think he does see. "I guess I just hadn't taken it in," he says. "Then when I did I tried to be just as polite as I could. I told him I wasn't asking Cyndi to leave the Church, and he said that didn't matter—'don't make no difference,' was what he said, and he said it pretty belligerently. The children have to be raised in the Church."

"That has a familiar ring," I say.

"You went through all this," he says, a little astonished. I am sure he never really thought about that circumstance before.

"It wasn't religion that caused trouble between Ted and me though." It seems important that he should know that.

He grins. "No, the kind of Catholic Dad is, I would guess not."

"And I don't think any of his family ever blamed me with your decision."

"Of course not," he says. "I think Grandmother blames Dad, but it's not the fault of either one of you. I just started thinking. I tried to explain that to Stanfield. He said he could understand that all right, and was glad to know I had sense enough to get out of that. Now he wanted to know if I didn't have sense enough to get into the true Church. I told him that at this time I couldn't see why there was very much difference, but I would certainly give the matter some thought."

"I was taught to think that Catholics were deluded by the devil," Mother says.

"Oh, Gran," Paul says.

"Well, I can't help what I was taught," she says. "Neither can Stanfield and Cyndi."

"But of course you don't believe it," I say.

"No," she says. "And yet it's there somewhere inside me still. It affects the way I think, I can't help it."

"Well," Paul says, "I ought to have known. But I was just sorting out my mind, kind of, trying to be honest. And of course he blew up. I think he was about to throw me out of the house—literally, bodily you know. But Tommye Jo intervened. I saw Cyndi turn to her and just whisper 'Mother.' Then Tommye Jo said in her quiet, kind of dry, way, 'Stanfield, we are supposed to be reasoning together.'"

"I know them words," Mother says. "Come let us reason together."

"I don't know whether we did that or not, but it seemed to calm Stanfield down a little. He talked some more about how important it is for the whole family to worship together. Then finally he came around again to asking me whether I wouldn't consent to worship their way [I think that was how he put it] and I said again that I didn't see how I could unless I underwent some change that I wasn't anticipating. I said I thought Cyndi and I, as two adult people, could probably figure that out for ourselves.

"Then Cyndi spoke up. She said yes, we were two adult people, and she was one of the two; so she thought it was time somebody listened to her. She said some of the things we had already talked out together—like my not having any objection if she took the children to Church with her. I remembered my own experience, and I thought I could depend on my children to find their own ways, as I've tried to find mine.

"Cyndi didn't exactly threaten them but I thought she was saying she would marry as she pleased, no matter what they said. I believe she will do it, but I admit she hasn't told me so. Anyway Stanfield finally simmered down a little, and he told Tommye Jo she could tell us what they had decided. It turned out to be a month's cure—if we promise not to see each other for a month, and if we still want to marry after that, they'll talk to us again and we'll see if we can work something out. Not that we could marry. Just that they would talk. Cyndi thinks we should go along with them, so what else can we do?"

"That don't sound too bad," Mother said.

"Just idiotic is all," Paul says. "They had already talked to Cyndi about it—they want her to invite some guy named Bob for a weekend, I suppose with the idea that if she sees him she'll realize what a mistake she's making, but she says she won't invite him. Not that it would really matter, to either one of us, but she wants them to see they can't force anybody on her."

"Well, whatever their purpose may be," I say, "it will give you time to think—maybe a little more clearly, being away from each other. Try to look at what has happened in the Messenger family already: your grandmother and Cyndi's grandfather both were part of mixed marriages of this kind. Think how things turned out for them."

"Yes, you might think about it, Paul," Mother says. "I know you don't see any reason to talk about whether Stanfield believes in divorce or not, because it won't happen to you and Cyndi anyway, but I wonder if some way in the back of their minds most young folks nowadays don't count on divorce if things don't work out right. You ought to search yourself and see if you might not have that in mind."

"You're right, Grandma," Paul says. "It just wouldn't arise, with Cyndi and me. But of course I think to force two people to live a literal hell of a life together because they don't *believe in* divorce—whatever exactly that means—is barbaric. Now you tell me: wouldn't it have made a lot more sense for Hugh and Estelle to be divorced than for all three of you to be as miserable as Mother seems to think you were?"

"I don't know, Paul," Mother says. "I didn't think so. And Estelle didn't think so. Hugh asked her to give him a divorce, even though he knew I probably never could bring myself to marry a divorced man. But she wouldn't hear to it. I think in a way I was glad, for it kept me from having to make a decision. For a time once, when we thought for some reason she might agree, I used to read my Bible every night; and search as I would, I couldn't find a place where Jesus approved of divorce for any cause except one. And that didn't enter into our case."

"How do you feel about Mother, then?" Paul asks her. It is something I have never asked, myself, and she has never told me.

"She's my daughter, and I love her, and I don't judge," Mother says. "But my belief in the Bible has never changed."

"Cyndi said something about like that," Paul says. "But it's a kind of double vision I'm not sure I understand."

"If you can't," I say, "you had better not marry Cyndi. Because as long as you live, there will be temptations to judge each other. It will be as hard for you to accept her belief as for her to accept your lack of it."

"That's true, Paul," Mother says.

"And yet," he says, "you love your daughter."

"At least you see the case will bear some thinking," I say, "and so maybe you won't mind the month so much."

"Oh I mind it," he says. "Of course I mind it. But Cyndi says we can do it. She says it really isn't such a big price to pay, and things will be easier if we go along with her parents' demands. And so I agreed; you see, I can be reasonable. Or at least—I'm not so sure it's reason, but I can compromise."

"It won't seem too bad," I say.

"Not too bad." I suspect at first he is mocking but he goes on, "There's a guy at Herley been wanting me to go on a fishing trip with him when I get laid by. I think I just may do that."

Meanwhile, perhaps my son and I will have a little of the companionship I came to Walnut Grove to find. I will cut my tongue out before I talk to him of Cyndi and marriage during this month allowed us.

Now Paul turns deliberately to the idea of hard work and getting his crops laid by. "But the hoe hands are coming in the morning," he says, "and it's time to go to bed."

II

About midmorning, Cyndi comes.

"He's over yonder, isn't he?" she says, pointing toward the north field where we can see the hoe hands working.

"Yes," I say, "but should you be here?"

"I told Mother I was coming," she says. "I told her I wouldn't see Paul, and she knows I'll keep my word."

"Would you like to sit on the porch?" I say. "It's still fairly pleasant out here, though I guess it'll be hot later on." The cuckoo, in one of its more articulate moments, is angrily crying, "Whip it!"

She sits down, her mind not on the meaningless words I am saying or even the cuckoo, which we have all developed the habit of commenting on.

"Where's Laura?" she asks.

"In the garden, I believe," I say.

"Could we talk?"

"I expect so."

"I want us to know something about each other," she says, looking into my face with serious searching brown eyes. She really is a lovely girl.

But I don't know what to say. I never know what to say when they come to me, those lovely serious students wanting to rap. They ask me questions about myself, as if they had a right to know: "What does your husband do, Dr. Stoneman? Is this a picture of your son?" Or, equally, they want to tell me about themselves—their pets, their parents, their sex lives. Theoretically, I am willing to accept their premise that I owe them what they're asking for. It will make a better relationship—

won't it?—in the classroom; and yet I feel myself closing up inside when they want so much of me.

("We don't expose ourselves to strangers," Mother said that time when—longing to be a schoolgirl—I stood out in front of our house and waved at the kids going by on the bus. "We don't stick ourselves out in people's view, where they'll be bound to talk about us and our ways.")

"Are you against us?" Cyndi asks. It's the kind of question they never mind putting.

"I don't think I'm against you," I cautiously say. "I understand the handicaps there would be inherent in your marriage." (Says Professor Stoneman.)

"Well, yes," she says. "Everyone understands that. We just have to get right on past them, right at the start."

"If you can."

"Of course we can. The main thing is to make all of you see that we really love each other and will have a good marriage."

"In spite of the differences."

"I will pray for him," she solemnly says, brushing a lock of heavy brown hair back from her broad forehead, "but I will never try to make him go to Church."

There is something familiar about that. I frown slightly, recalling it.

"You don't believe me," she says.

"Oh yes, Cyndi, I believe you. I was just trying to remember where I had heard something like that recently. Let me tell you who it was said it—you might like to know. It was my mother, telling me how she felt when she decided to marry my father. I don't know whether you have heard that my mother belonged to your Church then, but my father—like your grandfather—was more or less a Baptist, I believe."

She looks down at her blue-denim lap for a moment before answering. "Yes," she says, "I know about it."

"She thought she loved him so much it didn't matter," I say.

"Did it?"

"Do you really know what happened to them, Cyndi?" I ask.

"I think so," she says. "Paul hinted at it yesterday, and I made Daddy tell me."

"I believe," I say at last, deliberately thinking how much to reveal, "that she married my father before she knew him very well and then discovered she didn't love him as much as she thought she did."

"Then it wasn't the Church," Cyndi states—a conclusion arrived at.

She has me there. "Maybe not," I say, "but it might make you think what would happen if you discovered what she did—that you had made a mistake."

"Like you did."

"Yes, I made mistakes, too."

"Were you very, very sure?"

I try to remember. I honestly believe that, with Tony, I thought because we had kissed and embraced, and he had touched my breasts (had worshiped there, as he put it, at the shrine of my purity), we were practically the same as married already. I believe I simply thought it would be a sin if we didn't marry and I would turn out like my mother. I don't think I ever even wondered whether it would work. Ted and I talked and talked, and each thought we understood the kind of life the other wanted. This was the thing he thought we had to decide on—it wouldn't have occurred to him that sex would prove to be a problem, and I decided to believe either that my incompatibility with Tony was purely an individual thing, or else I was mature enough after five years to give a man what he needed.

"I think," I say at last, "I had rather an unfortunate background for marriage. I would certainly have said I was sure, but I might not have meant the same thing you mean."

"I think I know what it means to be sure," Cyndi says. "I was planning to marry Bob, you see, because we seemed to suit each other so well and Mother and Daddy thought it would be such a good thing. But then I took this course in marriage and family life, and I think I can see the mistake I was about to make with him. Really, Gail," she says, "I knew it before I even met Paul."

Oh God. She took a course. "Does Paul fit better into what you learned?" I ask.

"Oh of course they always warn you about differences in religion," she says, "but other than that, he does. We just *like* each other so much—and have the same ideas, you know, about what we want out of life."

"The difference in religion isn't that great, then?" I ask.

She looks puzzled. "Oh, you mean what we want out of life. I don't think it is. You see, we both want to live on the farm, and make as many of the things we use as we can. We're both into ecology."

"I thought you wanted to teach English," I say.

"Oh no, not really. I like the courses, and I had to be preparing for some kind of job. But I don't think I would be a good teacher. Like Paul. You know, he wanted to major in English, but not to teach, and his father couldn't understand why he would want to waste his time that way."

"I could understand," I say.

"Yes. He thought you would understand—about us."

"He has great faith in me."

"He likes you, Gail. I want to like you too."

Oh, she comes on so sincerely, but it's much too soon for that. They can put on sincerity and take it off again, like Tommye Jo's wigs.

"I'm glad you came." I can tell her that sincerely. I am glad to know more about the kind of girl that Paul has chosen. She has a charm, indeed, as I told Stanfield she did. But for Paul?

We hear Mother in the kitchen, and Cyndi waits to talk to her before she goes. Mother mentions the kitchen things.

"Oh I do want them," Cyndi says. "But I couldn't use them now, and if you don't care, Paul and I thought we'd just leave

207

them here. Seems like they kind of belong here—I just love your house, Laura; it's like part of nature."

After she is gone, Mother says, "Do you know what I suspect, Gail? I wouldn't be surprised if them kids think they're fixing to live right here with me."

"Maybe," I say, "they think you'll be living somewhere else?"

She fails to comment on that suggestion, but goes to get the black-eyed peas she has brought in from the garden. Then we sit awhile together, "fixing" them, talking of the ordinary everyday things we always do talk about. But finally, after a certain small silence, she goes back to what I have hinted.

"I know what you meant," she says, "about me living somewhere else. I know what you're asking me—and, Gail, I'd tell you if I knew."

"But, Mother—after fifteen years, how could you still be wondering?"

"It got harder and harder, year by year," she says.

"Well, I don't see why," I say, perhaps a little impatiently. The truth is, I don't see why Mother and Hugh should keep us all in suspense the whole summer through.

"She lived so long," Mother says, with a sigh. "Not that I ever wished her dead—I'm sure I never did, Gail—but I wouldn't be human if I hadn't wondered once in a while how things would be if something happened to Estelle. And you know she was always sick, or claiming to be. Even before they married, she used her sicknesses to get attention. I think, from something Miz Bailey told me once, even her own family knew that. But I prayed God not to ever let me think of such a thing as her dying, and I don't believe I very often did.

"But she lived so long, I got so old. Nearly fifty when she died, you know, and it had been close onto thirty years since the time I lived with your daddy." She looks down at the peas awhile; she is getting close to something she doesn't know how to talk to me about. I wait.

"You know I got to where I would go to Sloan City to the beauty shop twice a year, to get a permanent. I would never go to Net Bailey's little shop at Herley, because I was afraid things would be said there that I didn't want to hear. You know how it is in a beauty shop—how people under the drier talk, without always knowing who can hear. But then one time at Sloan City I heard something—no, not about me and Hugh," she puts in hastily. "About somebody I scarcely knew. You remember Iona Davenport, that lived with her folks so many years, took care of them through their last illness, till finally she was up in her forties when they died, and nobody knew what would become of her?"

"I remember *about* her," I say. "She lived over south of Walnut Grove, I think."

"That's right. Had a pretty good farm there—inherited it, of course, when her folks passed on. And then seems like two or three men come a-courting. Everybody thought because of the farm, of course, and I wouldn't be surprised if Iona didn't think so too. I knew her a little, when I first come here, and she was a sensible girl. Well, anyway, I don't really know anything about what went on; only, first thing I knew, Hugh told me she was married—to a man from up close to Herley that had lately lost his wife. And then, not hardly any time later—maybe two or three weeks—we heard she had packed up and gone home. All this is not the story a-tall, only you've got to understand it to see what I mean about the thing I heard in the beauty shop.

"It was a crude thing, not the kind of talk I was ever used to among women. And you know how I always was about jokes. I could see myself turning red, setting there in front of the mirror with curl papers sticking out all over my head. This woman in the chair next to me was telling her operator all about Iona and why she left her husband so soon. 'She told me she just couldn't take married life—said Derwood was on top of her half a dozen times every night.' That was the woman's very words. And then the thing that capped that—that set every-body in the shop but me just a-howling: 'Cain't no maiden lady hold up to that kind of treatment,' Iona Davenport said."

I know I'm like my mother about jokes, but I can't help smiling at this one, and Mother herself laughs ruefully. "Poor Mother," I say.

"Well, you see the thing was," she goes on, "I was well up in my forties, myself—like Iona; and I guess it struck me for the first time then that I might not be a very good wife, either. Still, I knew how I felt about Hugh, and he has always been a considerate person in every way. I knew I would never let a lit-tle gossip stop me if—for any reason, as I always expressed it to myself—we ever did get a chance to be married. All the same, I couldn't quite put it out of my mind; as you see, I never have.

"It wasn't so long after that—maybe two years—that Estelle took sick, and Hugh told me it was really serious this time. Nei-ther one of us ever said a word about what might be about to happen—what we would do if it did. Then one day he come and told me Estelle was wanting to see me. The doctors said she didn't have long to live—weeks, maybe, not months—and apparently she knew it herself. She wanted to talk to me. I didn't want to go. Hugh thought I ought to. I knew I ought to —you don't refuse the requests of the dying. Finally one morn-ing I told him to tell her I would come to see her in the evening of that day.

"She was in the new hospital at Sloan City—I don't guess you've ever seen it, it was built right after the war. It was where Mama died, and I knew the place well enough to go by myself to Estelle's room. It wasn't visiting hours, but there was people all over the place—always was. I know they had a sign up say-ing children under twelve not allowed on the floor, but the kids was running up and down the halls. It looked to me like about half of them was Stanfields: red sandy hair and big ears, like they've all got, even Stanfield. I guessed what I'd find in her room, and sure enough it was full of chattering women: her sisters and sister-in-laws. As soon as they saw me they all turned and walked out, looking right through me. I never expected anything else.

"Estelle saw me at the door and called to me to come in. Her voice was fairly strong. 'How nice of you to come,' she said, and I remembered how in the old days I never could tell what she meant by what she said. I asked her how she was—she said she was dying, just the way I had wanted her for years. I had started to set down—I stood up again. I didn't think I could stay and hear that kind of talk.

"She seemed like she was spread out all over the bed. Of course I had seen her once, at the graduation, and knew she'd got awful fat. But she was a lot worse. Somebody had made her a pink ruffled bed jacket, and she had on lipstick that seemed like it just jumped out at you from that slack, yellow face. Oh, and a string of beads. It was pitiful.

" 'Set down,' she said. I made myself do it. She wanted something; I decided I would try to wait and see what it was. 'You don't look that bad to me, Estelle,' I said. All I think I meant was that she didn't look to me like a woman that thought she was dying.

"She tried to prop herself up a little more against her pillows, and she hollered out in pain. I started to go to her, but she said again, 'Set down.'

"She said, 'You and Hugh have had a fine time all these years,' said it with that laugh of hers I remembered so well. 'Tuh-huh-huh!' Though I could tell laughing hurt her. I started to deny what she said, but she hushed me up. 'Just set down and listen,' she said. 'There ain't nothing you can tell me, nor nothing you can do for me. I wanted you here so I could tell you some things. Things I promised myself I wouldn't die without you knowing.'

"I didn't try to say anything else—I didn't know what to think. I just waited. She breathed a little bit and then started talking again. You'll have to believe what she said, for I tell you it's so. I remember the very words. I like to fainted when I heard them. She had that kind of a little sneer she would get sometimes, and she said to me: 'You didn't really think I ever believed you and him was breaking the Commandment, did you?'"

"Oh, Mother!" I gasp. "What a terrible thing."

"It was. I felt like she'd hit me. I couldn't say a word. Then she said, 'You never had the nerve to do that—I always knew that much about you.' I tried to say something then, tried to ask her a question—but she never let me speak. She knew what it would be; she answered it anyway.

"'Oh, but I saw you looking cow-eyed at him from the very first day,' she said, 'and him eating you up with them long gray looks of his.' She give me a long look herself, and she said a word. 'Lust.' She said it like she enjoyed the way it sounded. 'Lust was what it was,' she said, 'and it is just as bad a sin, the Scriptures says so.' It was just the same, she said, and so she hadn't told the elders any lie about it. She spoke pretty plain, Gail, and I guess I remember every word she said."

Mother pauses, draws herself in. "I want to tell you the very words she used," she says, "if I can bear to. I remember them so well. She said to me: 'I knew they wouldn't turn their backs on you if I told them the adultery was in your heart instead of your bloomers.' She laughed her old laugh. It hurt her though.

"She said a lot more. She knew I wouldn't stand up in public and deny anything, she said. And Hugh couldn't do anything because, as she said, he wasn't a Christian—just a Baptist, and not much of a Baptist, either. So she went on. He was going to hell anyway, and she wanted to make sure I went with him."

Mother's voice is shaking now. "I've never told you this before," she says. "You may not believe it—I don't hardly myself, but I remember it so well."

"She was evil," I say. I believe it as I say it.

"It's a scary word to use," she says. "I don't know. But she told me how she made sure I was delivered to the devil. And still she laughed. And went on talking. 'It hurts to breathe,' she said, 'but I got one more thing to tell you. You want to know how I knew you and him never went to bed together. Think I got second sight maybe, something like that, some miracle. No, the age of miracles is past,' she said. 'It wasn't a miracle, it was my brother.' And went on to tell me how her brother Will had spied on Hugh. 'He wasn't always going to see his mother and his dear little sister-in-law,' she said, 'when he left home at night.' What she told me was that for twenty years or more Hugh had been visiting a certain woman in Sloan City. She said she always knew when he'd been to her, and she said it was a comfort to her. 'Because,' she said, 'I'd always rather have lost him to a whore.'"

Again her head bends over the peas in her lap. I don't know whether I should speak to her, or perhaps go and touch her—for she is so still now, so pale—to see if she is all right. She lifts her head.

"It was true," she says. "I knew as soon as I heard it that it had to be true. And I don't blame him, Gail. What else could he have done?"

"I don't know, Mother."

"But I didn't understand his needs, you see. You would know because you're a modern woman. But you wouldn't believe how little I knew about the needs of men. And I never even knew women had needs. I used to read the articles in the magazines we took when you lived at home. I didn't hardly know what they was talking about, but then after all I begun to think. And you know it was funny, Gail. The reputation I had—what people believed about me—and I didn't even know what the word *orgasm* meant when I read about it."

"Don't, Mother," I say. (Do we have to start being frank about sex now, after so many years?)

"When I saw Hugh I was nearly out of my mind, it had been such a terrible thing to me. Because, at the end, she said to me, 'Did you ever think you had won?' I didn't answer, and she said it again, and then started laughing. Nothing like her old laugh that was so familiar to me. Hysterical I guess you would call it—half screaming. And I was so ashamed, and a nurse come in and said something sharp to me about what I was doing to her patient. I run out of there, down the hall without looking to see if there was Stanfields on every side. I felt like there was. And then Hugh was waiting for me at the car. There wasn't any way I could have kept from telling him what Estelle said. If I could have waited awhile before I saw him, I don't know. . . ."

"But you accused him."

"No, it wasn't like that—he got it out of me. I think he might have guessed that some of the family knew. But Estelle had wanted it kept secret. She told me that. She swore it was. She said it suited her purposes that way."

"But it wasn't exactly a secret?"

"Of course it wouldn't be, but I guess I thought then it was. I'm pretty sure now that Mama figured it out. Anyway, Hugh saw right away I must have heard something. He tried to explain to me how it was for a man to have a wife like Estelle and a—someone like me. Of course Hugh was always so nice about his language, but I did understand what he meant."

"Surely you and Hugh didn't fall out over this, after all those years?" I say.

"No. That's not what I mean to be telling you. No. He told me how it was—something about the woman. She was a widow that had a café in Sloan City, and really I guess not what Estelle said. Or he thought not. I think he had some respect for her. He said if we married—*when*, I think he really said—he would break off with her, and I believe he would have. But I couldn't marry."

"Because of the woman?"

"Not the way you think. No, I kept remembering what Iona Davenport said, and I was afraid. I finally come to understand why Hugh had to have that woman, and I just didn't know whether or not I could take her place. I put Hugh off."

"But for fifteen years?"

"One year after another, it got to be. Maybe Hugh understood what my trouble was, I don't know. And of course we both got older, and waiting got to be a habit. We are both very —well, fond of each other. Hugh is the dearest man in the world to me. But we've had our separate lives for a long, long time."

"But did he stop seeing the woman in Sloan City?"

"I never knew. I never mentioned her to him again, but I understand she's dead now."

But are they thinking of marrying now, Hugh and Laura? This is what I thought my mother started out to tell me, but I hesitate now to bring her back to it.

"Mother, he loves you," I dare at last to say.

"Can you use that word, at our age?"

"I can of Hugh," I say. "I don't know about you." Perhaps I can rouse her to some definite statement that she needs, for her own good, to make.

"I know one thing," she says. "Hugh needs what I can give him now, and the thing I want to do the most of anything in the world is take care of him, for whatever time the two of us have left."

"Then if you do, what on earth can you be waiting for?"

"The Lord's forgiveness," she says.

"Mother," I exclaim, "what can you mean?"

"If you don't know," she says, "I can't tell you." She rises, gathering up the peas—shells and snaps—in her apron. "It is time," she says, "to put on the peas."

TEN

I was unperceiving enough to feel at first a sense of relief about the month apart that Stanfield and Tommye Jo prescribed for Paul and Cyndi. Perhaps, I thought, just for this little while, the summer will take on the quality I imagined for it when I made up my mind to spend it at Walnut Grove: the uninterrupted quietness, the pleasant pasture walks in the cool of the morning or evening, conversations with Paul, ordinary companionship with my mother, untainted by the various kinds of guilt and resentment we have harbored so long toward each other.

I do have my walks; and in the pasture a midsummer quietness prevails, without, however, bringing the calmness of mind I had need of. More than anything, I want my mind to come as clear as the morning sky, under which I walk while the dewless pasture grass is still cool. I want to register nothing but a high hawk circling, the perfectness of a round, root-lined little nest in the grass, and the wholeness of the pure white egg contained there. I want uncluttered shapes and patterns, uncomplicated far-off sounds. I would listen to the raincrow if he called, but there is not a hint of humidity in the air, nothing to arouse him. Now I am not even hoping for a poem, only for peace. *Only* for peace?

Paul is working hard now. When he has finished hoeing (he

216

is out every day with the hoe hands, making a hand himself) and then plowing over the crops, he will be laid by and go fishing. Meanwhile, he has nothing to say to his grandmother and me—nothing but pleasant, cover-up greetings and comments on the obvious. He has apparently decided to read Proust, and every night as soon as supper is over he retires to his room with a volume of *Remembrance of Things Past*, chosen from a box of books he left for me to ship to him when he came to Walnut Grove.

"Why Proust?" I say, hoping for conversation.

"Why not?" he says absently, then perhaps feeling he has been too abrupt with me, adds, "I don't really know anything about Proust, Mother, but it was on a reading list at school—and it's something to occupy my mind." This is as close as he comes to talking about Cyndi.

He is unhappy, of course. I didn't want to see the signs of his unhappiness, but they are there and not to be ignored. It isn't that he never smiles; it is that he seems to say to himself, now I must work up a smile for my mother or my grandmother, so they won't begin trying to read my mind. The smiles come slowly, and never are reflected in his eyes. So we work very hard at mealtime keeping up a chatter about the crops and the weather and sometimes the headlines in the morning paper. But I might as well be in California as far as communication with my son is concerned.

It is almost the same with Mother. I keep remembering the strange answer she gave me when I asked her what she was waiting for, that day we talked about her marrying Hugh. The Lord's forgiveness, indeed! What has the Lord got to forgive her for? Well, I suppose we are all sinners, but if she equates the Lord and that Church, as apparently she does, then I would say He has a lot more to make up to her for. I would like some explanation of that answer, but now after having told me more than I had ever known about her troubled life,

217

Mother stays right away from the subject. If I seem to be approaching it, she draws in.

Well, it is her affair. Cyndi is Paul's affair. What I need (like Paul) is something to occupy my mind. The volumes of Renaissance poetry stand untouched on the shelf in my room, shoved in between *Pollyanna* and *The Girl of the Limberlost*. I read *The Girl of the Limberlost*, sitting on the porch with my chair placed so the evaporative cooler in Mother's bedroom blows cool air on me. Often I sit quite unseeing, and sometimes a tear falls on some page of my lost youth.

Hugh comes over every night or so to sit awhile after supper. Paul and I stay a little while on the porch for politeness and then excuse ourselves to go and read. I suppose he reads. I lie on my bed in the damp coolness induced by the evaporative air conditioners and study the water marks on the ceiling paper, which have not changed since my childhood because now Mother can afford to keep the roof in repair. If I should happen to stay at Walnut Grove (but of course there is no place for me here), I wonder if I would suggest to her that she have the ceiling papered. No—on the whole, I think I prefer to keep the mystic symbols of my childhold. They used to speak to me. Perhaps they will again.

Since I had my mail forwarded to Herley, Route 1, I do, of course, receive some. Most of it goes unopened into the wastebasket. But at last the big brown envelope arrives, as from time to time it must. I tell myself it couldn't matter less what the contents prove to be, and this is really true, yet still my heart palpitates and I tremble. These symptoms were perhaps a little more understandable in the days when I waited to see if my poems would come back. I always hoped they would come without a mark or a comment. I wanted no sign that any editor had looked at them; I sent them out praying they would never be read. This masochistic compulsion to give away unwanted pieces of myself was replaced with the necessity for producing what my trade calls scholarly articles. Now I grind out lines and paragraphs about the Countess of Liconbury's verse, and there is nothing of myself in them—not even the style is my own—and still my heart jumps when the envelope comes in the mail. Well, they have sent it back to me. It doesn't really matter. Perhaps I can simply burn it, unopened, in the trash barrel out next to the old outdoor toilet, where I burned the records of my childhood long ago.

Of course I can't burn it. Whatever I thought I'd find at Walnut Grove—the clarity, the insight, the wordless thing— still eludes me. There is no poem in me, and my life is not here. If there is a place for me anywhere in the world, I know where it is, and I had better see whether there is any criticism likely to be useful to me in preparing the article to send out again. My list is lamentably short anyway, and my tenure rather uncertain. I go to my room and rip the envelope open. There is a letter, rather a long one. The editor thinks he can use the article, but it will have to be rewritten. He has a great many suggestions for changes to be made, and none of them make much sense. The article will be all right the way he wants it. It would certainly be just as effective the way I have written it. But I will make the changes, so that I can add one more title to my bibliography in *Faculty Publications*.

This article in particular needs to be published because it will be a chapter in my projected critical biography of the Countess—undertaken because my institution has recently acquired her papers. I have never found anyone outside the English-teaching profession who ever heard of her, and only a few within it. But certainly a biography is wanted, as a Michael Innes character says somewhere, "—by workers in that field." I have even discovered a university press that is in accord with this philosophy. I now have something to occupy my mind, and my mother and Hugh are very much impressed with it. Paul works up to a laugh when I borrow his portable typewriter. "Good old publish or perish," he says.

"You aren't going to be using it?" I ask.

He takes this as a hint. "No, Mother," he says, "I didn't come to be a writer, I came to be a farmer."

"Well, there were Robert Frost and Louis Bromfield," I say.

"I never heard of Louis Bromfield," he says.

I don't tell him about Louis Bromfield. I suppose he might imagine, if I did, that I was trying to dictate his life.

I work an hour or two a day on the article. I can't feel there is any great hurry about it, as the editor has mentioned a backlog of somewhat discouraging proportions. Still, if it is going to be published—

Mother needs to go to town, and she says she won't insist on my going with her because she knows I have to work. I am glad she offers me my excuse, for I don't want to go to town, and I suspect she doesn't especially want me to. She guesses she will see if Hugh would like to go with her. I wonder how long she has been willing to be seen with him in public places, but I don't ask.

This is the day that Nadine comes to make her farewell visit and she finds me, of course, alone.

"Well, I'll be sorry if I don't see Laura," she says, "but I'll be expecting to see her next year. And no telling when I'll see you again."

"No," I say hesitantly, tempted for a moment to confide in Nadine what hopes I had. For I did hope; I might as well not try to kid myself, I wanted that fantasy to be real. But even with Nadine, I find I don't want to make a fool of myself by admitting I ever entertained the notion that you can go home again. "No," I say, letting a small sigh escape in spite of myself, "I don't know when I'll come to Walnut Grove again."

It is midmorning, and we sit on the porch in the shade of the honeysuckle vine, while the cuckoo comes and goes, fixing up the nest a little.

Nadine gives me a quick, hard look that I remember as a characteristic of hers. "Gail," she says, "you're not happy."

"Who is?" I say wearily.

"I am," she says, with vigorous certainty. "Oh, I guess anybody's crazy to say that nowadays, but I think it's just my natural way of looking at life. Do you remember that old poem?"

" 'Oh world I cannot hold thee—'?"

"Yes. I still feel that way. Oh I know, the world's in a pretty big mess and maybe always has been. But I like it. I've had some pretty hard times, but I've liked living in it."

"I envy you, Nadine. I always envied you."

"But what's wrong, Gail? You've got a good job that you like—"

I shake my head.

"You don't? Then quit it."

"Not possible," I say. "I have to eat."

"Do something else."

"There's nothing else." Only one possible thing, and I see I am going to tell her. Nadine always did affect me this way. "Only, for a little while, I almost imagined I could live here with Mother and Paul."

"Hide out from the world," she says, with too much understanding.

"Oh well, maybe so," I say lightly. "Anyway it won't happen. My mother and son evidently have their own lives to live."

"What's happening in the family, Gail? I know you thought something—"

"Yes, and I was right on both counts. Paul and Mother."

"Stanfield's girl? Paul's liking her too much?"

"They tried to announce their engagement. Stanfield and Tommye Jo mean to put a stop to it."

"And you?"

"Oh, I don't know, Nadine. I don't like it, but I don't think there's anything I can do."

"Of course there's not. It's their life, and their mistake if it turns out to be one. But I bet you it won't."

"Her parents may stop it though. I don't know Cyndi well enough to be sure."

"You're afraid for Paul because of what's happened to you, I think."

"To me—and to Mother. He doesn't have a very good background for marital happiness."

"He's probably tougher than you are. Laura's tough, too; maybe he takes after her."

"Mother's had a hard life."

"Of course she has. I doubt if you even know how hard it has been. But she lived it."

"Still is, Nadine."

"What's she up to?"

"I'm not sure. I believe she's going to marry Hugh, and I'm afraid she may be going back into the Church."

"Afraid?"

"Nadine, how could she?"

"I don't know that, exactly, but she's not like you or me that way. Gail, if she starts to go back, don't try to stop her."

"I don't suppose I could."

"No, but listen. I knew her when she was young—before all this happened. I know how much it meant to her then—she went every time the doors opened. She wasn't like some people about it—you know, self-righteous, looking down on people that didn't do just like she did. It just meant everything to her, to worship the way she thought was right."

"And yet she gave it up."

"And not only that. In a way, you know, she gave up the whole community. That meant a lot to her too. She was always wanting to be part of things, and wanting to be liked. I always thought maybe this was partly because she had already gone against her own family, to marry Earl; she'd left all her friends behind her. And she was liked here. My mama and grandma thought she was such a fine girl—an asset to the community, I remember Grandma saying. And what she said counted at Walnut Grove in those days."

"And Mother lost all that."

"So if she's finding some way now, some way she thinks she can get back part of what she lost—I don't know, it may be hard for her. She'll need your help, Gail."

"Sometimes I think I can just barely make it myself, Nadine."

"Oh, rot. You help your mother with whatever it is she's got to do, and let that fine young son of yours go his own way. And go back to California and find yourself a man."

"I've had that."

"Well, that's my prescription," Nadine says. "But then I guess I've always been inclined to oversimplify."

"No, you're probably right," I say. "On all counts. As I say, Nadine, I envy you—the way you meet the world."

"And do you know I envy you, too, Gail—your college education. Would you guess I wanted that more than anything when I was a girl, and my father wouldn't help me because he said all I'd do would be spend his money for four years and then get married. I've always thought of what I could have done if I had had an education."

"I guess we all have our handicaps," I say. "But I'd trade mine for yours."

"Well, I wish I could stay," she says. "I wish I could stay the rest of the summer. I wish I could help you all."

She really could, I think. I wish it, too. But Nadine is going now, leaving first thing in the morning to drive to Arlington with her brother Johnny.

"Write to me," she says. "Get my address from Laura."

"I'm not much of a letter writer," I say.

"I will want to know about Laura," she says. "Things she may not tell me."

"I'll write, Nadine."

"Give my love to Laura," she says as she leaves me.

"Nadine always has so much love to give," Mother says when I relay that message.

I am affected as a conduit might be by hot water flowing

through it. I am warmed for a little while by Nadine's passion for the world, and I think if I write her a letter it might be a thank-you note for that brief gift.

II

Paul gets through plowing, and there are still a few days before his friend at Herley can take off to go fishing. He is restless. He goes to town to buy some fishing gear. He works on the lot fence, which serves no purpose now that Mother doesn't keep a milk cow but ought to look neat—he says—until it's torn down.

"Why don't we make that visit to the cemetery in the morning?" I suggest to him at supper one night.

I think he starts to say no and then changes his mind. I know he is not much interested. "You'll come too, Grandma?" he says.

"No, you-all go on," she says. "I'm kind of expecting Hugh."

"We'll go while it's cool," I say, "unless you want to sleep late."

"Oh no," he says. He never does, now.

In the cemetery, a few flowers are still blooming but all the grass is dry. The three old arborvitaes huddled near the gate are dark against the sun-filled western sky, repeating the shape of the low round hill behind them. We stand up against the sky with the trees and the hill, taller than anything besides the clump of trees in that graveyard.

"You brought me here when I was little," Paul recalls.

"It hasn't changed much."

"No, but I have. I was down among the tombstones then."

I thought Death would speak to him there and explain itself. I was afraid he didn't really know people could die, and I wanted to show him the graves of our family. I wanted him to see where Mama lay, and read her name on the tombstone, for she was the one who of my childhood's population remained the most alive to me through the years when I seldom came to Walnut Grove and preferred not to speak of my mother. I wanted him to know how gently Death took away and how much it left behind. No, I see now it was myself I went there to comfort. Children understand death as easily as they do life.

"Was it scary?" It comes to me how like a horror movie it might have been for him, wandering in the old part of the cemetery where pillars of stone stand like bleached bones or whitened tree trunks.

"I don't remember it that way. I was interested in the shells, and the little reclining lamb—and you know, somewhere there was a little old iron locomotive, a toy I guess, by some child's grave."

Of course he wasn't scared. Nor did Death speak to him. He was just as I had been as a child—as I am now. Our minds select what we can comprehend and bear.

"Isn't it peaceful?" I want him to feel what I felt when Mother and I came for our visit, but I'm afraid of saying too much. There is a tinge of irony in this banality that is supposed to help it go down better.

"Well—cemeteries *are* peaceful as a rule."

"Not if they're right under a freeway."

"Oh, I know, Mother. It's remote and—I don't know, *basic* —and all that sky. It's the same feeling I get sometimes when I'm plowing, especially over in the back field. Then I have to admit I think I would have liked farming better when they plowed with a team."

"But you like it, even with all the noise and smelly machinery."

"Sure. Life is a continuing compromise with technology—I can make it. I *am* going to stay here, Mother. You do understand that?"

"Of course." I don't want him to begin making me understand what else he is going to do. "Let's look at some of the graves."

To our right is an enormous gray stone with the name STANFIELD in large block letters. Mother and I tacitly passed it by when we were here, but it seems to hold an interest for Paul.

"Look at all the little Stanfields," he says. He means the smaller gravestones clustered around the family monument.

"It was a large family. I think there were two brothers, of my grandparents' generation, and each one of them had a good many children."

"I didn't realize Stanfield belonged to such a monumental clan," he says. I mildly protest, as he expects me to.

"This must be his mother—Hugh's wife."

I have never seen Estelle's grave before. I never wanted to see it. I scarcely knew her in life, and now in death she breaks into the peace of the graveyard. For a moment I think I hear the high hysterical laughter that followed my mother down the hospital halls. But it is a bullbat, shrieking and swooping.

She is buried by "Papa" and "Mama," as the stone proclaims. There is no room for Hugh by her side, and anyway he is a Messenger. I wonder which part of Stanfield's name will determine where he gets buried.

"She was a bitch, wasn't she?" Paul says.

"I think she was a good deal more than that. I remember something Mother said—what she told us she said to the preacher. Evil is in the eye of the beholder. That might have sounded a little more profound than she meant it to. But I don't think she intended an ambiguity: Estelle saw evil because she *was* evil."

"Evil," he says thoughtfully.

"You don't believe in it."

"Well, something has to account for people like her, I guess." He kicks around some lumps of caliche. "I wonder what Stanfield thought of her though."

"I can't imagine. If you're saying her own people liked her, I suppose they did. But she was an awful person. I know that, because Mama hated her. And I never heard of anyone else in the world that Mama hated."

I lead him across several rows of graves to the Messenger plot. "Our place," I say.

"I like that," he says. "I'm farming the old Messenger place, and when I get through with that I'll have a place here." He reads the names. He comes to "Fannie Messenger," and he reads the dates and inscription. "She's the only one that's real to me."

"To me, too," I tell him. "I'm glad if she lives for you."

"I see her with bright black eyes. Did I make that up?"

"You've heard it, I suppose. They weren't exactly black, but deep brown—little triangular eyes. Uncle Nezer's were the same, and I think my father's were. I suppose it was a Kelso family characteristic. They were always lit up, twinkling—you'd think they were mischievous, but it really wasn't that. I think it was just the keenest possible interest in everything."

"You'd think she might have minded then—being sort of stuck at home, without much company or way of going anywhere. Or that's what it seemed to me you and Grandma were saying about the way you three lived after Grandma's excommunication."

"I don't know if she minded. I really don't think she did. Mother says she was always glad to see anybody that came visiting, but she never did go anywhere much, even when Papa was alive. It seems to me that she never really *sought* anything. She just accepted—things and people."

"Grandma's a little like her."

"I think she must have tried to be, after a while. But she cared too much about things—she was uptight pretty often."

I lead us down to the back of the cemetery where the grass and wild flowers grow. The flowers now are small daisies, star-

227

scattered through the browning grass. I draw him down beside me on the rock where Mother and I sat.

"Be still," I say, "and listen."

There are sounds to hear—little insect scrapings, small tinkling-voiced birds that sing from far away, an unseen cow bawling. I don't know whether he listens.

"Like Mama," he says.

"What?"

"Still, and listening. Accepting. Letting things be." He looks down at a trail of ants, racing along near our feet. His voice goes very low—I think, trembling. "Letting people love."

Can I reach him? I put my hand on his arm. "You care so much?"

He turns to me with a look that says he can't believe what he heard. "Of course I care so much. Did you think I would want to marry her if I didn't? I care so much that my chest aches because it isn't Cyndi sitting here beside me right now." I look up at him, trying to smile. There are tears in his eyes. "Cyndi can be stiller than anybody. She would sit here as long as I wanted and not say anything at all. And she would see what I see, hear what I hear."

Don't we see and hear the same things, my son and I?

"I thought you were taking it so well—being so mature about it, this month apart."

"Oh, mature! I want Cyndi. I need her. Do you think I've read any of that damn book? I just lie there imagining her there beside me. I wouldn't even have to touch her, you know. What's not mature is telling us we can't be together because I won't repeat some words somebody tells me to and be ducked under the water. What's not mature is thinking something that happened a lifetime ago can have any effect on what's happening to me and Cyndi now."

Maybe it's being here in this silence, surrounded by daisies and grass, that enables me to open myself to his meaning. Almost, I feel what's inside him. He is, simply, in love. The way

228

old poets were. A way I never was. Suddenly, I know that. It isn't something everyone experiences, growing up. It is something rare that comes to the believer, the accepter. Like Mama. I remember what she told me about Papa and her—how lucky they were that the Lord let them find each other, because she knew it often didn't happen that way. It came to my mother, too late, or at least Mama understood things that way.

But Paul and Cyndi are such little kids. Paul has never even imagined he was in love before, as far as I know. And Cyndi—well, she's supposed to have a sweetheart already. And Mama was sixteen when she married, and my mother had a husband when she fell in love. There is just no way to know. No way for me to know, and how can they themselves be sure? Such little kids. Surely, if they wait a little longer . . .

"But if you wait a little longer, to be sure . . ."

He jumps to his feet, not seeing the hurrying ants that he crushes as he wheels and walks away from me. I follow slowly, and he awaits me in the car by the cemetery gate. . . . For a little while there, we came so close.

III

Afterward, though, Paul doesn't seem to have changed. He is just as pleasant and polite as always—I suppose he never expected any better of me than he got in the cemetery, and so is not disappointed. He eats well at dinner and even sits on the porch with Mother and me awhile, favoring us with the superficial comments that he specializes in these days.

The little cuckoos have left the nest, and the old birds have simply added some sticks and started on a new family.

"Where do they all go?" Paul says. "You'd think we'd be in the middle of a cuckoo explosion."

"They must have a lot of enemies," is my surmise.

We hear a car on the road and see its dust cloud moving rapidly in our direction.

"Who was that comic strip character that always went around with a little cloud up over his head?" Paul says idly.

I want nobody here but the three of us on the porch as we are now, in seeming harmony. "I don't know," I say, "but if he's coming here, I think I'll just run off and hide somewhere."

"I used to do that," Mother says. "Literally."

I remember how sometimes when an unexpected caller came she would suddenly think of something she had to do outside and leave Mama to answer the door. But it was simply one of the familiar ways of my childhood, and I never wondered why then.

The car is slowing and will turn in. Actually it is a pickup—a blue Chevrolet with a quilted aluminum camper top.

"Who is it?" I ask.

"I don't recognize the pickup," Mother says.

"I think I may," Paul says, with an inflection that strikes me as ominous.

We watch while a middle-sized, middle-aged man in slacks and a knit sport shirt hops out and walks bouncily up to the gate.

Paul is gripping the wooden arms of the rocking chair he sits in. I can't imagine why he should be apprehensive—he can't be in any trouble, surely. I watch with dread as the bouncy little man reaches the gate, remembering how I used to feel when Paul got well into teen-age and began going out with the boys at night. Fearing the very word "teen-ager," because my reading had conditioned me to believe that my child at a certain age might turn into an unrecognizable monster, I trembled at every unexpected phone call or stranger at the door, imagining I was being called to the morgue or the police station. I really don't know why I am trembling now.

"How are y'all?" calls the man, with his hand on the gate latch.

No one speaks an answer. Mother nods—a quick little movement involving only her head; her neck and shoulders stay as set as a statue's.

He smiles on us all, and he says, "Sister Messenger?"

Mother can pull herself up no straighter, but she draws in— her mouth puckers ever so slightly, her eyes narrow almost imperceptibly, her legs press against each other; she grasps her right wrist with her left hand and holds her arms close to her body. I think for the first time—perhaps because I make a wrenching effort to keep my mind away from saying who this man is—I see what I always meant by Mother drawing herself in. I also suspect that I have made a series of movements that mirror hers. Drawn in and vertical, we await the next word.

He walks toward Mother, extending his hand. "I'm Cecil Files," he says.

I watch Mother stand up mechanically and put out her hand. There is something about her expression, or lack of it—I almost wonder if she is about to faint. Of course I know who this man must be—the "Sister" has revealed his identity—but surely her reaction is a little extreme. She knows the name, I think, and it seems familiar to me, but I can't think why.

"Sit down, Mr. Files," I hastily say, giving Mother a chance to drop back into her seat. (I don't know whether it would be correct for me to call him "Brother" or not, but it would be easier for me to call a priest Father than to say Brother to this man.)

Cecil Files pulls up a chair as she does so, and manages to make a circle out of the way the four of us sit.

He turns to me. "And this must be Dr. Stoneman," he says. (*Doctor?*) He addresses Paul; he calls him by name. "I haven't met you, Paul, but I've been looking forward to it."

"Yes, sir," Paul stiffly says.

Has he come to see Mother or Paul? At least I am out of it and can achieve a manner almost normal. "I am happy to meet you, Mr. Files," I lie.

"Let me explain who I am," he says.

231

"I know who you are," Mother says. It reminds me of the way Mama used to talk sometimes, coming so straight to the point you might think she was rude, although she never meant to be. I don't think Mother does now.

"I know who you are," Mother says again, "but I hadn't heard your name was Files. I wonder if you ever lived at Walnut Grove."

"You're right," he says, as if surprised and thrilled that she has caught it. "Not many people remember, but I lived at Walnut Grove when I was a small boy. You probably remember that my father was minister of the Church there."

"I remember," Mother says. (Here on this same porch, sitting maybe in this same chair, she heard Preacher Files speak the words that set in motion a chain of events fearful now for me to contemplate. I try not to.)

"I was in Minnesota," he says, "working with a small group just starting a Church there, when I was approached about coming back to this vicinity. And I remembered it with such pleasure—and with the certainty, too, that there was work still to be done here."

And here's your work cut out for you, I am tempted to say to Brother Files. But there is no need to say anything. He is the talker.

"Now let me tell you why I came," he goes on, attempting a sort of confidential rapport. "I want to extend to you—all three of you—a very special invitation to come and worship with us at Herley."

Paul gets up, a bit too suddenly. "Thank you very much, sir," he says, "I appreciate the invitation. I have work to do now, so I'm sure you'll excuse me."

"Oh I do wish you'd sit down and visit just a little while, Paul," says Brother Files. "I understand you plan to stay and farm in this community. You're a fine-looking young man, and from all I hear an extremely intelligent young man, able to think for yourself." (He knows Paul left the Catholic church.)

232

"I sure would like to get to know you better—and, frankly, have you with us at Herley."

"Well, I do appreciate that, sir," Paul says. "But you see, I have already gone through all this, and I find that church membership just isn't my thing."

"Surely salvation is everyone's thing," says Brother Files. I think he wouldn't mind a small debate now.

"Well, yes, sir," Paul says, "but I think the word is subject to a variety of interpretations."

Brother Files reaches for a Testament in his pocket, a reflex action which he seems to think better of right away. "We must have a good talk about this some time," he says. "There is a certain logic that you may have overlooked in pursuing your investigations."

Paul has risen from his chair again. He is determined to escape—before he says things he'll be sorry for. I have heard Paul on forms of religion before now. "There may be," he says. "I really have to go now."

His grandmother comes to his aid and says, "Yes, Brother Files, Paul is really a hard-working boy, you know. He came to me this year without a bit of experience as a farmer, and he's doing a fine job."

Brother Files has not really come to talk to Paul, I guess now. He wants Paul to come to him; he is determined on a logical discussion, tête-à-tête.

"Yes, certainly the kind of young man who belongs in our Church," he says; then, shedding his didactic manner, goes on: "And, Paul, if you should ever think of marrying one of our girls—you could never overestimate the satisfaction of the family in the Church. The only reasonable thing a man can do in a case like that is put aside his prejudice and accept the truth."

"Sir," says Paul. Somewhere he learned to adopt an almost military manner as a kind of shield. I am extremely proud of him for his restraint, because what the man is advocating is patently hypocrisy and Paul hates hypocrisy with all the zeal of youth. Without another word he steps off the porch and around to the back of the house. He will go and work on the lot fence, I suppose. When he needs the work, it is there.

Now Brother Files comes down to Mother. Literally, he seems to nestle down and the tone of his voice changes just perceptibly, in the direction of unctuousness. "Sister Messenger—?"

"Brother Files," Mother says. I think she has forced herself to say the name. I think she is not surprised that the preacher has come, she may even have been expecting that Tommye Jo and Stanfield would send him; but she has not been prepared for him to bear this name. They should have told her.

He looks a long moment into Mother's face, as though deciding something. He may have been planning a long introductory speech, or perhaps he simply intends to give this impression. He shakes his head slightly, smiles broadly, and declares with a sort of coziness: "Sister Messenger, we want you back in the Church."

"There are reasons why I haven't been to Church for a while, Brother Files," Mother says.

"But we needn't speak of these reasons now, surely," he says. "All hard feelings are gone long ago, so I pray and believe."

"It was not just a matter of hard feelings, Brother Files," Mother says.

"Oh of course not," he says, "but I see no reason to go into all the details of it now. Some of the elders are persuaded you are sorry for what happened many years ago."

"I always have been," Mother says.

"Of course," he says. "So come back. Let it be known that you are sorry, and worship with our fellowship again. Believe me, Sister, there would be great rejoicing."

"I thank you for coming, Brother Files," Mother says. "I have not yet reached my decision."

It is a definite answer, almost a cold answer, it seems to me, and I am glad to see the preacher takes it as dismissal. "Let us pray then," he says, and we all bow our heads. I imagine Mother enters with fervor into that prayer, but I am quite outside it, thinking only: "Is she praying to a God that would let her sacrifice her whole life for a principle and then recant in the end?" For I do not see this Church as one that will offer terms any different from the ones she rejected forty years ago. The Church is constant and unchanging.

The cuckoo in the mesquite at the corner of the yard is singing its sputtering song as the preacher takes his leave. We watch him drive away, gathering his little cloud, the sun glinting on the quilted aluminum of his camper top.

"What would you have to do to go back?" I ask now.

"I suppose," she says, "I would simply have to ask their forgiveness." An obvious and easy thing, her calm and gentle tone seems to suggest.

"My God, Mother." She draws in a little at my use of the Name. "After the story you've been telling me this summer, it seems to me that they should come to you. Every one of them, on bended knees, and begging for *your* forgiveness."

"No," she says with the same gentle, almost infuriating calmness. "For I know I have sinned against them."

"Mother, what can you mean?" I think I have asked this before, but I am importunate now for an answer.

"I'll tell you," she says. "You thought, I know, I turned against the Church, or ought to have. And with part of my mind I think I wanted to. I know I have changed some about it, too—I don't believe I think any longer that it is the only way, but I do know that it's my way. Outside the Church, I feel like I'm setting myself against God and the whole world. I have always been having to prove myself beyond reproach. I don't know if you see why. I set myself apart—almost, you might say, above the Church. In my own mind, I did. And so I lived continually thinking I felt all eyes always upon me. I

235

chose my own way, and that way had to be—what?" She frowns, searching for the word. "Immaculate." She nods. "Yes, immaculate. This is why I treated Rosabella the way I did, why I was less than a true friend to Nadine when she came back divorced and was angry the time she left with Buck. You see, I told myself then it was on account of you. I couldn't bear to have attention drawn to us, more scandal heaped upon us, because I was afraid it would lead to you finding out what the community thought of me."

"Was it really that?"

"I don't know. I don't know now, and I don't suppose I really knew then. But you see if I had been in the Church I could have been kind to Rosabella, been a real friend to Nadine. For I couldn't have been smirched by what I took to be other people's sins."

"This may all be true—I think it is and I know it's sad—but I still don't see how it proves you sinned against the members of the Church."

"Not the Church alone—I think I mean the community."

"Walnut Grove? Good grief." It would not be strange, I suppose, if her forty years in the wilderness outside her Church have affected her mind a little.

"I've thought of that in the last few years—since I've begun to feel like maybe the community is turning back to me. Oh of course, like you've said, you can't hardly say there's a community here any more. Sometimes it makes me nearly cry when I think how it disappeared in the years when I lived outside of it. I wanted so much to be a part of it—like I told you, joining the home demonstration club, visiting around, trading garden stuff and dress patterns. You know how it used to be." She pauses. "No, you don't. You couldn't, and it's one of the things I'm sorriest for."

"I never wanted to be part of the community, Mother," I assure her, "least of all after I found out how they ostracized you.

236

I'm *glad* Walnut Grove disappeared while its back was turned. It was all it deserved."

"Well, I'm not glad. It was a nice place, with good people. It still is, and in a way, you know, there still is a Walnut Grove."

"I would have thought it had been absorbed by Herley."

"Not quite. Of course there's the Community Center—and actually still a Walnut Grove home demonstration club. Tommye Jo goes to that, and I notice she still visits around the old community, and takes food when there's sickness or death in the family. And, you see, I want to do that too."

"And you never have?"

She shakes her head. "I never thought I ought to, but I think if I get through all this—" She breaks off.

"All this?"

"Find my place again, you know. As I said, ask forgiveness—but what was I going to tell you?"

"Why you are."

"Well, you may not see it. It may sound silly. But I'm going to tell you about a thing that happened to me about two or three years ago. You know, for several years now, I've had the feeling that in some way I was getting to be part of the community again—some community, anyway. Just being more like other people, maybe is all that I mean. At Piggly Wiggly in Sloan City one day I was going along, pushing my cart down the aisle, and I got to talking to another woman shopping there—just about the price of something, I guess, I don't know what, but talking along, a way I never used to do. She asked me where I was from and without thinking I said Walnut Grove. Then another woman stuck her head around a corner to see who I was, and it was Cora Bailey, one of Nadine's cousins, you know. I knew her a little, never well, when I first come to Walnut Grove, and she recognized me, and called my name. She seemed glad to see me. We drifted together, rolling our baskets along, talking of this and that—Stanfield's house mostly; I think it was still pretty new then, and a subject for discussion in the community. Then she begun to talk about another new house in the community, built by a fairly young couple I didn't know at all, though I had seen the house and knew their name. 'It's too bad they're separating, so soon after getting such a nice house built,' she said. I simply agreed that it was, not wanting to ask questions, but she went on. It seems the story in the community was that she had been actually living with another man, her sister's husband (though I think the sister was divorced from him). I'm not sure I followed very well what she was saying, because I begun to get a terrible feeling like I was folding up inside. I wanted to stop her, or walk away and leave her, but still I felt like anything I could do would just serve to remind her who I really was. I knew nearly she had forgot who she was talking to, and I expected her to remember any minute. I expected her to remember any minute."

In a pause, while she discovers her hands clenched in her lap and then spreads them, sighing, I say, "And so she suddenly remembered and turned red, and went off and left her grocery cart."

"No," Mother says. "No, I think it might have been better for me in a way if she had. She never did give any sign that she remembered. I really don't believe she did, not then, not in the store, although I suppose it must have come to her later."

"But, Mother—"

"You don't see." She is disappointed in me, studying me with her eyes wide and serious.

"I'm sorry. No."

"No, you don't. But wait till I tell you how I felt. In the store, while I was talking to her, I was scared to death she'd remember, embarrass herself. Really, that's what I was mainly thinking of—her being embarrassed. But later, on the way home, I got to thinking. There was something else about the way I felt, and it seemed suspiciously like I was disappointed about something. I felt—oh, I don't know what you would say

—overlooked. Neglected, maybe. And you know what come to me? What the truth was?"

"No, Mother." I am beginning to suspect though—an understandable thing, one a person less sensitive than my mother would fail to discover.

"You see," Mother explains, summing up. "She didn't really know who I was—she'd clear forgot, at least for a little while. She called my name, but she didn't know—well, who I was." There is something eluding Mother, something she really doesn't understand yet.

"She'd taken away your identity—your place in the community," I suggest.

"That was it. I didn't put it to myself exactly like that, but that was it. And I was ashamed of myself when I saw how it was with me. I accused myself of pride, and I couldn't deny it. For so long I had laughed in my secret self at the people that pointed at me and called me names. [For so I thought they must do.] Yes, pride. That was what I found in myself, and from that day I begun to think how I could save myself from that sin. Because some way it seemed worse to me, the more I thought of it, than any sin I'd ever been accused of. I even wondered if it could have been the true reason why I didn't marry Hugh."

"I guess people don't always know the real reasons for the things they do."

"No," she says, slowly shaking her head, "I guess they don't. But I know what I have to do, to live with myself in the future."

"Go back to Church, and confess," I say.

She frowns, I think really puzzled. "I don't know if that's quite how it is," she says. "But go back. Belong among Christian folks again."

"And yet it seems to me you put off giving an answer to the preacher."

"I need your support, Gail. It's one reason I wanted you this summer. I want you to tell me it's right, and I want you to go with me."

(And stand with her—little Pearl to her Hester—on the scaffold in the market place?)

"Dear Mother," I say, "I can't even save myself."

ELEVEN

It is as quiet as I ever wished around my mother's place now with Paul gone fishing. But it is not a quietness I care for because it is born of Mother's constant preoccupation with this step that she is determined to find the strength to take. I know she believes I could help her, but I swear I don't know how. Sometimes I wonder if she would like for me to compose a statement explaining what sin it is she repents of.

"What will you say when you go back?" I ask.

"Oh, nothing much," she says.

But of course she will want to make clear that she is not submitting to that ancient accusation against which the elders allowed her to make no defense. She could not possibly go back on those terms. I don't want her to go back at all—I don't see how she could bear to go, or feel it necessary—but I can keep from telling her that. I don't see what else I can do for her.

My thoughts, I admit, are not so much on my mother's problem as my own—what I consider my own. Shall I really sit calmly by while my son commits himself to this life so far removed from the one he is capable of so brilliantly living? Don't I have some responsibility to guide him toward the fulfillment he seems to have lost the perception of? Sometimes I even wonder if I should call his father and see if he would come and talk to Paul. But I know Ted washed his hands of him; he told me that himself. And in recent years his talking doesn't seem to have had much effect.

I don't know whether there is anything I can do either for my mother (who wants help) or my son (who defiantly doesn't). Neither do I know what I can do for myself. I continue to plug along on revising my article, for I see it is not very likely that my future holds anything else.

I work most of the morning, while it is still cool in my little northwest-corner room, but I spend an inexcusable amount of time looking out at the bare dirt yard that is shaded by the elm trees, across my old orange crate desk that still sits beneath the north window. Tommye Jo catches me in my idleness this morning; I think she has come tiptoe through the kitchen to my open door and has stood looking at me for some little time before I sense her presence and turn around. She is wearing a red Orphan Annie-style wig.

"Is this how writers work?" she says.

"Very often," I tell her. "Come in and sit down." I indicate my white-counterpaned bed—I never did have a comfortable chair in this room.

"I saw Laura heading for the chicken house," she says, as she sits in the place that I offer, "so I just came on in."

"Did you come by yourself?" I ask.

"Kevin came with me," she says. "Yonder he goes now."

Looking out toward the barn, I see him slipping along with his twenty-two over his shoulder.

"I hope he knows where Mother is," I say.

"Oh sure," Tommye Jo says. "He knows how to be careful with a gun. Stanfield saw to that before he ever let him fire one."

"Is that a new wig?" I ask, as she doesn't seem inclined to start a conversation.

"Oh no. I don't wear it much, just sometimes for every day. It kind of tickles Stanfield."

It seems to me it doesn't tickle Tommye Jo. There is a hard edge to her smile today and a rather grim look in her eye.

"Is everything all right with your family?" I ask.

"Oh sure, fine," she says. "Do you realize that month's about up, though?"

"I didn't know exactly what the last day would be."

"Next Sunday," she says. "That was the day they decided. Paul said he wanted to know exactly what the first day he could see Cyndi would be, because he aimed to be sitting on the doorstep when she woke up that morning."

"Do you imagine they feel any different?"

"I can't tell. Cyndi won't talk about it."

"Neither will Paul. I expect they're both pretty stubborn."

"I thought I could get her to invite Bob to visit for a weekend; I thought that might make some difference to her."

"I think she told Paul she wouldn't," I say.

"I think she's afraid to. I think she knows if she saw him she wouldn't be all that sure about Paul. Because she always has cared a lot about Bob. I don't know but what I think she's acting so stubborn just because Stanfield and I like Bob so much, and—"

"And you don't like Paul?"

"Oh, we *like* Paul, Gail. You know that. And Stanfield says you don't want them to marry any more than we do. That's why I came today, really."

"What would you think I could do?"

"Can't we make Paul think Bob and Cyndi are engaged?"

"Lie to him?" To keep Cyndi in line with the Church, perhaps a lie would be justified.

"Well, I wouldn't think about it exactly that way," she says. "They'as just about the same as engaged, before Paul came along."

"She's probably told Paul all about Bob," I say. "I doubt if you could make him believe anything he didn't hear from Cyndi herself."

"I don't know," she says. "I had an idea."

Her idea is that she will call Bob and tell him Cyndi wants him to come. "I thought I'd call from over here," she says, "because seems like it's hard to find a time when Cyndi's out of the house. And then, too, Hugh's always listening in on our party line. If he hears a ring, he picks up the phone and listens. And even when we're doing the calling, seems like he's apt to just happen to pick up the phone. And if anybody's talking, he listens to every word they say."

"I had an idea listening in wasn't too uncommon," I say.

"Oh no. Stanfield and Kevin do it too. But I don't think there's anybody on Laura's line that would get the word back to Cyndi, if they did happen to hear something. You reckon Laura's fixing to be outside awhile?"

"I have no idea," I say. "Do you want me to watch for her?"

"Would you, Gail? And if you do see her coming, maybe you can think of some way to keep her outside till I get through talking."

As I stand at the kitchen door watching the paths where I could expect Mother to appear, I wonder. Am I actually involved in a conspiracy against my son? And what are we conspiring to do, anyway?

I listen while Tommye Jo makes her call, from the wall phone in the kitchen. She has no trouble reaching Bob, who she seems to know will be at home this morning. Cyndi wants him to come this weekend, she says. Well, yes, she was, but that didn't work out. It's all over. (I wonder if she is telling herself this is not exactly a lie.) Yes, they would all be glad to see him. Kevin was asking about him a day or two ago. He wants to do some target shooting with Bob again sometime. Well, sure, if he could get in Friday night that would be just fine. Yes, Cyndi will definitely be glad to see him. She just hated to call after what she wrote him.

"How will this help?" I ask Tommye Jo, as she turns away from the phone.

"It may not," she says, "but I think it's worth a try. When she sees Bob again, she'll know what a mistake she's making."

"Well, you know her better than I do." If she's as fickle as Tommye Jo seems to think, I'll certainly be glad I have done my part by watching at the door.

"And I thought—why don't you tell Paul when he comes in that Bob has come to see Cyndi and brought her a ring."

"Is he bringing a ring?"

"Well, I know he did last time, and she didn't take it. I'm just as sure as anything that he'll bring it again."

"Anyway I can tell Paul so."

"And maybe, you know, make it sound like Cyndi knows—like that's why she wanted him to come. You wouldn't exactly have to tell him anything that wasn't true."

"But, Tommye Jo, I don't think you're going to break up our kids that easily. Paul would go straight to Cyndi and find out soon enough it wasn't true."

"You tell him that," she says. "I'll work it on the other end."

Tell her what lie about Paul? I don't think I want to know, and anyway Mother is coming, through the back gate and across the yard.

"Trust me," says Tommye Jo, and she turns to greet Mother. "Hi, Laura," she says. "Did you see Kevin anywhere?"

"Out behind the barn," says Mother. "How are you this morning, Tommye Jo?"

She says she is fine. She just stopped by a few minutes, on her way home from Johnny Carlile's house. Johnny sent word he had some cantaloupes to give her, had more than he could tell what to do with. Sent Laura some, too; she has them in the car. I suppose all this is true, but I can't help wondering if she went to town and bought the cantaloupes, having planned well and deviously ahead.

"I'll go call Kevin," she says. "And then we'll go get you some cantaloupes out of the car."

She calls, and Kevin promptly comes, and we go to the car

where there is indeed a box of cantaloupes, mud-caked from the field. Mother takes two, and appears very pleased at Tommye Jo's thoughtfulness.

"It's good to have friends," she says, when Tommye Jo has driven away.

No doubt it is, if you can tell who your friends are.

II

The days of the fishing trip go slowly with us at home—perhaps all too fast for the boys at Lake LBJ. I finish my summer's work—the rewritten article on the Countess of Liconbury—and one morning place it in the mailbox. As I raise the red metal flag advising the mail carrier that there is something in the box for him, I realize this is the first thing I've had to mail all summer. Here at last is my message to the world—at least the part of it that regularly reads the *Journal of Fannie Burney's Epoch*. Mother, I suppose, may be preparing her message, too, for I have little doubt that she is strong enough to do whatever she feels called on to do.

Toward the end of the week, the weather changes. There is a chance of rain in the forecast, a hint of moisture in the air. Outdone by modern science, not the first with the news, the raincrow hollers. The calls come to me first from far down the creek on a morning when I awake to walk at sunrise, but in the evening we hear them close to the house.

"We could use some rain right now," Mother says. "Three weeks later I wouldn't want it, but it would sure be good for the crops right now."

As we sit on the porch, we watch lightning flash far in the south.

"Them boys may have to come on home," Mother says.

"I hope they don't get caught in a storm."

"Well, it's not fixing to rain here—not tonight."

She is right. This night we never even hear the thunder. But about two o'clock we are awakened by heavy footsteps on the front porch and male voices trying not to be too loud. By the time I wake up enough to realize this is the fishermen come home, Mother is already in the kitchen making Stuart some coffee and Paul a cup of tea.

I draw on my light cotton robe and go to join them, begging coffee for myself. The scent of it cuts through the air, which is warm and heavy in the house, for we never sleep with the air conditioners going. They are sitting around the table: Mother, crisp-haired and rosy, wide awake, and the boys, bearded and bleary-eyed, in clothes that have been wet and are not quite dry yet.

I greet them.

"Rained out," Paul says.

"Aw, we'as done fishing," Stuart says. "But we aimed to stay all night."

"They had good luck," Mother says.

"Congratulations," I say. I suppose that is the right thing.

"We've got the big ice chest full," Paul says. "They're fresh, too—we caught every one of these in about two hours, just before we decided we had better come home."

"What will you do with them?" I ask.

"If y'all don't care," Paul says, "we thought we'd have a fish fry."

"We could build a fire outdoors," Stuart says, "and save messing up the kitchen and smelling up the house."

"I don't see why not," Mother cheerfully agrees.

"I thought we'd ask Stanfield's family," Paul says, "and Stuart will bring his girl."

"Is the month over?" I ask.

"It's a day early," Paul says, "but I thought maybe if we asked the whole family it would be all right."

"Tommye Jo said Bob is coming for the weekend." I might

as well tell him that much, at least, for he is certain to find it out when he issues his invitation.

"I don't believe it," Paul says. His face looks drained and gray, but maybe it looked that way all along, the result of the long night's drive. I just hadn't noticed before. Stuart's face is too sunburned to look gray.

I don't know what to say. I wasn't expecting Paul home so soon, and I am not yet prepared to enter into Tommye Jo's scheme. I haven't thought about it enough yet, and I don't know whether I am capable of taking that risk. To save my son by breaking his heart, perhaps, is what I am contemplating.

"Cyndi didn't invite him," Paul says. "I know that."

"I didn't hear Tommye Jo say he was coming," Mother says.

"She mentioned it to me the day she brought the cantaloupes," I say.

"Well, if Bob's here, invite him too," Mother says heartily.

Paul laughs—really amused, I think. "Good for you, Grandma. That's exactly what we'll do."

"No—wait, Paul," I begin. But what do I think I am going to do—blurt out now in the wee hours of morning, with him wet and tired, and his best friend and his grandmother listening, that Cyndi and Bob are engaged? Tommye Jo expects me to be more subtle than that. No, let it go; I don't have to make up my mind yet. I will see what I think in the morning.

The boys sleep till about ten, and after a cup of coffee and scrambled eggs Stuart departs, saying, "I'll be back about middle of the evening, and help you get things set up."

"I've got to see about the fish," Paul says, but his grandmother has already taken care of them, pouring the water out of the chest and adding more ice, from a supply she keeps in the freezer. She has joined us in the kitchen, and we all stay sitting at the table after Stuart has gone.

"Hugh always used to be bringing in fish," she says. "I learned what to do with them."

"Hey, we've got to invite Hugh, too, for the fish fry," Paul remembers.

"Why yes, he'll be tickled," Mother says. She is going along with the plans as if there were no doubt that Stanfield's whole family, including his hoped-for son-in-law, will be thrilled at the invitation.

"Don't you think you might be taking a little too much for granted?" I ask Paul. After spending the sleepless hours since three o'clock going over what Tommye Jo told me, I still don't know for sure what to say. I won't lie to Paul, but how do I know, anyway, that Tommye Jo isn't right about Cyndi's feelings? As I said, she knows her better than I do.

"I don't see why," says Paul.

"Well—they might have other plans."

"Cyndi and Bob, you mean? I don't think so."

"And of course the month's not quite over."

"Oh the month," he says. "How I ever agreed to such a ridiculous thing I don't know. But I promised not to see her, so I'll simply call her on the phone. I don't suppose I can injure her much that way."

"Don't, Paul," I say. I don't think he hears me.

He goes to the phone by the refrigerator and dials a number without looking it up. "Two longs and a short," he says, nodding and grinning as he hears the ringing of Stanfield's signal. Paul is still pleased as a child at the rural party line.

"Of course they may not be at home," I say.

"I'll let it ring," he says.

And who will answer? If anyone at all is at home, won't it be Tommye Jo, telling Paul Cyndi is out with Bob somewhere, getting her ring? I imagine Paul's face when he hears it. I feel my heart twist in my bosom, and I know I won't be a party to this deception. I have always been weak where Paul is concerned; I do think I am right to oppose the marriage but I know now just how far I can go.

"Who?" Paul finally says. Someone has answered. "Oh, sure,

Bob," he says. "Well, could you have Cyndi call when they come in? No, wait, let me tell you what I called for. This is Paul Stoneman." A pause, then, while Bob says—who knows what? Mother and I both unashamedly listen. "A friend and I just got back from a fishing trip," Paul says now, "and we've got more fish than we know what to do with, so we thought we'd have a fish fry. What I wanted was to ask Cyndi if she and her family could come, and we'd be glad to have you, too, if you-all can make it." Another pause. "Well, sure, you tell them when they come in, and let me know. Okay?"

Paul hangs up laughing. "Good ol' Bob thinks a fish fry sounds like a lot of fun," he said.

"Does he know about you and Cyndi?" I ask.

"Sure," he says. "Cyndi wrote him a long time ago." (Of course I knew that.) He laughs again. "I guess she's been telling him more since he got here—he says he's real happy about us, and wants to meet me."

"Well, I wonder what good old Stanfield and good old Tommye Jo will think about coming to the fish fry," I say.

"I think they'll come," he says. "Bob said they'd all gone down to Hugh's for a little while. He slept late, and was shaving when I called. I expect they'll call back in a little bit."

"We'd better figure how to manage this affair," Mother says.

"You don't have to do a thing," Paul says. "Stuart and I have got it all planned. We'll build a fire outside somewhere and use a big Dutch oven he's got to fry the fish in."

"Have you got plenty of grease?" Mother asks.

"Grease? Oh yeah, sure, Stuart's got that. And he's bringing some pickles his mother makes—mustard pickles of some kind, he says they're real good with fish. And he'll pick up some frozen French fries—we didn't plan on anything very complicated or fancy. Just fish, mostly."

"Well, I'll make the corn bread," Mother says.

"Corn bread?" Paul and I both question that.

"You always have corn bread with fried fish," Mother says.

"I've known that all my life. When I was little, and a child got a bone in its throat, somebody always said 'chew some corn bread.' Anyway, we *had* corn bread, and Mama was the same way."

The phone rings—two longs—and Paul jumps to answer it. "Hello?" . . . "Cyndi!" . . . "Yeah, I've got a lot to tell you too." . . . "Gee, that's great!" . . . "Oh, about five-thirty I think." . . . "No, I don't think you need to bring anything." "Well, if you've made a cake . . ." . . . "Sure, I know, not a mix. Did you grind your own flour?"

He hangs up laughing and happy. "Cyndi wants to bring a cake," he unnecessarily tells us.

"They're all coming?" I ask.

"Sure—the whole family. And good ol' Bob."

"Well, I guess everything's working out then," Mother says.

"I'll make the tea," I offer. "I ought to make some contribution."

"And can we eat on the porch?" Paul asks.

"I've got a few TV trays," Mother says. "Not enough, I'm afraid."

"The kids can sit on the floor and eat picnic-style," I suggest, and Paul says that's what he had in mind.

"All very well if it don't rain," Mother says.

"Well, there's not a cloud in sight," I observe.

"They settled back in the night," Mother says, "but I heard the raincrow again this morning."

"Hey that reminds me," Paul suddenly says. "I think I'm onto that raincrow."

"How's that, Paul?" Mother asks, much interested.

"Well, I heard one down on the lake, and then I think I got a glimpse of it. I'm not sure it's the same bird—I'll check it out when I get a chance to go to town and get to the library."

"But what is it then?" I insist.

"No, I'll tell you when I'm sure," he says. "It's been a mystery so long—I'll wait and bring everybody together and go over all the clues when I'm absolutely sure of the solution."

"Nothing we need like more suspense," I say.

Leaving the table, Paul pauses and puts an arm around my shoulders. "Don't worry about things, Mother," he says in his gentle, little-boy fashion. He has always been a forgiving child, and I think he may have forgotten how angry he got in the cemetery. "Don't worry," he says again. I suppose he just means him and Cyndi: I wonder what those two are going to think if Mother has to expose the dirty linen when she goes begging her way back to Church. I wonder what Paul would think if he knew the very idea of having a fish fry provides almost more suspense than I can manage. It takes me so utterly back to the dark days with his father, when it seemed to me that for Teddy the sole reason for acquiring a house and wife was to be able to Entertain. Afterward, I realized I should have known this before we married; but what I still can't understand is why he ever thought I could be the hostess for the home in the foothills, with the pool and patio making what he considered the perfect setting for our own luau. Really he was talking about it on our honeymoon: the first thing he wanted us to do was entertain a back yard-full of his friends and business associates, and for some reason (I suppose it was fashionable then) he had his heart set on a luau. It was, now that I think about it, a little like a fish fry. Only his idea of entertaining (no matter what the occasion) was that he mentioned the idea to his wife, thus setting in motion a machine that would provide all the proper food at the proper time with the proper service, as well as registering charming smiles and suitable comments to each guest.

The truth is, I suppose, that what he wanted was entirely within reason and entirely to be expected of at least 75 per cent of the women he might have married. Nor is it fair (I see this now, though never through all the long and senseless quarrels did the concession even occur to me) to say he was looking for a wife to be an adjunct to his house. He could have found a great many women better qualified for the post than I was, located comfortably within the confines of his family friends and church. I thought he never loved me, but I don't know—perhaps he did. And I know I myself thought in those days when he was courting me that what he wanted of a wife was what I wanted to be: my life centered around the home and family but admitting (as soon as I had mastered the fundamentals like Entertaining) some sort of volunteer work and club membership, which would represent my contribution to society and be as well an asset to his business career.

I was twenty-four years old then (back in college working on my B.A., and Ted had come back for a master's in business administration). I should have known better, and my only excuse to myself is that I supposed I was normal enough to assume and enjoy those wifely duties that, according to the magazines I still read, were the natural lifestyle (a word just beginning to be noticed in print at that time) of the average American woman.

Oh, it is all very well for me to offer such knowledgeable suggestions about Saturday night suppers and fish fries. I am almost as well versed in the theory of entertaining as Amy Vanderbilt. It is all very well as long as no one expects me to stand up in the middle of things with my hair set and sprayed and my long dress on, saying, in effect, look at me—I am the hub of all this marvelous activity, the spark that makes the party go, the source of all this nourishment of body and wit being offered here. It was just that position that made me forget to offer the right dish to the right person at the right time, but Ted never could see that.

Oh well, I am not the center of this affair, and surely I can make the iced tea.

Stuart arrives in midafternoon, as promised, and sets the work of the fish fry in motion. (Ted would have admired his efficiency.) Around five o'clock, with all the preparations made, he goes to get Sue and we are ready for the party to begin.

The first guest is Hugh, who comes in time to sit on the porch with Mother and me awhile, and watch the lighting of the fire. The fire has burned low, and the boys have set their fish on to fry, when Tommye Jo's Continental pulls in and stops near the yard gate. Now here is the athletic and short-haired Bob, bounding out of the car and around to open the door on Tommye Jo's side, then bounding back in time to offer assistance to Cyndi, who lets him take and hold her hand. I wonder if Paul had much reason to be so carefree after the phone call this morning; but as I watch her lead Bob a few steps to where Paul stands waiting, and observe her introduction of the two young men, I conclude that if there is a ring it is still in Bob's pocket. I don't think Paul could put on such a show of heartiness if Bob had been presented as Cyndi's fiancé.

Now Kevin (without his rifle, thank heaven) goes prancing around the fire like a morris dancer, getting in the way of Paul and Stuart frying the fish, and Cyndi brings Bob to the porch to meet Mother and me and deferentially greet Hugh before they join the group around the fire. Mother and I retire to the kitchen, leaving Tommye Jo apparently content to sit on the porch with the men and watch Bob.

Really, I do well enough with the tea, having carefully calculated the proper amount and remembered to look to the ice supply. I offer glasses of it, trimmed with lemon slices and mint from the patch by the leaky faucet in the back yard, while the frying fish smokes in its kettle.

Stuart and Paul have offered beer, from the six-pack of long-necked Lone Star bottles left from their fishing trip. Only Hugh and I accept, having a bottle apiece, for the paragon visiting Cyndi for the weekend does not, of course, drink, nor do any other members of the Church, including my mother.

"This is goat-ropers' beer, Mother," Paul tells me with apparent pride.

"Goat ropers?" I have not heard the term before.

"Cowboys. This is what the real tough cowboys keep in their pickups all the time."

I ask Stuart if he is a cowboy, but he says, "No, ma'am, I just help my daddy do carpenter work."

The young people gather now around the fire where the fish cook, and I go to sit on the porch with the old folks. Tommye Jo eyes me and my long-necked bottle with disapproval and scolds Hugh, who assures her the doctor said a little beer now and then wouldn't do him any harm. I suspect her dissatisfaction with me is due less to the beer than to my failure to follow her directions and keep Paul away from Cyndi, but we have not yet found ourselves in a situation where she can privately speak her mind.

"Look at ol' Bob," she says, loud enough for everybody on the porch and around the fire to hear. "He knows just what to do wherever he is, and he can talk to anybody—from the college president on down."

I do not doubt that this is all true, for Bob undoubtedly is an admirable young man—at home, as Tommye Jo suggests, in all societies. He reminds me of Ted. Now he insists upon his turn at the fish kettle, while Paul and Stuart stand finishing their beers.

Stuart may not be a goat roper but I imagine he looks like one, in his skinny Levis, barely hanging on over his hip bones, and his wide-brimmed straw hat and boots. Paul is the farmer, with his John Deere cap and his regular blue jeans and open-throated plaid shirt. Bob is wearing well-faded jeans and a blue knit shirt with a sailboat emblem on the front of it. It is amazing what different effects these boys produced in their jeans.

Of course the girls and little Kevin are all in jeans too. This universal costume allows for great individuality. There is no use in wishing girls would dress in a more feminine fashion. There is nothing much more feminine than the hips, busts, and waistlines emphasized by the faded tight jeans and T-shirts worn by Cyndi and Stuart's friend Sue.

A car approaches, slows somewhat, passes on. Fortunately, none of us recognize the car or the people in it.

I say fortunately because of Tommye Jo's complaint: "And there they stand, right out there in plain sight, drinking beer."

"They oughtn't to embarrass you that way, Laura," Stanfield says.

"Oh, they don't embarrass me," Mother says.

"When you're back in the Church, you'll feel different," Tommye Jo says.

"If I get back in the Church," Mother says, "I'll feel just the same as I do now. If they don't want me like I am, then they'll just have to tell me."

Now the girls come toward us with platters of fish, and it is a good time for Tommye Joe and me to go to the kitchen. All that is left is to bring out the corn bread and French fries, keeping warm in the oven.

"Well, it didn't work," Tommye Jo says. "I guess you never had a chance to tell him about Bob and Cyndi."

"Not really, Tommye Jo," I say, "but I couldn't have done it anyway."

"Well," she says, "you couldn't care as much as we do, I reckon."

Perhaps she really doesn't blame me as much as I expected, but puts my failure down to some weakness I can't help.

"Seeing them together this way," she says confidently, "may make a lot of difference to her. That's why Stanfield and I decided to come on over here with the kids tonight, even if Paul wasn't keeping to the time he agreed on."

When all the food is ready and everybody gathered on the porch, Stanfield says, "Wouldn't you like for Bob to ask the blessing, Laura?" And although it has never been the custom of this house, at least in my time, to say grace at meals, Mother accepts Stanfield's suggestion. Tommye Jo and Stanfield smile beatifically while Bob, with the voice of a preacher or a lawyer, performs. Cyndi, I suppose they think, is seeing the difference. It appears to me that she is looking at Paul all the time.

After the meal we all stay lounging on the porch, and the talk, appropriately, is of the futures of the young: Bob's plans for law school, Paul's farming, the house Stuart hopes to build for him and Sue. We touch lightly upon Cyndi's major in English, Sue's job in a store in town, and Kevin's hesitation between becoming a detective and a surgeon.

Stanfield doesn't want things to sound too easy for the kids, though—especially not for Paul.

"Farming's not ever go'n be what it has been," he says pontifically.

"How is that, Mr. Messenger?" Bob dutifully asks.

Stanfield rears back and prognosticates. "Just all kinds of ways," he says, a bit belligerently, as if he expects to be doubted. "For one thing, there's just not any more land. Now you take this place right here, for instance. Say you take it over, Paul, and you aim to make a living on it, support a family. Maybe you can do that much. But what if you want a little extra? Say you want to build a good house—just an ordinary brick house with three or four bedrooms, like I got, like a good many around here. Of course it's go'n cost you at least twice as much to build as it did me, and the only way you can hope to do that is by getting more land. And where's it fixing to come from? It used to be a joke to say you didn't want much land— just what joins yours. Don't nobody make that joke any more. Don't nobody even expect all their land to join. What you want to do is get maybe a thousand acres in cultivation, say in a radius of twenty miles. With a little help you can farm that, the kind of equipment we got nowadays. You can farm that, and you can make a little money. But you know how many places has come up for sale in twenty miles of Walnut Grove the past year? Not a blame one. By the time anybody dies, their land's done spoke for."

257

He stops and looks around to make sure everybody is hearing the lecture. The children are respectfully silent.

"And now I'll tell you something else," he goes on. "Say you could get the land. What are you go'n use to run your tractors with? It's go'n be just as hard to farm without fuel as it is without land. And this is gonna happen. It probably won't happen next year, but it may be a lot sooner than anybody thinks. And then just say you have got a thousand acres—what you go'n do with 'em? I remember Grandpa Stanfield used to tell about his daddy farming a thousand acres back in Mississippi—and I reckon we all know how he done that. But I don't figger we're goin' back to slave labor either."

"Maybe we'll go back to what it was like when I first come to Walnut Grove," Mother says. "Folks made a living on the little farms—plenty didn't have more than a quarter section then, and of course didn't have to have gasoline to plow with a team. The store and school was close enough to everybody, that you could run a car for weeks on a gallon of gas. Of course Walnut Grove was already a consolidated school, with bus routes, but the miles them buses traveled wasn't much compared with the distance children around here have to go to school now. And I hear they're thinking about closing Herley, to consolidate with Sloan City."

Now in the soft gold sunlight we sit and listen, and although the talk is serious, I don't think anyone feels aroused. The kids sit leaning against porch posts, listening I suppose as youth does to its elders without paying very much mind to what they say—but Cyndi sits suddenly erect, her hands clenched in her lap, her little breasts pushing against the letters on her T-shirt.

"Paul and I are against that," she cries. "We want our children to go to a community school."

"Your *children?*" Tommye Jo says, not really a question but more of a comment, with the dry laugh that reminds my mother of Estelle.

"Yes," Cyndi says calmly, patiently, like a teacher answering

258

the question of a child who is a little retarded. "We do mean to have at least two, and if we can afford more than that we might adopt them."

"Hmph!" says Tommye Jo. She has not really expected an answer.

"I was against Walnut Grove going to Herley," Hugh says, reminiscently, not as though he wishes to participate in any discussion involving population control or the further consolidation of schools. "There was a good many of us against it, but it cost a lot to keep a school going then, when so many of the young folks failed to come back to settle after the war."

"We think we can do something to stop the trend," Cyndi says. "We've already talked about this, and we mean to find out just how much it really costs to run a good community school and what kind of taxes we would have to pay to have it. We think most people care about keeping their schools close to home, but just don't know enough about the public school system to see how it could be done."

"Well, I think you're absolutely right about that," says Bob. "If you're going to live in a community, you want to understand the laws that affect the way you live and the kind of education that will be available to your children."

Tommye Jo is surprised into a slight gasp, and Stanfield stares. I wonder if the triangle of lovers have been discussing Paul and Cyndi's future all evening.

"But of course," Bob continues, "there may be a question of whether your children can have quality education if you cling to the small community school concept. I know Cyndi has told me science courses at Herley were little more than a pretense, due to lack of laboratory equipment."

"I believe they can," says Paul. "With a different kind of planning—say, with a school board that really understands what education is all about—I believe they could have the basics. I believe the small school, the small farm—even maybe the small country store—can still succeed, if people learn to readjust their thinking a little. You were saying I might never be able to build a brick house, Stanfield, but why would we want a brick house? I've lived here with Grandma and been pretty comfortable. I even like the looks of the house, and so does Cyndi. The only question, it seems to me, is how long it will last, provided we take reasonable care of it. How old would you say the house is now, Hugh?"

"Why about seventy-five years, I would guess," Hugh says. "It was a fairly new house when Papa bought the place. I figure if it's looked after it'll last at least another seventy-five. You might have to put some kind of siding on it sometime."

"I love it just like it is," Cyndi exclaims. "It looks like it really *lives* here on the land, instead of being set down like a toy block or something."

"Cyndi's right," Bob says. "You wouldn't call it exactly distinguished architecture, but it has an organic look about it. I bet if you have to put on siding you can find something that won't detract from the effect."

"Effect?" says Tommye Jo.

Hugh, with the little grin that lurks almost secretly just curling his lips, reaches over and puts a hand on Mother's knee. "When are you kids figuring on moving in?" he asks.

Cyndi jumps up and runs to Mother, putting her arms affectionately around her neck. "Oh, Laura," she says, "what did we sound like? Did you think we meant to just move you out of your home?"

Paul joins them, and the children stand behind Mother's chair, with their arms around her and around each other. Paul is flushed, I suppose at the realization that they have let themselves go so far in the presence of their unsympathetic elders.

"Grandma understands—don't you, Gran?" he says.

"Of course I do," Mother says, "and you kids can move in with me any time you're a mind to."

Stuart says to Paul, "You and me was gonna clean up all the mess, remember?"

Soon all the young people are trouping into the house, carrying trays and dishes. We can hear talking and laughing, mingled with the kitchen sounds, and I do not think there is any embarrassment among them. On the porch no one seems to know what to say.

"Paul and Cyndi must know something the rest of us don't," Stanfield at last observes.

"They're jumping the gun a little," Hugh says.

"We may marry," Laura says. "We're not trying to hold out on you kids. I've got to get satisfied about the Church before I change my life that much."

"Well, then," Stanfield says, "I don't think there's any doubt about what's fixing to happen, and I want you-all to know that it suits me and Tommye Jo fine."

"I just hope Hugh's planning to go to Church with you, Laura," Tommye Jo says.

"I may go sometimes," Hugh says, "but you'll have to understand that I'm not like Laura." He pauses, then adds with a softness that does not conceal the firmness. "You see, I'm satisfied."

"And I'm satisfied that he's satisfied," Mother adds. "So we won't any of us be going on at Hugh about the Church."

"No," Stanfield agrees. "He's made his decision, and if that's the way he wants it, it's all right with me. But if you're thinking we ought to feel the same way about Cyndi and Paul getting married, well it's just not the same thing a-tall."

"You're not fixing to raise a family," says Tommye Jo with her Estelle laugh.

"I'm not trying to tell anybody else what to do about getting married," Mother says. "Goodness knows, I wouldn't have any right to. But I will say that if Cyndi and Paul do marry I would be glad to know they want to live in my house."

"I told her I'd move over here if she wanted me to," Hugh says.

"Well, I'd think anybody would rather have Hugh's house than this thing," Tommye Jo says.

I wonder if Tommye Jo knows what she has just accepted. I wonder if she thinks she will have any more luck telling Cyndi what to do about the house than she did about a man.

When the kids come out onto the porch, Cyndi and Paul and Bob are in a little cluster, but Cyndi is holding onto Paul's hand. Bob and Paul are talking earnestly, and the subject seems to be public school law. I have the wild notion that Bob is planning Paul's campaign for election to the school board.

As Stanfield's family prepare to depart, Cyndi still holds onto Paul's left hand. At the car Paul and Bob shake hands cordially while Cyndi still hangs on.

"I wonder what Stanfield and Tommye Jo will try next," Hugh says.

Mother moves her chair closer and puts her hand in his. "I expect they saw the writing on the wall tonight," she says.

Paul returns from seeing off Stuart and Sue and sinks down in a chair beside mine. "Well, old Stuart and I put on a pretty good affair, if I do say so," he says.

"Is Bob fixing to be best man at the wedding?" I ask.

He leans over and takes my hand in both of his.

"No," he says warmly, "that'll be old Stuart's place. But I hope Cyndi sends him an invitation."

We know what we have said to each other.

TWELVE

The weather continues hot and humid, but the promises the raincrow makes are not fulfilled. On the Sunday morning after the fish fry, we take our breakfast trays onto the front porch where we find some freshness in the shade of the honeysuckle vine. The whole world seems silent and still, until the cuckoo comes quarreling around in the trees to the west of the porch. "Whip it! Whip it!" it cries.

"That silly cuckoo," Mother says. "It never is satisfied."

"Just like people," Paul says.

"Always kicking up a fuss," Mother says.

"Do you know what Tommye Jo tried to do?" Paul asks.

"No, but I bet she was the one responsible for Bob being here this weekend," Mother says.

"Mother knows about it—don't you, Mother?" Paul says.

"A little," I admit.

"Cyndi thought she tried to get you to help her in some scheme she had. She heard her talking to Stanfield about it."

"Was she trying to break you kids up?" Mother asks.

"I guess so," he says. "Cyndi was pretty mad at her—she told me about it last night. But she said she'd decided to go on as if she didn't know. She says her parents will see soon enough that we have a lasting relationship. Mother does—don't you?"

"I'm willing to admit I think there's a good chance of it," I say. "In my day, I think we would have called it being in love."

Paul laughs happily, jumping up to come behind my chair and hug me. "I knew you'd be okay, Mother, I told Cyndi you'd be okay." He goes on to hug his grandmother for good measure, then—I suppose because he's too happy to sit still—paces up and down the porch. He pauses to look into the cuckoo's nest, which has, as I know, two or three bluish-green eggs in it.

After a little time of silence among us, Mother sighs and says, "I ought to be getting ready to go to Church."

"Mother, you're not going today?" I cry.

"No," she says a little sadly. "I only mean I ought to be."

"Why wait then, Grandma?" Paul says.

"It's hard," she says. We don't discuss it further.

Later on, though, Paul and I do, because he comes to me for the purpose. What I am doing when he finds me is sitting stock still at the desk by my window, staring out over the yard, into my future. What I am thinking is that it is about time for me to pack up and go home. I haven't found what I came hoping for at Walnut Grove; sometimes I feel it was here and I just missed it. But at least I know more about some things in the past than I did. I don't really hate Stanfield any more; perhaps I am even able to think of myself as a member of the Messenger family again, if only an associate member. It is not what I came for, but it is at least a change.

"Mother," Paul says, "what are we going to do about Grandma?"

"About Grandma?" I say. "And what about me?"

"You? I don't see you wanting to make any new commitments."

"No," I say, "I was joking. But, Paul, I don't see what we *can* do about Mother. Isn't this something a person has to do for herself?"

"I think she wants our help." He stands tall and firm in the doorway, challenging me.

"Well, come in then," I say, "and come down to my level." I pat the white bed where my guests always sit. "What is it you think we can do?"

"What you could do, Mother, is not be disapproving."

"Why, Paul, I haven't said a word against what she wants to do."

"But you are against it, all the same. You don't see your expression—not just your face, but your whole body—every time she mentions going back to Church."

"Well, I'm sorry to be against it; I'm sorry if it shows. But I don't think I could ever truly change. I've got over some old hates this summer, but I don't see how I could ever get over what that Church has done to my mother—and of course through her, to me."

"But if *she* can—?"

"And if she does—how do we know what will happen to her now? I don't know what she is going to say when she stands before the congregation. I don't suppose that after all this time she is going to confess to a sin she never committed. She told me she has realized she sinned in cutting herself off from the Church and the community—as if she could have done anything else. But suppose she does go back, and she tells them that. Then how do they know—how do Stanfield and the preacher know—that backs won't be turned on her all over again? If they demanded her confession of adultery forty years ago, why will the situation be different now?"

"I think we just have to assume," Paul says, "that Grandma knows what she's doing. But it's hard, like she said. Of course it's hard. All that seems so long ago to us, but don't you imagine it hurts her almost as much as if it were yesterday?"

"And so what do you think we should do?"

"I think we should tell her go on, and we'll be right there with you."

"You'll go?"

"Of course. And if you don't, I will anyway. I don't want her worried by this from now on."

"Well, then—if you feel this is what she's waiting for."

"Let's go and tell her now."

We find her in the garden, picking some squash for Hugh.

"Mother," I say, rather loudly, so she can hear me inside the tunnel of her split bonnet.

She straightens and, loosening the strings of her bonnet, pushes it back off her face.

"Oh hi," she says. "What mischief are you two up to?"

"Paul and I have just been talking," I say, "about you going back to Church. Of course he'll be here to go with you whenever you decide to go, but I was just thinking—I'll have to go home in a week or two you know, and if you don't go ahead next Sunday, I may not be here to go with you."

She stands with staring eyes for a moment, her mouth slightly open as though she is starting to speak but not sure what to say. Finally, she comes to me and throws her arms around me. Her "Oh, Gail" turns into a sob, and she gives way to weeping.

I stand letting her hold me, letting her tears fall along my cheek. At last I have done what I came to Walnut Grove to do.

During the week showers come—enough (Hugh tells Paul) to help the cotton, but also to interrupt the combining of maize. Enough, as well, to lighten the air, and perhaps even the atmosphere in the Messenger household. We do not talk to each other very much, but we move with lightened loads. I think my mother is praying a great deal. She also makes several unexplained trips—I think to see the minister of the Church and possibly the elders. Paul is gone most evenings, dating Cyndi again.

One showery afternoon the whole Stanfield family comes to visit. It is between showers when they arrive, and the three of us are sitting on the porch admiring the sky—patches of pure blue among the purple-tinged masses of thunderheads.

Except for Kevin, who as usual goes off with his twenty-two over his shoulder, everyone settles down on the porch. Cyndi comes to sit on the floor by my chair, whispering as she bends near me, "Gail, you're sweet—I knew you wouldn't let us down." She holds my hand a moment, and I feel myself pleasantly warmed. I even wonder, "Could she love me?" We will have one more good talk before I leave, and I shall try then not to close myself against her.

"Laura, we're just tickled to death," Tommye Jo says loudly, claiming everyone's attention. Stanfield echoes, "We sure are."

Mother murmurs thank you. No one needs to say what it is they are tickled about.

"I guess Gail and Paul are going with you, aren't they?" Tommye Jo says.

I am glad that Mother can say of course they are.

"Then what I would like," Tommye Jo says, "is for us all to go to our house for dinner after Church."

"Well, I appreciate that, Tommye Jo," Mother says, "but why don't we all come back and have dinner here. I was thinking Hugh could come on during the morning and watch things."

Hugh is not going to Church, of course; I have already asked Mother about that, and she has said she never means to ask him to go with her. It would be too much, I agree.

"I was planning big on everybody coming," Tommye Jo says.

"I'd just like to come home, when it's over," Mother says. "I'd like for us all to be together here."

"Then that's just exactly what we'll do, Laura," Stanfield says, giving Tommye Jo a look that simmers her down under her exuberant red wig.

Our conversation moves on to other subjects—mostly the cotton and the rain, and the imminence of another shower, which is the thing that—before an hour's visit is over—sends Stanfield calling Kevin to go home. We have not spoken of Paul and Cyndi or what their plans may be. I suppose we are not so tickled about that.

II

Getting ready for Church on Sunday is more like preparing for a funeral than anything else I can ever remember doing. Something (I am not sure what) will be dead and buried before this day is done. No one smiles, or speaks any more words than are strictly necessary to get us into the car and along the road to Herley.

The bare brick box is Puritan in its décor—or the lack of it. I remember hearing somewhere that this Church, like the early New England Puritans, allows into the meeting house only what the Bible specifically permits. They have not gone quite as far as the Puritans though (those who shivered through long hours in unheated church houses because the Bible didn't mention stoves), for—though lacking an organ or other instrument for music—they do have central air conditioning, a welcome if worldly addition on this hot, humid day.

Paul takes Mother's arm as we walk down the aisle to a pew near the front, where Stanfield and Tommye Jo have saved three places. I am probably more in need of support than Mother is; though silent and unsmiling, she has emanated some inner assurance from the beginning of this day.

The sounds of the service—the songs, the prayers, the sermon—pass me by like the soughing of wind or the songs of birds whose messages I never decipher. At last I realize the time for my mother's ordeal must be near, and I make a wrenching effort to focus my mind on the words being said.

"Sister Messenger. . . . Long lost to us, and to God. . . ."
[How dare he presume to think he knows about my mother and her God?] . . . "Will come forward. . . ."

She is rising from her place at the end of the pew, walking toward the pulpit with her back straight and her head high. (Whatever she may be about to say, she hasn't lost all her pride, and however unchristian my attitude may be I thank God for that.)

The minister comes forward, extends his hands. Will this be the moment, I try to guess, when she will make her public confession? But no, there is something else first: something I do not understand at all. She takes his hand, leans forward, and whispers in his ear.

And then Cecil Files, standing before the congregation in a leisure suit about the shade of his blue pickup camper, speaks in loud and matter-of-fact tones, as if he were announcing the date of some Church function. Sister Laura Messenger confesses that she has sinned against God and Christ's Church and will earnestly try to correct her fault. The elders, having been so informed, have restored her to the fellowship of Christ.

She stands and looks out over the congregation for a moment, her eyes bright with tears, a soft smile playing about her lips. Something like a long sigh moves through the congregation, and she comes back to her place and sits down.

I grab Paul's hand, holding hard. I am almost afraid I will rise and shout, "Let her speak! Let her tell her sin!"

I do not, of course, rise. I turn and smile at my mother, as if this were what I expected all along. Now there remains only Communion—what they call, simply, the Lord's Supper. My mother is to partake of the bread and grape juice that is being passed from hand to hand. No kneeling at the altar in this plain meeting house. I pass the plates to Paul, he passes them to Mother, and now the tears roll freely down her cheeks. It is finished. These words come to me from far back in time, when on Sunday mornings at the kitchen table my mother read the

Scriptures that she said my soul thirsted for. I can't remember the context now, but if the expression means what I think it does, I hope it has come to me truly. My mother has suffered long enough.

On the Church grounds the brothers and sisters gather around her, and then they come to me, where I stand with Paul and Cyndi. "We are so happy," they say, and their tears fall down, and at last mine do, too, though I bitterly resent them.

Now the spell is broken, and on the way home we can talk.

"Mother," I demand, "why on earth didn't you speak for yourself? Why didn't you tell them what sin you thought you were guilty of?"

"Don't you know?" she says softly. "Don't you remember the Apostle said 'Let your women be silent in the churches'?"

"But surely," I said, "no church nowadays thinks his words still apply. Why there are women active in churches everywhere—even women ministers."

"We still believe the Bible," Mother says simply.

"Do you mean that this is the only way a woman can ever speak in your Church—have what she says relayed by a man?"

"Of course," she says.

"But then there is no way you could ever make yourself understood. I thought you would be allowed to explain—you know, all you told me about what you thought your sin really was. Why, there's no knowing what they think you were confessing. Or rather—I don't suppose there's really any doubt about what they think you were confessing."

"I sinned, I repented, they have taken me back," Mother says as if reciting a litany. "Nothing else matters."

"Nothing else really does, Mother," Paul says. "Can't you see, and let Grandma alone?"

I suppose I see. If pride was her sin, then surely she is absolved of it.

Stanfield and his family are already at Mother's house when we get there. Having left well ahead of us, they have come by their place and picked up a freezer of ice cream, a tall layer cake, and a cloved and pineappled ham. Our little beef roast that Hugh has been watching for us seems rather pitiful in comparison, but I don't blame Tommye Jo. The occasion is certainly worthy of a great display of her culinary ability, matching the high-piled blond wig and shiny white polyester dress.

Asking the blessing, Stanfield thanks God for Mother and (perhaps filled uncommonly full of loving-kindness) fails to mention the rest of her family. The meal proceeds amid much happy talk and laughter and—about halfway through—the cries of the raincrow.

"That takes me back," Mother says.

"Some forty-odd years," says Hugh.

"What is it?" asks Tommye Jo. "I never heard anything like it before."

"Why I remember that," Stanfield says. "It's the raincrow."

"It only exists at Mother's place," I say fancifully, "because what it really is is a myth."

"Oh, Gail," Kevin says scornfully. "That's silly."

I look at Paul and he shakes his head. He hasn't had a chance to get to Sloan City to the library.

"It's a sign of rain, anyway," I say. "But no one seems to know what it looks like."

"I remember how we run outside to look for it," Stanfield says, "one day at Sunday dinner. But we never got a glimpse of it."

"Well, I never heard all this," Tommye Jo says. "I don't know why you wouldn't find raincrows any place but here."

"I remember we talked about that," Hugh says, "that first time we heard it. It was on account of Papa's trees, we decided, and I imagine too it's because they stay along the creeks and this place is closer to the Breaks than where we live."

"I'm going to find it," Kevin announces.

"You'll finish your dinner," Tommye Jo says. "I don't know what your daddy and Gail might have got by with when they were little, but you're not running off from this table."

As soon as she decides he has eaten all he is likely to, she lets him go, and soon we see him with his faithful companion, the twenty-two rifle, treading lightly across the back yard.

"Stalking a tiger?" says Paul.

"No, he's usually after something real, with that gun," Stanfield tells him.

"Paul and I will wash the dishes," Cyndi announces as we begin to leave the table.

"Let them, Laura," Tommye Jo says.

Mother says, "Well, I'll just stay and help them put some of the stuff away," but Cyndi insists she know how to do that.

"I know just where you keep everything," she says.

As usual we go to sit on the porch, and again this afternoon the sky is piling up with shadowed-silver clouds.

"There's something to that raincrow," Hugh says.

"I'd just as soon it would hush," Stanfield says. "I figure the cotton could stand some dry weather about now."

Tommye Jo turns to Mother, with a question as to how she makes her chow-chow. "Because it looks to me like we're apt to have a whole lot of green tomatoes this fall."

Hugh and Stanfield talk man talk; Mother and Tommye Jo talk woman talk. I imagine this going on now down through the years—I hope it lasts a long time, this family harmony, but there is no part in it for me. I lazily watch the cloud piles and think my own thoughts. They are not particularly happy ones, but I find I can say to myself I am glad of this summer at Walnut Grove.

272

Dishwashing sounds die down after a while, and we hear the children—coming to join us, probably, for a little while before going off to wherever they may be going.

The screen door is thrown abruptly wide, and they appear hand in hand. I am reminded of their appearance before us the last time we all ate a meal together at Mother's table. Then they both wore jeans and a tousled look. Today they are sleek and beautiful—a beautiful couple; there is no other phrase quite so right. Cyndi's long, shining brown hair and Paul's well-brushed pageboy; Cyndi's cool green print dress, Paul's white open-throat shirt with the trousers of his brown sport suit; their glowing cheeks, their shining eyes—they have made themselves match, somehow, or perhaps it is nature that has done this. They do not resemble each other in any discernible way, unless in the shade of their burnished brown hair, and yet one might almost, glancing at them, guess they were twin brother and sister.

"Well, Sebastian and Viola," I greet them.

They laugh and turn to each other saying *"Twelfth Night"* at exactly the same time. Oh, well matched indeed.

"Not exactly that, Mother," Paul says. "We have an announcement to make again that makes your allusion just slightly inappropriate."

"Another announcement," says Tommye Jo with her touch of irony that reminds Mother of Estelle.

"No, not really," Cyndi says. "The same one. We thought we'd try again."

"We're going to be married," says Paul.

"We really are, this time," says Cyndi.

"We've been good children," Paul says, "and we've waited, and this time we really are."

I think I am about to rise and go to them, to say I hope they'll be happy. Stanfield is clearing his throat—I don't know what he is about to say, but I remember Hugh wondering what he and Tommye Jo would try next.

273

Neither of us says anything at all, for while we are still hesitating Mother gets up, goes to stand by Hugh's chair, and says, "We have an announcement too."

The company dissolves into a chucking, twittering communal exclamation, like a tree of cuckoos singing.

Cyndi reaches Mother first, and throws her arms around her. "Oh, Laura, I'm so glad," she cries. "We'll have a double wedding."

"That would be awfully nice," Mother says, "but I guess we have our plans made. Hugh and I thought we'd get married here at this house, with just you children here, sometime before Gail goes back to California."

Now I rise and go to them too, to Hugh and Mother, and all I can think to say is "Thank you for that, I want to be here." And Hugh smiles on me, and I know that after all our summer porch talk we have spoken to each other at last.

"Oh of course that will be best," Cyndi says. "It will be a lovely wedding."

"And when do you kids think you're gonna jump the broomstick?" Hugh says.

"Do *what*, Grandpa?" Cyndi says, laughing.

"It's just an old saying, child."

"Well, we plan to get married Thanksgiving, if that's what you mean. We thought that would give us lots of time to get ready, and Gail will have a holiday so she can come back for the wedding."

"I would have to fly, you know," I say.

"We'll meet you at the airport, and then after the wedding, Daddy will take you back. Won't you, Daddy?"

"I expect we can work things out," Stanfield says gruffly. That may be as close as he ever comes to consenting to this marriage, but whatever he may say or do, it is going to take place. I know that now.

"Well," Mother says, "I think that sounds like a real good

date. You'll have three months to fix up this house the way you want it."

"So you'll be moving in with Hugh," Tommye Jo says, and is beginning, I think, some further comment, when we all notice Kevin coming around the end of the porch, with his gun over his shoulder and a dead bird in his hand.

"Why, Kevin!" Mother's voice rises out of the murmur still going on. "You've killed my cuckoo!"

"Why, son," Stanfield says.

"You know better than that, Kevin," Tommye Jo says.

He puts down the gun and comes among us holding out the dead bird, an offering for which it is clear he expects to be praised.

"But it's the raincrow," he says. "I tracked it down, and it's the raincrow."

"No, you see, Kevin," Mother says, trying not to let her hurt show [and not succeeding, for she loves her birds], "it's a cuckoo just like the one that built in the honeysuckle. I imagine it's one of that pair."

"But I know it's the raincrow," he insists, nearly crying. "I saw it in the elm tree when it hollered, and it flew, and I followed it all the way to the china grove down in the pasture."

"Okay, Kevin, okay," says Paul, going to him, putting an arm across his shoulders. "You're right, and they're right. You see," he says, addressing us all, like the detective revealing the secret in the last scene, "the raincrow is the cuckoo."

"It can't be!" I hear myself cry. "The raincrow can't be this silly, sputtering cuckoo."

"I guess it can," Paul says. "I never did get to go to the library, but now with Kevin's evidence, I don't think there's much doubt. You see, I saw one down at the lake when we were fishing. I was just about as sure as I could be, then, because I heard this raincrow one morning in a tree right over where I had my sleeping bag. Then I sat up to look for it, and it hushed; and then immediately a cuckoo flew out of the tree."

"Well, that's a sight," Hugh says. "Finding that out after all these years."

"But why did you want to shoot it, Kevin?" I shouldn't ask that—it's not my place to criticize Kevin. I only want to know.

"I just wanted to show you-all what it was," he says.

"Just the same, Kevin, I wish you hadn't shot my bird," Mother says.

"Well, he oughtn't to've done it," Stanfield says, "but you'll have to admit he was the only one of us that was ever able to spot one and track it down." He is proud of Kevin; this is almost like shooting his first buck at the age of ten.

"What should I do with it?" Kevin asks.

"Bury it," Cyndi says, "and have a funeral. That's what I always used to do. I had a bird cemetery in our back yard."

"We're not having any bird cemetery in our back yard now," Tommye Jo says.

"That was before we moved to the new house, Kevin," Cyndi says. "Of course you couldn't bury it in our back yard now, but Laura might let you bury it here."

Mother nods and Paul says, "Sure, why not? I'll go and help you find a shovel, and you can have its grave right under the elm trees where we always heard it cry."

They rush off hunting a shovel, as though they were all three Kevin's age. I wonder what the rest of the family would think if I went too—I wonder if it isn't my duty to be present at those rites.

Tommye Jo sighs and shakes her head. "And these kids think they're fixing to get married."

"I'm afraid I think so too, Tommye Jo," I say.

"Of course they are, and why not?" Hugh says.

"Well, I'm not gonna fight it any more," Stanfield says.

"I thought you were against them marrying too," Tommye Jo says to me.

"My reasons were not the same as Stanfield's," I say, "but I am like him now: I don't plan to fight it any more."

"They're too young," Tommye Jo says. "In a few years they'll forget all about each other, if we can keep them from making this mistake now."

"Sometimes, Tommye Jo," Hugh says, "people's feelings about each other don't change."

"Not in a lifetime," Mother says.

"Hmph," is all Tommye Jo can think of to say to that. After a pause she says, "Well, I hope you don't think they're fixing to live here in this house."

Nobody bothers to answer that. In a little while she says, "I'll gather up our things. We'd better go as soon as the kids get through with that funeral."

IV

Mother has gone to the evening service at Herley Church. "No," she assured us, "I don't expect anyone to go with me. When I move to Hugh's, I'll be close to Tommye Jo and Stanfield, and I expect they'll come by for me."

Paul and I sit on the porch alone. There won't be many more times like this.

"So the raincrow was the cuckoo all the time," I say. "There it was pretending to send me secret messages, and all the time it was really that silly cuckoo, sputtering in the honeysuckle vine."

"I sort of thought you felt that way about the raincrow," he says, "but after all, how do you know which one is the real bird?"

"What did you put on its tombstone?" I ask.

"Would you like to see?"

We walk around to the corner of the yard nearest my bedroom window, and Paul shows me the tiny mound there. On a shingle set up at one end of the grave, Kevin has printed RAINCRO.

"You see," I say, "that answers it. The raincrow's dead."

"Oh, Mother," he says, with his loving, teasing laugh that I have heard him laugh at Cyndi, "there must be dozens of them around, out of that one nest in Grandma's honeysuckle."

I shake my head. "No, it's dead. And the darn kid was so proud of himself. And Stanfield too—proud of him. Oh, Paul, how can you want to stay at Walnut Grove and be a Walnut Grove man?"

"Trust me to be myself, Mother," he says. "I believe you think as soon as your back is turned I'll start taking on Stanfield's characteristics and Cyndi will put on one of Tommye Jo's wigs and turn into her mother."

We have walked on through the back gate, without any mention of the direction we're taking, across the barnyard to the pasture trail.

"No, you'll be okay, Paul. I really believe you're going to be okay. About myself, I'm not so sure."

"Dear Mother," he says, "you've had a hard summer, in a way, and I think you expected something more than you got from it."

"Some word," I say. "I really wanted a poem, but I would have settled for a word."

"We've all been too noisy about our lives," he says.

We are walking now on an old, old trail, deep as tear-worn furrows in an ancient widow's face. The sun goes down in a flaunted splendor, too public to touch the heart.

Paul takes my hand. "Maybe there needn't always be a word," he says. "Or the whispered one we never hear may be enough. Grandma got along all right in Church this morning."

"I was shocked at that. You know, I almost asked her to let me write something for her to say—some statement that would clear up the misunderstandings and let her say what she really felt about her sin. I didn't know she wouldn't be allowed to speak."

"This was a braver way," he says. "She won through at last."

Thinking of all her wasted years, I heave a sigh.

"She'll be all right, Mother," Paul says. "I'll see to that."

"Dear Paul."

"And you'll be?"

"Let me tell you what I mean to do when I get home again," I say. We have come in view of the gnarled mesquite at the head of the shallow draw, but it does not invite us and we turn back, walking slowly toward the faded gold where the sun went down.

"Tell me," he says, and I begin, making it up as I go.

"Some evening I'll be walking in the garden, and I'll hear Mr. and Mrs. Zimmerman, with their murmuring voices, come out for a breath of air. I'll have the key in my pocket, and I'll unlock the door in the wall and look through it at them strolling among their camellias. And I'll say 'Good evening, won't you come and sit with me awhile, and watch the fountain play?' And they will come, gravely smiling, and sit together on the stone bench, and I will have a folding chair. And there won't be very much that we can say to each other, but they will politely wait, and in a little while it will be time, and I will ask the question: 'Do you know what the little brown doves in the palm trees are saying?'"